THE TASTE OF TOO MUCH

CLIFFORD HANLEY

CORGI BOOKS

THE TASTE OF TOO MUCH
A CORGI BOOK 0 552 13597 6

Originally published in Great Britain by
Hutchinson & Co (Publishers) Ltd

PRINTING HISTORY
Hutchinson edition published 1960
Mainstream edition published 1989
Corgi edition published 1990

This book is set in 10/11¼pt Plantin
by Busby Hannan & Busby (Printers) Ltd, Exeter

Corgi Books are published by Transworld Publishers Ltd,
61–63 Uxbridge Road, Ealing, London W5 5SA, in Australia by
Transworld Publishers (Australia) Pty. Ltd, 15–23 Helles
Avenue, Moorebank, NSW 2170, and in New Zealand by Transworld
Publishers (N.Z.) Ltd, Cnr. Moselle and Waipareira Avenues,
Henderson, Auckland.

Reproduced, printed and bound in Great Britain by
BPCC Hazell Books
Aylesbury, Bucks, England
Member of BPCC Ltd

Clifford Hanley is something of a Scottish institution. His working life began in journalism, and branched into radio writing, the music hall, the legitimate theatre, song writing and television. His first published book, *Dancing in the Streets*, an affectionate evocation of Glasgow childhood, was hailed as a classic, and in a score of novels and works of non-fiction he has acquired a mass of happy readers. His thrillers under the pseudonym of Henry Calvin have a cult quality.

Still popular on radio and television and as a journalist, Clifford Hanley was responsible for the lyric to the ancient pipe tune *Scotland the Brave*, now undoubtedly *the* national anthem of Scotland. He is married and has three adult children.

Praise for *Dancing in the Streets*

'Mr Hanley is no phoney. He's danced in the streets, he's necked in the parlours. He's done all this in Glasgow and he's written the best book about Scotland that I've read in years'
James Kennaway, *New Statesman*

'Affectionate and highly amusing . . . an autobiography of great gusto and enjoyment'
Sunday Times

Also by Clifford Hanley

DANCING IN THE STREETS
ANOTHER STREET, ANOTHER DANCE

and published by Corgi Books

THE TASTE OF TOO MUCH

1

Nearly fifty years of life and nearly twenty-five years of marriage, and nothing to show for it except a houseful of people who had come from God knows where. Samuel Haddow often said the country was overrun with people.

It was a remark that had started as a fresh joke and flattened into a habit. There was a pair of socks in his chair, even.

'They're your own socks,' his wife told him, before he could complain. 'Peter hasn't got any black socks.'

'What do you mean, Peter hasn't got any black socks? Does he think he's taking these? He can go out and dirty a pair of white socks. My God, nothing's private.'

His son Peter stood in bare feet and underpants, with his back to the living-room fire and when Samuel glared at him, the boy shrugged his bony shoulders as if he was pleading innocence. Samuel didn't know whether this was more irritating than words. The boy seemed to have a genius for driving him over the edge of exasperation even by doing nothing at all.

'Oh, take the damn socks,' he muttered. What was so important about a pair of socks, that he should go mad over them? He had promised himself he would let it all flow over him and keep his temper. Fathers were supposed to be fond of their children, but a great deep well of irritation always opened up inside him as soon as he came home and found them there; especially Peter. The boy can't be as bad as that. I would give the damned socks away to a beggar and never miss them. But a beggar wouldn't take them for granted, that's the truth.

'You don't want him to look wrong when he's going to

the school dance,' Mrs Haddow said apprehensively, trying to sound casual and businesslike. Her manner merely underlined her anxiety to avoid an outbreak of Samuel's temper, and this somehow irritated him even more.

'I said he could have the socks, I don't care about the socks, you're ironing that crease squinty.'

'Now you're not going to tell me how to press trousers after all these years,' Mrs Haddow said testily. 'Men don't know everything.'

'Here,' said Peter, 'I'll press the pants, and you can go and make the tea, Mum.'

'*You'll* press the pants!' Samuel's well of irritation bubbled again. 'You'll look sweet dancing wi' a hole the shape of an iron on your backside.'

'I'll be careful, Dad,' Peter said, quite reasonably.

'Aye, sure, you'll be careful.' Samuel forced himself to look at his evening paper. The boy *would* be careful, he wasn't in the habit of doing things badly. There was just something about the way he did them.

'I've got some nice spiced beef ham for your tea, Samuel,' his wife said brightly. Appeasing the monster. It was so transparent that a grin twitched at Samuel's mouth. What a bloody life. I'm a monster. Emily surrendered the iron to Peter reluctantly, convinced that he would ruin his good trousers. Men didn't have the touch for jobs like that.

But in the jumble of thoughts that lived in her head, she never lost sight of the need to take care of Samuel, even if Peter *did* arrive at the dance with his backside showing. Men were like babies, especially fathers, and it was important to let them see that they weren't being neglected in favour of their children. She had read it somewhere and its beautiful simplicity had startled her like a revelation of the Light.

The trousers were laid on a folded bedsheet on the living-room table, and Peter was pressing the iron on a damp cloth in a one-two, one-two-three rhythm and humming to himself. His feet began to twitch in sympathy. Samuel caught sight of them, past the edge of his newspaper, and grinned again. The boy was a bloody clown.

'You'd be better goin' in your bare feet,' he remarked. The derision in his voice was mere ingrained custom. 'Socks'll just hide that fancy toe stuff.'

'Yes, I do have rather pretty feet,' Peter said in a thoughtful, yah-yah voice, and Samuel looked to heaven and muttered, 'Oh God, he's got modesty like a wasting disease.' Julie, ten years old, came into the living-room, skinny and self-contained, and stared at Peter with a sneer.

'You look stupid,' she said. Peter answered with a wolfish smile and laid his right foot flat against his left thigh.

It was always the same, there was always something going on, kids spilling over the whole house. Who were they? Christine, twenty, came home from work to find Peter dressed except for his shoes; wriggling the waistband of his trousers to try to make them hang lower. She swooped on him as if she had just created him and started tweaking his tie.

'Dere's a handsome wee brother,' she cooed. 'All nice and clean for his first dance.'

'Dere's a nice wee sister asking for a belt right in the chops,' Peter said. Samuel looked up sharply and then shrugged his shoulders.

'Who's taking you home tonight, Petesy-wetesy?' Christine asked. 'Whose heart is going to be broken?'

'Whose teeth are going to be broken in a minute?' Peter asked her, and she chuckled merrily.

'There, doesn't he look handsome, Mum?' Christine insisted. 'I think our wee Peter's too good for any of these schoolgirls.'

'Don't be silly, Christine,' Mrs Haddow said sharply. 'Peter's too young to be thinking about girls.'

'That's right, Mum—' Peter was saying patiently, when his father answered, 'He'll be dancin' wi' whippets.'

'—Corporation buses.' Peter finished, and his father grinned at him triumphantly. 'You're no' the only comic in the world,' he said. And Peter cried, 'Everybody gets inta de act!' Mrs Haddow looked vexed and uncomprehending, and Samuel and Peter exchanged a rare smile of collusion.

Peter insisted on leaving the house thirty minutes too early, choosing to walk the cold streets rather than suffer family fussing beyond the limits of endurance. He was unbearably embarrassed. There was frost on the ground.

His father said, 'Well, at least you look clean,' and turned back to his paper with the air of a man who is not going to be further bothered. When Peter had left, Samuel reflected sourly that he might have thought of giving the kid some money, his first school dance and everything. The omission nagged at him and spoiled his pleasure in his spiced beef ham.

Peter walked quickly and took deep breaths. The only light showing in the school came from a window of the janitor's house. The wooden gym annexe was in darkness. There would be red crêpe paper shrouding the white lamps. He had tied some of it on himself a few hours earlier. Six of them, the dance committee, had been excused the last two periods to get the gym ready. They had all been slightly hysterical, for no good reason. He thought back to try to savour the strange flavour of the afternoon.

Coming back from the gym they were all talking at once, and one of the girls slipped on the frozen path and fell into his arms and knocked him down, clutching him as they tumbled. As they lay absurdly on the path, laughing, he had had a sudden consciousness of the present, of living with unnatural vividness for a moment. The laughter, the crisp cold, the gathering darkness, the tingle of anticipation, glowed inside him.

* * *

During the last half-hour the dance started to lose its sense of confusion. Peter saw the gym clock showing a quarter

10

to eleven and reminded himself that he was dancing with Honey and that he must be enjoying it. He stumbled and muttered sorry.

'My fault,' Honey said. 'You dance very well, for a school-kid.' Peter felt hot and pink, and ran his tongue across his front teeth to stop his lip from sticking on them.

'I should never have used that word,' he said. 'It gives you a weapon against me.'

'And don't I need it,' Honey muttered. 'You dance divinely, for a schoolteacher,' Peter said. Honey laughed and said, '*Touché*'. Peter tried to look casually round the gym. He couldn't pick out Lily anywhere.

'You're terribly beautiful, for a schoolteacher, too,' he said, and when Honey started to groan in protest, he went on, 'Well, you are, aren't you? You're much prettier than Mr Long.'

'As you were,' Honey said crisply. 'Don't start seducing me into disloyalty to the headmaster.' The word seduce hovered briefly in Peter's mind before he dismissed it. He gave up trying to pick out Lily in the crowd.

'It makes everything difficult,' he said, 'when you use your no-nonsense voice. It inhibits communication. What's the point of being a human being if human beings can't communicate with other human beings? Life becomes stale, flat, weary and unprofitable.'

'Is this the way you frighten all the girls away?' Honey asked, and added hurriedly, 'I didn't mean that, it was just a joke. I find your conversation highly stimulating, Mr Haddow.'

'For a school-kid.' But they both smiled. The music stopped and Peter stepped back and bowed. Honey said, 'I can't tell you how much I've enjoyed dancing with you, Mr Haddow.'

'Try.'

'Oh, beat it,' Honey said, amused and exasperated. She dropped into a chair beside Gutty Greer and caught his eye.

'Kids,' she said, shaking her head. Peter overheard the

11

word as he walked away, and smiled to himself. 'That Haddow's the worst,' Honey went on. 'He makes me feel like an old crone.'

'Astonishing, astonishing.' Gutty's thick lips barely moved, the sound came from somewhere in his chest.

'Where do they get the patter?' Honey wondered despairingly. 'Especially Haddow. Thank the Lord I'm stuck with first-year brats, I could never stand the pace with these adolescent wolves.'

'Glands, a matter of glands,' the words trickled out of the small space between Gutty's lips. 'You simply represent . . . um . . . a stimulus to the . . . mm . . . endocrine system.'

'Why, Mr Greer,' said Honey, 'are you paying me a compliment?'

Anxious not to look anxious, Peter still couldn't see a trace of Lily. He couldn't see Big Joe Chadwick either. By the gym clock, there were ten minutes to go. What was the point in bothering? He had had the dance, and any minute people would start pouring into the cloakroom. There were some people there already. Peter backed casually towards the cloakroom to find his coat unobtrusively and disappear. One of the people already there was Jimmy Webster, whom Peter would fain have avoided.

'You chuckin' it as well?' Jimmy asked him; short, thin and shrilly aggressive, ramming himself into his coat. 'Catch me gettin' lumbered, it's a mug's game.'

'Oh?'

'For God's sake!' Jimmy was vicious in his contempt. 'Walkin' two miles wi' some bird just for a cuddle.'

'It's a nice night for a walk,' Peter said blandly.

'With who?'

'Mind your own wee business,' Peter said amiably.

'Well, it's your funeral,' Jimmy said, toning down his derision. 'There's nothing in there that would keep *me* out of my bed.'

It would have been easy to make an unkind reply to

Jimmy, but Peter felt sorry for him, and disliked him, and wished he would go away quickly. He did, and Peter watched him from the door until he left the playground and disappeared, walking with short, belligerent steps, before he himself left quickly in the opposite direction. There were three taxis at the school gate – for teachers, probably. Or could one be for Big Joe Chadwick? It was the kind of thing Big Joe could do, he always had money. Peter contemplated the idea of Big Joe in a taxi with Lily and found he could raise no emotion from it. This discovery irritated him slightly.

Big Joe was wearing a new suit tonight. He always had new suits. Peter looked down at his own feet. His trousers had crept up on him during the past months and no longer sat elegantly on his shoes. 'Durn you boy, your socks don't match,' he sang in an undertone. They did match.

He took the path across the waste ground, away from the housing scheme where he lived, and walked up and down streets to pass enough time to convince his sister Christine that he had taken a girl home, because Christine would be waiting at home for a cosy talk about it, and it never crossed his mind not to deceive her. The truth would only annoy her.

As he approached his house he saw two girls standing at the gate. One was Christine. With a small lifting of the spirits, Peter saw that the other was Jean Pynne.

'It's the conquering hero,' Christine said. 'This is my baby brother, Peter.'

'I know,' said Jean Pynne. She was probably the same age as Christine, about twenty. Seeing her seemed to diminish the importance of the dance. She was the legendary Jean Pynne, the fixed standard of comparison in all discussion on feminine beauty between Peter and his friends. She was dark and slender and gorgeous.

Christine tucked her arm into Peter's and leaned on him, and the display of sisterly warmth irritated him mildly because it seemed to signal the end of the conversation with Jean. She's only a girl, after all, Peter chid himself. But it wasn't true.

'Go on talking,' he said, and cleared his throat. 'Go on talking.'

'Come on, I want to hear everything about the Big Ro-Mance,' Christine said. Her air of self-conscious ownership was flattering but bothersome.

'There are some things a gentleman doesn't discuss,' he said, and Christine shook him impatiently. Jean Pynne said, 'Well, it's time I was away home. Cheerio.' She hung momentarily on her farewell. Just imagine, Peter thought, his mind racing. Just imagine taking Jean Pynne home. She's standing here talking to me – Jean Pynne. I'll never get the chance again.

'I'll walk you home.'

'What?' Christine was indignant. 'Two in the one night?'

'You must be freezing,' Jean said. It was mere politeness.

'Oh, I'm young and strong.'

'You're the limit,' Christine said. She was annoyed.

'I don't mind.' Jean Pynne laughed doubtfully, and Peter disengaged his arm from Christine's grasp.

'I'm not going to the moon,' he said. 'Women shouldn't be about at this time of the night without protection.'

'Ho, ho,' Christine scoffed. 'You get straight back here. I'm putting the kettle on now.' Peter fell into step beside Jean Pynne, wondering how it could have been so easy. They walked in silence, awkwardly, looking straight ahead.

'Did you enjoy the dance?' Jean asked him. Was there a hint of condescension in her voice? Peter shrugged.

'It was all right. Dancing is a rather lowbrow pastime, actually. I'm more of the intellectual type. You know, chess, Hindu philosophy, all that trash.'

Jean gave a delicious little giggle. Her cheek was impossibly smooth and transparent and her teeth flashed white in the lamplight.

'You talk funny,' she said.

14

'It's because I'm adolescent,' Peter told her. 'I'm precociously immature. I talk too much. Sometimes I have to listen to myself making dopey jokes when I wish I would shut up or say something else. It's a disease.'

They walked on in silence.

'You see what I mean,' Peter said. 'The kind of things I say, nobody can say anything back. I bore me.'

'I don't mind.'

'You would if you were me.' This seemed funny, and he started to laugh. Jean laughed too, and a jolt of pure pleasure went through him at the sound, and at the prickling consciousness of her presence. It was mixed with a wild, terrible resentment that she couldn't realize how beautiful he found her; that telling her would merely sound like more words; and that her beauty could wring him while he had no effect on her at all.

'I mean,' he said, 'that in this situation I should start talking about the stars and the velvet curtain of the night, you know, that muck. For instance, the light from the star has taken two thousand years to reach us.'

'That makes me feel frightened,' Jean said, shuddering, and Peter instantly protested.

'Why? Stars are just bits of furniture, no matter how far away they are. It's human beings that matter. A hell of a lot of good it would do that starlight if it travelled for two thousand years and then we weren't here to see it. Don't let it browbeat you.' Jean laughed again, helplessly, and put one of her arms in his to support her. Peter squeezed tight on it and imprisoned it as they walked on.

'How did you ever get home?' Jean asked him, '—if you've been talking like this to somebody else?'

'Can I talk seriously to you?'

'If you like.'

'I didn't see any girl home from the school dance. I didn't have the nerve. I talk a lot, but I'm a coward.'

'That's a shame,' said Jean. 'Imagine how the girls feel

15

that nobody took home. It's awful, you don't know how awful it is.'

This novel view of the situation startled Peter, who had hoped for warm sympathy.

'I didn't think of that,' he admitted. 'I suppose I'm a rat, as well as a coward.'

'I would probably be just as bad, if I was a boy,' Jean said.

'Ah, it's a terrible business, sex,' Peter said, and added, 'I don't mean sex, like that. I mean, having two sexes in the world. It truly baffles me. I bet you're fed up listening to me.'

'No, honestly, don't be silly.'

'Well, half the people are one sex and half the people are the other sex. *All the time*, I mean. When you think of all the trouble it causes. What if everybody was the same sex most of the time, and then just a different sex occasionally, or if there was no sex most of the time and just sex now and then, like dressing up for Hallowe'en. Do you know this? I've started to talk absolute nonsense again.'

'I don't quite get it.'

'Good. I don't either. But it truly baffles me anyway. How do I *know* some girl wanted me to take her home from the dance? If some girl did. There should be some better system. I don't even know what to say to a girl. I talk a lot, but I don't know. I don't know what they're thinking.'

'They're just ordinary, they just think ordinary things.'

Peter gave a short, bitter laugh.

'All right,' he said, 'say I had taken some girl home from the dance—'

'What's her name?'

'She hasn't got a name,' he blustered. 'It's just a hypothesis. So I take her home. I still don't know what she's thinking, and she doesn't know what I'm thinking. Does she want me to kiss her good night? The way we talk in the class, we're all big guys, men of the world, we've done

16

everything, but that's what it boils down to, does this girl want us to kiss her good night? And how do you start?'

'I don't know,' Jean said helplessly. 'It's up to the boy.'

'Well, do I break off in the middle of a sentence about trigonometry and woof! Probably land in her eye, or her ear,' he added glumly.

'It can't be as difficult as that, if she likes you. It shouldn't be difficult for you, anyway. Most of the boys that used to take me home couldn't say anything at all, and neither could I. You can talk.'

Peter brightened at once. 'Could I have talked you into kissing me good night – if I was taking you home from a dance?'

'What is this leading up to?' Jean looked sideways at him and saw him shake his head and saw his bony baffled face and felt that she had been elected to the status of a woman of the world. How old was Peter? And how was a sophisticate supposed to act in this situation? They had reached her gate, and Peter still had her arm in his.

'There's nothing to it,' Jean said shakily. She raised her free arm to touch his cheek and turn his face towards her, and kissed him lightly on the mouth. 'See?'

'Hey,' Peter said. 'You kissed me.'

Jean disengaged her arm firmly.

'It was just a demonstration.' She opened the gate and moved to the inside of it. 'Now you'll know next time.' She giggled in spite of her determination to be calm and controlled. Peter was standing with his arms hanging limply by his sides.

'Well, good night,' he said. Jean ran up to the front door, but he called after her, and she turned round.

'Thank you!' he called in a whisper. Jean waved her arm and vanished into the house. Inside the front door she stopped to find that she was blushing and breathless. Soft as a jelly, she accused herself in irritation. For God's sake, I'm nineteen.

Peter walked home briskly, looking thoughtful, and now

and then gravely jumping sideways to kick his heels together. He went in by the back door to find Christine in the kitchen making a fine show of annoyance.

'This dancing's gone to your noddle, my boy,' she chid him. 'Just who the blazes do you think you are, Casanova?'

'Can I help it if I'm rugged and handsome and irresistible to women?'

'You conceited little pig,' said Christine, ramming an Abernethy biscuit into his mouth while he grinned vacuously without resisting. 'That's the last time this kid waits up to make your supper. Well, what was the dance like?'

Peter spluttered cheerfully through crumbs of biscuit. 'It was all right,' he said.

'How was your dancing? I hope you relaxed, for God's sake.' Peter waved a dismissal of such trivialities. 'Nothing to it,' he sprayed.

' "Nothing to it," he says. God, my aching feet after the way I shoved you round the living-room floor. How did David do?'

'David did all right,' said Peter, in world-weary tones. 'For a Clydesdale. I know you think Davie's a sweety-pie, but he's no advertisement for your training. He'll never dance like your brother. Earnest but clueless, that's our Davie.'

Christine was determined to wring everything from him.

'Did you take somebody home? Who was it, after all? Lily?'

'What do you know about Lily?'

'Oh, give us strength. You've had Lily coming out of your ears for weeks, whoever she is. Even David thinks you're daft about her.'

'My pal Davie,' Peter said bitterly, 'and his big Severn-tunnel gub. All right, I took Lily home. A nice wee thing, but immature, immature.'

'Don't come the big-man stuff here,' Christine crushed him. 'Just because you walked Jean Pynne round the block.'

'Jean's nice,' Peter said thoughtfully, and Christine threw another biscuit at him, crying, 'She's out of your class, infant!' She would have said more, but Peter fielded the biscuit and threw it back, and Christine had a fit of the giggles. Peter went to bed and lay on his back with his eyes open.

2

Peter had been carrying on a silent, inactive, unsuspected love affair during most of the autumn with Lily Enterkin. The nearest it ever got to breaking out was in the maths class, where he shared a desk with Davie McAllister, three rows behind Lily. From this position he could peer through the intervening heads and watch the back of her neck and the top of her blouse. In the seat beside him, Davie had the habit of crouching low over his books in such a position that he could stare under his forearm at the desk at the other side of the room where Alice Jackson sat. These activities provided most of the pleasure of the maths class, in defiance of the acid atmosphere that lived round Aitkenhead, the maths teacher. Davie despised Peter for his wishy-washy adoration of Lily Enterkin, Peter despised Davie for his tongue-hanging inarticulate lust for Alice Jackson. Mutual contempt bound Peter and Davie together. It was a happy arrangement.

Davie also needed Peter beside him in the maths class; to mutter answers to him when necessary, and to direct his attention when Wee Aikie was looking at him. The sight of Alice Jackson's legs stimulated Davie to a degree of concentration that needed physical pain to break it, and there was a tender spot on his left ankle that Peter usually kicked to warn him that Aikie was approaching.

'She must have a sunray lamp,' Davie had a habit of crooning. 'Look at that tan, in this weather. Hey,' he would mutter, 'Peter, do you think she's sun-tanned all over?' His eyes would go glassy.

'What, you mean her bum and everything?' Peter would ask innocently, knowing from long acquaintance how to goad Davie, and Davie would clench till white showed at the sides of his nostrils and mutter, 'You're a filthy-minded swine!' Sometimes, after saying this, he would reconsider the matter, and choke into a helpless fit of sniggering till his eyes bulged and tears streamed down his face from the effort of suppressing it. He rarely noticed, but Peter did, that during these fits, Alice Jackson would glance coolly across the room with self-satisfaction lurking in her cool sallow face, and sometimes rearrange her feet to show a different section of brown leg. On the morning after the dance, Peter and Davie met for the first time in the maths class, and Peter could see that Davie was boiling up for an attack on him.

'How did you and Alice get on last night?' Peter asked, to forestall whatever it was.

'Don't act the bloody innocent,' Davie grated savagely. 'You know damn well Big Joe took Alice home.'

'Tch, tch, did she give you the well-known waggle? I'm sorry.' Peter meant it. Davie shut him up with a chopping gesture of the right hand. 'What's the diff?' he demanded. 'Oh, you're a right champ. Talk, talk, talk, you'd sicken anybody.'

'Hey, pick a fight with Big Joe, it was him that stole Alice,' Peter complained.

'Who cares? Know who I got?'

'No, who?'

'Wee Enterkin.' Davie spat the name out and glared at Peter as if he had been mortally insulted. Peter stared back at him without saying anything, and after a short spell of this, Davie turned away and mumbled, 'Well, it was your fault – where were you?'

'*Quelle* difference does it *faire*?' Peter asked nonchalantly.

'You mean you don't mind?'

'Me?'

With the load off his conscience, Davie abandoned his display of fury and went on in coaxing tones.

'Aw, come off it, Haddow, you know you're crazy about

21

her. Mind you, I don't blame you,' he added defensively, 'she's a bit of all right.'

'Good. I hope it turned out nice for you.' Odd, Peter thought, how stunned he might once have been to think that Davie of all goons could have succeeded with Lily. I must be getting better integrated. Besides, while it would have been frustrating to think of Lily going home with somebody like Big Joe Chadwick, to think of her going home with Davie merely diminished her.

'Well, who did you get?' Davie asked, truculence struggling with relief and plain curiosity. Peter curled his hands and shrugged his shoulders in a Gallic pose, and Davie said with sour satisfaction: 'I knew you'd got nothing.' Peter didn't answer, and irritation returned to Davie. 'You're not fooling anybody, I know you got nothing, but if you look bloody smug you think I'll think you got something good.'

'You're so right, Davie,' said Peter, and the reasonableness of his voice started worry nagging at Davie again.

'Who did you get?' he snarled finally.

'Ssh, here's Aikie.'

'Don't give us that! Who did you get?' In a frenzy of curiosity Davie grabbed one of Peter's hands and started to squeeze the fingers together. Provoked to titters by his friend's desperation, Peter picked up a pencil and started to bore the blunt end of it into the back of Davie's hand, without rancour, till Davie let go and looked pathetically at the circular mark.

'I suppose you took Honey Parish home,' he muttered. 'Bloody bighead.'

'A teacher? Now what could have made you think of that?' Peter laid the innocence on thick.

'Aw, shut up . . . Well, at least it wasn't Honey.'

'Just a minute,' Peter said, 'I'll have to answer that very carefully.'

Wee Aikie's voice cut in on Davie's strangled rage.

'Do you suppose you could devote a small piece of your

22

tiny mind to geometry, McAllister?' he twanged. 'If it's not too square for your taste.'

Tom Arthur, who had a rare appreciation of teacher's jokes, guffawed. Davie straightened up and looked at Aikie with an expression of burning intelligence, and muttered without moving his lips, 'I'll kill that wee rat one day.'

Under Wee Aikie's sharp eye, Davie abandoned his inquisition and affected a devout interest in square geometry, but habit was too strong, and inch by inch he fell into his maths-class crouch with his eyes fixed on Alice Jackson's legs. Peter kicked him from time to time when Aikie was near. In the end, he would have to tell Davie about Jean Pynne, and he feared that he had goaded him so far that Davie would refuse to believe him. He wouldn't exaggerate the story. The truth was too unlikely and bewildering to need embellishment. He was right, Davie refused to believe him, but was stung to admiration all the same.

'You know, you're a terrible liar,' he said, 'but you make it sound good. I couldn't even *make up* a story like that. Start at the beginning again. But could you not make it a wee bit better at the end this time? Since you're a flaming liar anyway? Oh, Jeannie-Peenie. What a beaut. Ay-ay-ay.'

Peter realized too late that nothing could stop Davie from blabbing his story to everybody. But what harm could it do? It made him uneasy, all the same. If it ever got back to Jeannie-Peenie she would despise him utterly. In the meantime, though, it gave him a pleasant sense of notoriety, and he felt that even Lily Enterkin must notice the new character he had acquired – quietly confident, a bit on the blasé side.

In fact, when he bumped into her in the corridor between classes and she asked him how he had enjoyed the dance, he answered with a nonchalance that made him marvel.

'It was okay, as far as it went. Never saw much of you, though.'

23

'Well, you could have if you had tried,' she said reasonably, and without a twinge of self-doubt, Peter answered, 'Well, would you like to come dancing with me yourself and have a monopoly of my well-known charms? We could go to the Locarno or somewhere. Except,' he added, 'that it occurs to me I've only got elevenpence. My munificent remittance hasn't come through from the old pater type. Have you any dough?'

'What a cheek!' But Lily giggled. She spent quite a lot of her time giggling, a habit that Peter had often defended to Davie. 'Do you play badminton?' she asked. 'I always play badminton on Fridays.'

'I don't know, I've never tried. Can I come?'

'All right, if you like,' Lily said, suddenly going uninterested in case Peter might think it mattered to her. 'Meet me at the school gate at half past six and I'll take you along. You'll be absolutely useless if you've never played before.'

'I'll beat you senseless,' Peter warned her levelly, and they stared at each other briefly like wary enemies.

3

The Haddows lived in a four-apartment downstairs Corporation house in a two-up, two-down block of four houses in Whiteknowes in the north-west of the city. It was one of Glasgow's older housing schemes and Samuel regularly pointed out, when people spoke about 'new' Corporation houses, that three generations of Haddows had lived in this one. His wife Emily said it even oftener, at irrelevant moments. Emily had her roots dug as deep into her little house as any matriarch in a manor. She was used to the silent, correct ageing couple in the upstairs house and the prolific Dougans through the wall. But sometimes she felt that it might be nice if the whole house could be bodily moved farther away from the Maryhill Road, because her sister Sarah lived in Maryhill Road, and Sarah terrified Mrs Haddow.

The two sisters resembled each other physically; both short and inclined to tolerable stoutness. But Mrs Haddow's essential being lived apprehensively inside her stoutness, peering out through timid eyes at a world that refused to be manageable and nice all the time, as it was supposed to be. Sarah carried her stoutness like a club. Sarah carried everything like a club. She knew that life was hostile and that was fine with her. If it came to a showdown, she would get in the first clout and grab life and tear its hair out by the roots.

One afternoon just after four o'clock, Peter was sitting in the living-room over a French exercise, and his father, home from an early shift at the gasworks, was at the fire, with his shoes off, reading the paper, when Emily clattered through the door, heavy with shopping and so much more flustered than usual that after one glance, Samuel turned back to his paper with gritted teeth and muttered:

'Somebody's met your Auntie Sarah.'

Peter said nothing. Saying nothing was the best way to cope with his father, though even that was no guarantee of a quiet life.

Emily went straight through to the kitchen and spent some seconds banging shopping bags and packets down before she came back to the kitchen door and said, 'I was speaking to Sarah.' Samuel raised his eyes to heaven and muttered, 'Oh Jesus.'

'Is she as fat and murderous as ever?' Peter enquired, and his father shot him a warning glance crackling with exasperation.

'That's no way to talk about your auntie!' Mrs Haddow complained, and Samuel said, 'What other way in God's name is there to talk about Sarah?' This was said not in support of Peter, but rather in irritation at everybody. 'Well, what was Sarah saying to it?' he went on, in his familiar voice of long-suffering patience, with a hint of mental breakdown tightly controlled.

'She was asking how . . .' Mrs Haddow pursed her lips and gestured with her head towards Peter, '. . . how *somebody* was getting on at school.' She fought back tears of vexation. 'And she was talking about her Joseph having a good steady job in a builder's. Quite the young man, she said.'

'Quite the young illiterate pig,' Samuel corrected her.

'Oh, you haven't heard the half of it! She asked me if I thought we were doing the right thing keeping . . .' Emily gestured with her head again, '. . . on at school.'

'I like that secret code you've invented, Mum,' Peter remarked from his chair at the window. 'Nobody would ever know you were talking about me.'

'Will you shut up?' Mr Haddow asked in his excessively calm voice.

26

'So Sarah was saying,' Emily went on, going deep red, 'that Jeannie Frizell had told her—'

'Who the hell is Jeannie Frizell?'

'I don't know! Oh. That rhymes. Who the hell is Jeannie Frizell. Oh, I wish I had thought of saying that to her face. You know how Sarah keeps on talking about people as if you knew them as well as her and you've never met them in your life. She said that Jeannie Frizell told her that she knew a woman that kept her son on at the school and he—' Emily's voice dropped and she narrowed her lips to a slit so that Peter wouldn't understand, '—got this girl in trouble.'

Samuel leaned back and gave a roar of laughter. He had a rich loud laugh. The sound confused his wife, who hadn't realized that anything funny had happened.

'I bet,' said Samuel, 'I bet this woman was a poor widow?'

'That's right,' said Emily, startled. 'A God-fearing widow.' Samuel went into another roar of laughter, and Peter stood up from his chair and put his hands on his hips and cried in a sharp falsetto,

'And this is no' a word of a lie – this boy broke that poor helpless widow's heart!'

'That's exactly what Sarah said!' Emily gave a bewildered titter.

'Hurry up and make some tea,' her husband told her. 'You know by now Sarah is just a scruff. I don't know why you listen to her. Her and her bloody helpless widows. She's never heard about anybody that hasn't got three husbands in the cemetery, and a terrible cross to bear. God, you would think to listen to her everybody in the Maryhill Road was staggering up and down from St George's Cross wi' bloody great trees on their backs.'

'And nobody'll ever know what I've suffert!' Peter cried.

'I don't care,' Emily complained. 'It's all right for you, you can laugh at her. I never know what way to turn when she starts talking to me. And you shouldn't imitate her,

Peter — she's your auntie, after all. Anyway you don't understand what we're talking about.'

'That's right,' Peter said. 'I only understand about dogs and rabbits.'

'There's a hell of a *lot* you don't know, so don't get cocky,' his father warned him.

'I knew it,' Mrs Haddow wailed, 'I've forgotten the bread and the salt. It's that Sarah, she scatters my wits. I never heard anything so stupid in my life, her and her widows, it's true, isn't it? Everybody she knows is a widow.' Mrs Haddow invariably grasped an idea that was forcefully explained.

'I'll go for bread and salt, Mum,' Peter offered, weary of French, and his father muttered, 'I should damn well think so, you do little enough.'

'You get on with your homework, son,' his mother said firmly. 'You've got to get your Highers.' And his father added, 'Aye, and just see that you do.' Peter shrugged his shoulders and picked up his pen. French and maths and the Highers were sacred mysteries to his parents, and it was no use explaining that the Highers were months away and that he was doing the French exercise only so that he wouldn't have to do it two days later. Understanding little about his school work, his father insisted on visible evidence that he was toiling at it.

But his mother had barely left the house when there was a shriek from the Dougans' house, through the wall. A few seconds later somebody started to hammer on the Haddows' back door, and when Peter opened it, one of the tiny Dougans was on the step — Tommy? Alexander?

'Ma Gran, ma Gran!' he sobbed. 'She's burnded she's self!' While Peter was still taking it in, Samuel dived for the first-aid box and pushed past him, and Peter followed him next door. The small Dougan trailed behind them, breaking into a wail of sobs. Mrs Dougan was lying back on a sagging brown chair with one of her prodigiously fat legs stretched out bare in front of her, and a terrible

28

flaming patch of red on the ankle. She was moaning quietly with one hand over her eyes.

'A scald,' Samuel muttered, and knelt beside the leg and opened the box with swift, confident movements. Mrs Dougan continued to whimper to herself in a quiet monotone. 'Oh, thank God you came, oh it's you, Mr Haddow, oh my God, oh my God, oh mammy-daddy, mammy-daddy, oh my God, oh *Christ*, oh mammy-daddy, mammy-daddy.' Wrung with horror and pity, Peter had to clench his teeth on his tongue to keep back an hysterical laugh. It was some minutes before she subsided into sniffs and gazed gratefully at Samuel through her immensely thick glasses. She was short and very fat, like a two-tier doughnut and she wore her grey hair short and askew.

'Oh, you're awful good, Mr Haddow,' she moaned. 'Naebody ever had a better neighbour, you've been that good to me this day, it was a bilin' kettle, I was just makin' a wee fly cup, oh it's terrible sore, no, it's a lot better. I would just have deceased all my lee lane if you hadn't of come, Mr Haddow, wi' naebody but the poor wee wean frightened out his wee wits. There son, don't greet, your poor old Gran's aw right. Aw shut your girnin' face, you snivellin' wee get,' she added, as the pain gave a jump. A choked titter broke through Peter's teeth, in spite of his father's warning glare.

'Aye, you can laugh, son, it's no' you that got burned to death. Oh dear God, naw, it's awright son, I know you never meant it, you're awful good to me. I thank God this day we've got a nice family like the Haddows next door. Oh, Mr Haddow, Mr Haddow, they'll no' have to take the leg away, will they? I would look sweet wi' a widden leg.' She giggled tearfully. 'Oh, my God, how will I make their teas? They'll be comin' in starvin'.'

'Now don't you worry yourself, Mrs Dougan,' Samuel soothed her. 'Maybe the wife can come in when she gets back, and help you. Just don't you move. And if she's no' back in time they can make their own teas.'

29

'Oh, my God, it's sore, naw, never, they couldny so much as wash a dish not one of them, the rotten lazy pigs, they've got me about demented.'

'Never mind,' Peter said contritely, 'I'll make their teas.'

'Aye, you'd better do something useful for a change,' his father said testily. 'I'll better see if Emily's not back. But you'll need to get the doctor to that, Mrs Dougan.'

When his father had gone, Peter masterfully prevented Mrs Dougan from getting up and asked what he should make for the tea. She lay back gratefully enough, but she shook her head.

'Oh, son, you'll never manage, you'll never understand my way o' workin'. Well—' she grimaced with pain as she moved her bandaged leg, '—Paul never has anything to do wi' meat, he's took a scunner at it, so that's the first thing, and Ria's on her fish diet, but Paul doesny like fish either, and Joe's all right, he'll take Spam to a band playin', so that's the second thing you don't need to cook, and not one a the boys'll touch spuds, bar they're chips, but Ria doesny like chips wi' her fish and Veronica just takes one wee biled spud because she's gettin' fat, she says, and Daddy never touches bar mashed tatties and mince for his teeth.'

'Is he having trouble with his teeth?' asked Peter, dazed.

'Naw, naw, he hasn't got ony. Oh, dear God, this is terrible, I've been on at him for thirty years but will he wear them? Not him. Not a bite's passed his lips for thirty years bar tatties and mince. Oh, I've got a wee chop for Andra, nice and fat. Andra's nae trouble, a chop and an egg'll suffice him any night. Don't bother about the weans, they have theirs standin' up in the kitchen. Chips, an' plenty of mayonnaise and marge to spread on them.'

'What?'

'Well,' she moaned resentfully, 'they'll not eat them any other way, and they've got to eat something. They've got me about delirious tremens.' She closed her eyes and

30

moaned very softly. Peter went into the kitchen, where he found pots everywhere, on the table and the draining-board and the cooker. There were two in the half-open oven and three under the sink. Some were empty and clean and others had layers of food in the bottoms, including one which had a light grey speckled lamina that turned out to be cooked mince with grease congealed over it. There was a piece of uncooked white fish in one of the clean pans.

Under the kitchen table, almost hidden by boots and shoes, he found Micky, the Dougans' dog, a dingy-white smooth-haired terrier arrangement. Its little eyes snapped and it growled hatefully when he bent down, and he reached behind the shoes and dragged it out. It had just started to eat a raw fatty chop, and its eyes rolled as he prised its teeth open and took the chop away. He was in no mood to be fussy. Once the chop was wiped and fried, Paul would never notice the toothmarks. Or was it Joe? Or Andra?

Micky snarled with its lips drawn back showing as many fangs as a crocodile, and when Peter ignored the snarl, it jerked forward and tried to bite his calf. He turned round without anger and kicked it under the chin, whereupon it immediately recognized a familiar manner and wagged its tail at him, and followed him round the kitchen bleating.

Then he pulled out a barrel half-full of potatoes, emptied about forty into the sink, and looked for a knife. He felt it would be nice if he could get the whole thing right, since he was doing it at all, but he couldn't force himself to worry too much if the wrong Dougan ended up with a chip instead of a slice of Spam and mayonnaise. Then he thought of the chip pan. There was no sign of a chip pan. He searched the kitchen and finally found it standing doubtfully outside on the window-sill, either to keep it away from the dog or to let the birds have a peck. It was about the size of an Army soup-pot and had five or six pounds of fat in it. He wondered how Mrs Dougan had

31

survived a week without boiling herself to death or taking a brainstorm.

He had never cooked a fish, but he knew all about potatoes and chips and the egg and chop presented no difficulties apart from how to find room for so many pots on the cooker at once.

The small Dougan joined Micky the dog in following him round the kitchen hopefully and when he left the kitchen to look for plates the little boy stood behind the dog, which stood upright with its legs against the cooker and sniffed joyfully at the crackling chips.

When the Dougans started to arrive home from work, he had succeeded in setting the two tables in the living-room with five different designs of dishes, including the brown earthenware pint mug for Daddy's tea, and four different kinds of sauce bottles. You would think the greedy pigs drank sauce, Mrs Dougan complained, not without wry pride. There was a pile of chips drying out hard in the oven and another pile of potatoes cooling in a pot on the draining-board, and he had the chop in the frying-pan, pressing the edge of it down with a knife in an effort to smooth out Micky's toothprints.

The Dougans – he could separate them into individuals and put names to them if he tried, but he was too harassed – reacted with a noisy theatrical babble to the news of Mrs Dougan's accident, and it got louder and louder as new Dougans arrived and the early arrivals repeated the story to them. Two new Dougan children emerged from the front bedroom where they had been playing throughout the afternoon without noticing any commotion. They burrowed underfoot between Mrs Dougan's chair and the kitchen, where they stared without expression at Peter. One of them said:

'You don't live in oor house.'

'Hey, lookit the chef!' Jimmy Dougan cried. He was the same age as Peter, but he had a job as a message boy, and he was wearing a black shiny jerkin and narrow wrinkled grey jeans.

'You shut your ignorant mouth, James Dougan,' his mother called stridently from the middle of the crowd scene. 'If it wasny for Peter and his Da you would have nae tea this night, and your poor auld mother would be lyin' dead.'

'Aye, you're right, Maw. Sure, Peter's the wee boy. Hey, where did you learn to cook? Did he mind to make the mince for Da?' It was a confused chorus from several Dougans.

'You'll have to get the doctor to look at your mother,' Peter said, to cover his pleased embarrassment. Jimmy Dougan dropped to his knees beside his mother and said, 'Aye, that's right, Maw. You'll have to take care of yourself.'

'Aye, that's right, son,' said his mother. 'You'll better go and get the doctor the night.' Jimmy instantly looked evasive and said:

'Och, you'll be all right, Maw.'

Mr Dougan, who was even smaller than his wife, but thin and stringy, and who had been standing silent during the disturbance with his lips pursed over his toothless gums, barked sharply at Jimmy.

'You'll go and get the doctor when you're telt.' Jimmy looked sullen and muttered: 'Okay, Da.' Andra, the eldest son, who stood a head taller than his father, broke in,

'Och, it's just a wee burn, Da.' With the slickness of a striking cobra, Mr Dougan slapped Andra on the cheek.

'Don't interrupt your Da,' he said coldly. Andra shrugged his big shoulders, and nobody else paid any attention to the attack except Henrietta, who cried in vexation:

'Your Da shouldny hit you. It's no' right, Mr Dougan, so it's no'.' Henrietta, Peter suddenly recalled, wasn't a Dougan, but merely Andra's wife. Mr Dougan ignored her, and Andra threw her a glance that begged her to shut up.

Mr Dougan cut short the babble by ordering everybody to sit down and start their tea, and Peter went to the kitchen to ponder on how to serve it. Cooking was easy enough, but he had never felt capable of dividing food on to plates. It was only after a sharp order from Mr Dougan that any help was offered to him. Jimmy and Veronica came into the kitchen and started to shovel food on to plates with their hands.

'Hey, that's nearly as much chips as the old lady makes,' Jimmy said admiringly. Veronica added, 'Aye, you'll make somebody a rare wife, Peter,' and gave him a seductive sidelong glance that brought the blood rushing to his face.

'This'll dae for the weans,' Jimmy said, heaping chips on a single plate. 'They can feed the dog as well – Micky's daft about chips and mayonnaise, aren't you, my wee son?' Micky flailed his tail, stood up with his forepaws on the kitchen table and craned his ferrety face towards the chips.

The Dougans loudly pressed Peter to sit down and have his tea with them, and he refused firmly until Mr Dougan cut the noise short and ordered him to sit down. Peter barely prevented himself from declaring that he was only sitting down because he didn't want a leathering from Da. Jimmy, who had been noisiest in his invitations, went sullen again when Mr Dougan ordered him to give his chair to Peter, because there wasn't a chair to spare, and Jimmy spent the meal leaning over the back of Peter's chair to eat his chips. Spam, chutney, tomato sauce and Worcester sauce. Somebody praised the strength of the tea.

'It's a wonder to me how Peter got it made in time,' Mrs Dougan called from her chair. 'That gas is terrible slow.'

'Oh, there was good hot water in the tap,' Peter explained. 'It was practically on the boil when I put it in the kettle.'

From the other table, jammed into the bay window, Ria Dougan uttered a terrible wail.

'An' I've went and drunk mine! We'll get lead poisonin'.'

Consternation burst upon the Dougans. Mr Dougan paused with his pint mug half-way to his lips. Peter was aghast.

'Did you never know that?' Veronica's eyes were wide

34

with horror. 'The water in the hot tap's full of lead.'

'Why?' Peter stammered. 'Is there something wrong with your tap?'

'No, no, no, you don't understand, Peter.' Joe Dougan's face was patient as if he were speaking to a backward child. '*Every* hot tap's got lead in the watter. It's the heat that biles the lead off the tank into the watter.'

'But, but . . . it's no' true!' Peter floundered to find a story that would convince them in their barbaric ignorance. 'I've studied plumbing in the science room.' The boast sounded pompous and childish and hollow.

'Aw, the school!' Jimmy Dougan's voice throbbed with sophisticated contempt. 'Shut your lip,' his father told him. 'If you had stuck in at the school it would suit you better. Let the man speak.'

'Well,' Peter swallowed. 'It's the *cold* tank that is lined with lead. Look. The cold water comes into the boiler and then flows up to the hot tank – that's all *copper*. The boiler, the tank, everything.'

'Oh, save us, watter flows *up* next,' Jimmy muttered, but almost inaudibly, with one eye on his father. A lively argument broke out: Sure the *pipes* are made of lead, or was there no lead inside the hot tank? Or maybe the cold water got lead in it but it wasn't poisonous till it got boiled in the boiler and brought the poison out? An element of doubt had entered some of the Dougan minds, but nobody was drinking tea. For a spell Peter found himself ignored while separate discussions raged at both tables, and various Dougan voices tried to translate the mysteries of Peter's theory into plain language for other Dougans. From the table at the window he heard Ria demand of somebody, 'Well even if it's copper, is *copper* no' poisonous just the same as lead? I mean, if you et copper you would die as well. Oh, shut up – did you ever eat copper? If you canny eat it, it stands to reason it must be poisonous.'

'Well,' Mrs Dougan said finally, 'it's maybe all right if you're used to that way of workin', but I like my ain system, and I've been mashin' tea for fifty years, no offence to you, Peter, son. Joe, son, just you put on the kettle for another cup, this cup of mine's cauld anyway.' Joe got up willingly. Mr Dougan sipped gently from his pint mug. He seemed to feel that his authority was obscurely challenged, and he didn't want to make any mistakes.

'I've never heard of that.' His voice still had the trace of its flat Belfast beginnings. 'If Peter here got it in a book it's maybe right enough, it would be an educated man that wrote the book. I'll look into that.'

'Ach, you get your heid filled wi' trains and rails at school,' Jimmy Dougan muttered in the respectful silence that followed Da's announcement. 'It's for the birds. Except for the holidays. When you get to be a man you should be workin'.'

Peter was conscious of Jimmy's envy and resentment and contempt, and sympathized with it.

'Oh, here, Maw,' Veronica Dougan wailed. 'Did you no' iron that black frock? I'm wearin' it tonight.'

'Aw, hen, I never minded, wi' the kettle an' the bilin' water an' everything,' Mrs Dougan said placidly. 'Never mind, I'll can put the board across my knee after.'

'You'll do nothing of the kind,' Mr Dougan said coldly. 'She'll iron it her bloody self or she'll go jiggin' without.'

Tears sprang to Veronica's eyes.

'What do I know about ironin'?' she cried. 'I'll just ruin it.' Henrietta offered to iron it for her, and Veronica fell on Henrietta with cries of gratitude and love.

'She'll iron it herself!' the old man barked, and Henrietta's face set aggressively, while Andra her husband tried to catch her eye with a pleading expression, and Veronica burst into passionate weeping. Whether Henrietta would have made a frontal attack on the Da's tyranny Peter didn't discover, for there was a knock at the front door and the family sat silent and grateful for the interruption while Jimmy went to answer it. He came back grinning and said to Peter:

36

'Here, you've got a visitor, Peter, it's your lumber, they've sent her in from next door.' To his alarm Peter saw Lily coming into the living-room behind him. She had one hand stuck in the pocket of a camel coat, and a badminton racket swung from the other. Veronica ran over her with greedy eyes pricing everything. Lily returned a hard stare. Without rising, Mr Dougan ordered Joe to give the young lady his chair, but somehow Peter succeeded in getting up and getting out with Lily. They stood together at his gate.

'You said half-past six,' Lily said. 'I got cheesed off waiting.'

'All right,' said Peter. 'Wait a minute and I'll get a coat and shoes. You don't seem to realize that I've been the hero of a great disaster.'

'Ha ha ha,' Lily said huffily. 'If you're not polite enough to keep a date, I can always go myself.'

It was a shame to see an infantile pout on so pretty a face.

'Don't talk banal, Lily,' Peter said brutally. 'You're too good-looking for that kind of patter.'

'What's that supposed to mean?'

'Just shut up and wait here till I get a coat and shoes, that's all.'

'I'm freezing.'

'Well, I'll cuddle you later, not now.'

Lily was seething as he left her and abruptly went into the house. It could have only been his little sister Julie who had sent her to find him at the Dougans'. Julie was looking at him with a self-satisfied smirk as he raked about in the kitchen for his sand shoes, and he told her she was an evil little changeling. His father automatically muttered that he wouldn't have that kind of language in this house.

Stamping her feet at the gate, Lily was thinking hard to boil up some perfect squelch for Peter. She had reason to feel aggrieved. For months she had known that he spent the maths period staring at her like a sick calf.

Maisie Corbett, who sat beside her in maths and shared giggles, could see Peter with a hand mirror and keep her posted about the duration of his stares. It had only been an act of kindness, after all, to let him come to the badminton club with her, and now instead of staring at her and giving her something to giggle about, he was trying to be funny. Being a girl who was accustomed to obeying her impulses, she thought of obeying the impulse to walk away and abandon Peter, but she still remembered her earlier impulse to turn up with a new boy friend for badminton, and this one proved stronger.

She was still anxious to punish Peter, however, and when he came out again she was ready to begin without preliminary.

'Do you know what Maisie and I call you?' she demanded. 'Peter the Haddock.'

'Oh? Oh, very finny.' Peter was still riding on the crest of his new trouble-shooter personality. Lily giggled and said that she thought it was very funny too.

'Finny, not funny,' Peter coached her. 'Finny, fish, Haddock, see? If you're going to make a joke you have to cover all the angles. You can tell Maisie that one on Monday and have a good yell.'

At the same time as he was cynically reflecting that Lily would never be anything more than a laughing doll, well suited to Davie McAllister, Peter was still hopeful that they might be seen by somebody he knew. She had the looks. She would be wonderful if you were stone deaf, he thought. Cuddly and nice to look at. But not in the same class as Jeannie-Peenie, naturally. Jeannie-Peenie, Jeannie-Peenie, you're fabulous. Dear Jeannie-Peenie, I adore you, especially your feet, I must dig up a bit of ground you've trod on and worship it some time. Ah, *si Jeannie savait*. Jeannie has a brain, too, how is it possible for anybody like Jean to exist?

Peter had a rigid rule that the ideal woman must be intelligent as well as beautiful. It never occurred to him to question the fact that Jean Pynne was intelligent. She had spoken to him and listened to him, and that was enough. And none of his reflections on Jean, and on Lily, diminished his pleasure in walking beside Lily with her curls blowing and her turned-up nose turning up. It turned up quite a bit. She'll probably look like a monkey when she's old, but that won't be this week.

'You're awful quiet,' she said peevishly.

'I have a tragic secret on my soul, that's why. A secret that no other human being may share.'

'Och, you're a nut,' she complained. 'What tragic secret?'

'Oh, my great-grandfather was a dogfish, or something.'

'You're absolutely daft.' She giggled.

The badminton club was in a church hall, and Peter looked around suspiciously in case anybody looked like asking him to sing a hymn. When he mentioned this, Lily assured him that Mr Garside, the minister, was a nice jolly man who only looked in to say hallo and sometimes have a game, and at this Peter felt even more trapped and wary. The only people he knew were Big Joe Chadwick and Alastair Rule, who was sometimes known as the Stool. Everybody else knew everybody else, and their conversation was all light-hearted talk about one another and other people whom Peter didn't know either. He became convinced that the evening was going to turn out drably, and his mind was made up when Lily, looking cute in white ankle socks, made him look foolish in his first attempt at badminton.

'What's that, thirty-love?' he asked, and a beefy youth sitting on a bench at the side and wearing shorts cried disgustedly, 'Two-nil. It's not tennis. You play till somebody's got twenty-one.'

'Oh. Like ping-pong.'

'Oh, *ping-pong*!' the beefy youth shouted, making it sound like a perversion, and Lily wrinkled her nose and said, 'It's table tennis.'

'You can play table tennis,' Peter remarked icily to the

39

beefy youth. 'It's still ping-pong.' He kept on staring after he had spoken, and the beefy youth stared back. Peter realized that he was being childish, but he couldn't think of a way out, and he decided he disliked the beefy one anyway.

He had already decided that the evening would produce no joy, and he was apathetic when Big Joe offered to play with Lily, and she left him sitting alone watching. Some of the other people seemed disposed to be friendly, but to his disgust he was cornered by Alastair Rule, one of the few people in his class who sickened him without reservation. Alastair was flabby without being fat, but his hips were broad and bulging like a middle-aged woman's, and he had small hands, and minced when he walked. When he talked, his little mouth went out in a little sneering pout.

'I see you're improving your company,' he sneered chummily. Peter had the feeling that he was trying to snuggle up, like an importunate slug.

'It's suddenly started deteriorating again,' he said unkindly, but no unkindness registered on Stoolie, who went straight on:

'I never expected to see you in church.'

'I came to play badminton,' Peter said, his hackles rising.

'But you're in the house of God, all the same,' Stoolie said complacently.

'What are you trying to do?' Peter demanded. 'Give me the boak?'

'Oh, it's easy to scoff,' Stoolie intoned, with a trace of sulkiness. He was, Peter realized, giving some kind of imitation of the absent Mr Garside or some other parson, and Peter found the spectacle obscene.

'We have a youth meeting on Sunday evenings,' Stoolie said. 'There's often a good argument – that would suit you, with your funny ideas.'

'What's the use of arguing?' Peter asked, 'with a bunch of Bible-thumpers? Nobody could ever teach that crowd

40

anything. They've got prejudices like . . . like God knows what.'

'Remember where you are!' Stoolie said snappishly. 'Oh, you've got no prejudices, of course, you know everything, high and mighty. You don't know how many people there are like you that found out they were wrong.'

'Ah, death-bed repentances,' Peter said disgustedly. 'Just chuck it, I came to play badminton, that's all.'

'That's right, change the subject,' Stoolie said triumphantly.

'Okay, okay.' Peter was conscious of a thousand great thoughts hiding somewhere in his mind that would demolish Stoolie's fatuous piety, but none of them would come to him. He sat trying not to glower as Lily danced back and forward laughing merrily to Big Joe, who was as good at badminton as he was at everything else. Well-co-ordinated sod, Peter thought, but without dislike. Big Joe was so satisfied with himself that it was impossible not to like him. The evening passed, Peter was relieved to find, without a visit from the sanctimonious Mr Garside and his jolly Christianity. When Lily picked up her coat, Joe was still there, and Peter said:

'Will we go to the café, if I've got any money?'

'Sure thing,' Lily said, but Big Joe protested.

'Think I'm a goosegog? You came with her, you can buy her an iced drink.' Big Joe had certain fixed rules of social behaviour.

'We're only going to the café,' Peter said. 'You can buy your own iced drink.' There was some satisfaction in making it clear that he wasn't worried about his proprietary rights over Lily, and he was nettled to see that she wasn't worried either. There was a crowd of the crowd at the café, and the three of them squeezed in at a table that already included Davie McAllister. He raised his eyebrows and exchanged a secret glance with Peter at the sight of Lily, and then grinned at Lily stupidly.

'Hey,' he said to Peter, 'you'll never guess who's here.'

41

'Who?'

'Oh, just somebody and her boy friend.'

'Cease thy senile stutterings,' Peter said uncomfortably, and when Davie started to dig an elbow into his ribs and mutter, 'There, quick, she's leaving!' he shoved the elbow away and cried desist.

'Quick, you'll miss her,' Davie said desperately. Peter turned his head, grumbling, and saw somebody holding the door open for Jean Pynne. He couldn't see what she was wearing. His eyes at once focused right down to a point on the side of her face, and something leapt inside his chest. She turned her head just before she vanished, and smiled to him, but she was gone before his hand could come up to wave.

'Did you see that?' Davie was stunned. 'She *blushed*. Hey,' he muttered under his breath, 'was it the truth, right enough? Come on.' He dug Peter viciously in the ribs again, unconscious of anybody's presence. Peter kicked him under the table on the usual ankle bone, and Davie cried indignantly, 'What is it? Oh.'

'You can have a real expensive drink, Lily,' Peter said. 'Absolutely anything you like up to one-and-six. Everybody else pays.'

42

4

Even in the English class, which always had more entertainment value than the maths class, Peter's mind tended to wander. It always had wandered slightly. From his seat he could see a third-floor kitchen window in the gable-end of the tenement that bordered one end of the school playground, and he had a habit of staring up at it as a prisoner stares at a thin glimpse of ordinary, free life from his cell window. Sometimes the woman in the kitchen would look down and wave sympathetically to him, and he had a practised gesture of raising a hand to pat his hair which allowed him to wave back without stirring Gutty Greer's suspicion.

Now it was worse. Since the night of the school dance he had kept staring up at the window, but with his eyes out of focus while he thought about Jean Pynne. His domination over Davie McAllister was total from the moment Jean blushed at him in the café, but Peter had no illusions about his standing with Jean, he just liked to think about her.

'. . . and out of his visible cerebral activity, Haddow will now give us another example of the misrelated participle,' Gutty was saying. Where Davie would have started to attention and given the show away, Peter subtly kept staring up at the window and narrowed his eyes; a very smooth performance, he considered.

'Bolting out of a doorway, a tramcar knocked me down, sir.'

Gutty leaned back, balanced his paunch and nodded his head like a jointed doll.

'One can hm hardly blame it.' He twitched his thick lips

43

to let the class know it could now titter, which everybody did; except for Tom Arthur, who was sitting in front of Peter. Tom Arthur guffawed.

'One imagines, Haddow,' Gutty went on, 'that your mind was mhm still in the empyrean. You are, mhm, entirely with us?'

Peter made a show of examining and counting his limbs and said, 'Everything seems to be here, sir.' Gutty twitched his lips again to signal for a fresh titter, but Tom Arthur turned and said, 'Aw, very funny!'

Gutty balanced himself back and forward. He was tall and tubby, and apart from his flat nose, he looked rather like the picture of Doctor Samuel Johnson at the beginning of Boswell's *Life*. But his hair was cut short, and there was a perfectly circular bald patch right at the top. He had a habit of standing with his left hand in his trouser pocket jingling his change while his right hand, palm down, rubbed round and round the bald patch.

'I wonder, um, Haddow,' he said, 'what in heaven's name you're going to make of yourself.' His trick of keeping his lips quite still and pouring the words out through the middle was widely held to be the result of twenty years' training in stir.

'The best I can, sir,' Peter said, 'with the material available.' Tom Arthur turned to Peter and groaned, 'Oh, you're killing me!'

'You seem to be upsetting Arthur, Haddow,' Gutty said, and Peter answered, 'I don't think he likes my jokes, sir.'

'Jokes!' Tom Arthur made the word filthy.

'Ah, be warned, Haddow,' Gutty said chummily. 'The fate of the um humorist is to live out his um ways among people who don't like his mhm jokes. You must consider the teaching profession, boy. Everybody laughs at teachers' jokes.'

Everybody in the class groaned, and Gutty gave a short bow of appreciation. Later he settled his gowned bulk on a corner of Peter's desk and murmured, 'What *are* you planning to mhm make of yourself, Haddow? Time's winged chariot is going like the mhm hammers of mhm hell now, you know, boy.'

'I don't know,' Peter said uncomfortably. 'Miss Cumberland's got me half-persuaded into science.'

'Um, the new men, Haddow. Read C. P. Snow. Write it down, boy. There's lolly in making squibs. C. P. Snow, write it down, you'll get him in the library. Frighten yourself to death. Opposite end of the shelf from Havelock Ellis.'

'Havelock Ellis?'

'Never mind, only get you mhm confused. A bit of a bore, old Ellis.'

'I didn't find him boring, sir,' Peter said innocently, and Gutty twitched.

'Matter of endocrinology, boy. You've got mhm glands instead of taste. Only natural, only natural, control, control.'

'Naturally.'

'You're a dangerous man, Haddow. Gallow's meat, boy, Gallow's meat.'

'Good-oh.'

Tom Arthur was ostentatiously fidgeting, and when Gutty ballooned away he turned round with his jaws clenched and muttered, 'Oh, helluva funny. Bloody sook.' Peter gave him a nauseated look and bent his head. He had been disturbed in the act of picturing Jean Pynne. The penalty of being at school was the number of interruptions and they couldn't be evaded. Gutty and teachers in general, and incidents like Tom Arthur, who had always been chummy in his glowering style but had suddenly conceived a murderous hatred of Peter. There was no visible reason for it, but it was there all the time, on the fringe of Peter's mind while he pictured himself in a white laboratory coat, looking intellectual and confident. There was somebody else there, a girl also in a white lab coat, with her hands stuck deep into the pockets and her hair shining against a frosted-glass window. Slim and clever, but respectful.

45

Comradely, though, affectionate. Who was it, Jean Pynne? He couldn't make up his mind. He washed the picture out and stared again. The feeling of the school building round him was oppressive. He felt a hunger to be old, thirty, no twenty-four, on his own with money.

Money was the biggest trouble of all. How could you get to know somebody like Jean if you had no money? She had a job, she knew people with pounds to spend, maybe even with cars. He hated them all: all people with money and a lot of suits and cars, who could do anything and didn't have exams to pass.

At four o'clock he walked to the Public Library with Davie, to look for C. P. Snow and Havelock Ellis. Davie was apathetic until Peter suggested that Ellis was probably kept in the basement for special customers.

'Is it dirty?' Davie asked eagerly. 'I'll bet old Gutty's got a filthy mind.'

'Tuts tuts, boy, you find filth everywhere you look,' Peter chastened him. 'There's no sign of it anyway.'

Davie had gone automatically to the file copy of the *Autocar*. 'This is what you need to do Jeannie-Peenie in style,' he whispered. 'A Porsche. No, a Merc, it's got more style. A 300 SL.'

'No, that,' Peter said, pointing to a caravan. 'Wired for hi-fi.'

Davie was growing restive at the lack of developments in Peter's affair with Jean Pynne. 'When are you seeing her again?' he demanded, still in a whisper, and Peter shrugged.

'You're useless!' Davie grated at him. 'Talk, talk, talk. What's up with you? She likes you, doesn't she?'

'Well . . .'

'She must, unless you made everything up. If you did I'll kill you.'

'Right.'

'Phone her up, make a date.'

'Where?'

46

'She must have a phone where she works.'

It wasn't unlike a conversation in Wee Aikie's class, apart from the absence of such distractions as Lily Enterkin and Alice Jackson. They spoke with their heads bent over magazines and without moving their lips. From time to time a librarian at the counter in the corner looked up vaguely disturbed by the faint buzz and jealous for his silence.

'I don't know where she works.'

'She works somewhere in Hope Street.'

'That's a big help.'

'Well, find out!' Davie's voice loudened in exhortation, and the librarian stared hard at them across the reading-room.

'Christine knows her, ask Christine,' Davie muttered.

'Not on your life. And don't you mention it to Christine, blabbermouth.'

'You might as well forget the whole thing, you'll never get the guts to do anything about it.'

'Silence, vassal.'

But his inactivity was irking Peter himself. The brief conversation he had had with Jean Pynne and the briefer kiss were becoming overlaid with recollection and project-ing and imagined developments until it was hard to be sure they had ever happened at all. He had gone over his meeting with her so often that he had worn it out.

He knew he could never have the gall to phone her with-out provocation, but the prospect of arranging something more accidental appealed to him and quickened his excite-ment without exposing him to any outright danger of going too far.

He interrogated Davie on where Jean worked, and demanded to know how Davie knew. Davie didn't know how he knew, he just knew. Jean Pynne was the kind of person people knew things about, and remembered them. Peter was suddenly jealous of everybody. Until a few days ago Jean had just been a girl in Whiteknowes, a perfectly sensational girl but just a girl, and he had never considered the fact that a whole lot of people, ordinary people like Davie, might know things about her that he had never heard. There must be people in her office too, who knew things like when she went for lunch, and whether she took sugar in her tea. Ordinary dull people who hardly existed, but who saw her every day. It was hurtful to think about it.

He finally decided that the cleverest thing to do was to meet her accidentally on her way home. He could wait near the bus stop and hail her with glad surprise. Or maybe just with surprise, and not too much surprise, or it would look obvious.

'Well, don't forget to ask her where she works,' Davie insisted. 'Then you'll be able to phone her any time.'

'Take it easy, Superman,' Peter said, 'I'm young, time is on my side.'

'Aw, hurry it up. I think you've crapped it.'

An even cleverer idea would be to watch the buses at about half past five as they passed the corner of Faroe Street. Then, when he saw her on one, he could race across the waste ground and catch it at the next stop, and get right on the bus with her.

'Oh, God, *that'll* not look suspicious, spending thruppence to travel two stops,' Davie cried.

'I'll not let her see me till she's getting off,' Peter explained.

'I don't believe you'll do anything. If it was me I would do something.'

'Don't get above yourself, bub, Lily Enterkin's your stretch.'

'What's up wi' Lily Enterkin?'

'She's quite an amusing cretin, for short periods,' Peter sniggered. 'Alice Jackson's a better cuddle, I can tell you.'

Instantly Davie fell into the trap, and was frantic.

'How do you know? Come on, tell us, or I'll punch you. I don't care if we do get flung out. How do you know?'

Davie was in murderous earnest, and Peter was over-come with a sniggering fit, which infected Davie without diminishing his fury. He was too easy to torment.

Peter did force himself to stand guard at the corner of Faroe Street. On the first evening he saw no sign of Jean. On the second it started to rain and he gave up in disgust. On the third outing he was practically sure he had seen her on a bus a little after six o'clock. By this time he had fallen into a dull, cold torpor with standing staring at buses, and had forgotten everything he had planned to say when he met her. He raced across the waste ground stumbling on its uneven surface in the dark and barely caught the bus at the next stop, slumped on a seat near the door, downstairs, and panted.

His morale was assisted by the reflection that he was committed to spending thruppence on what might after all be a wild goose chase. But two stops later, when he stood on the platform listening to passengers coming down the staircase, he knew by the prickling in the small of his back that Jeannie-Peenie was indeed there. He got off the bus and stood in abstraction for a moment, looking round as if deep in thought, and she stepped straight into him.

'Oh, hallo,' he said. 'Were you on that bus? I didn't notice you.'

'Neither did I.'

'Going my way again?' Peter swallowed and tried to stop showing his teeth, and Jean said, 'A bit of it.' That was right, she would branch off just about halfway, but she could hardly stop him from branching off with her. The distance was only three hundred yards altogether, and it seemed pitifully short. Then somebody touched Peter's arm, and Veronica Dougan said, 'Oh, it's Peter, I thought I recognized your back.'

'Oh,' said Peter, limp with shock. 'Oh. Oh, hallo. This is Jean Pynne, Veronica Dougan. We live next door to each other.'

49

'Well,' Veronica said briskly, 'where does everybody go? You'll can give me a butty, Peter.'

'Oh, everybody goes thisaway,' Peter said feebly, and they started walking together. 'When a gentleman is escorting two ladies,' Peter said, 'should he walk in the middle or on the outside? Answer, No, the ladies should walk in the middle.'

Veronica said huh? and Jean gave a little snort of amusement which Peter found delicious.

'How's your mother, Veronica?'

'Aw, all right, still moanin'. Here, she thinks you're the mostest, but. Never done talkin' about that boy Peter Haddow, you're the old wife's pin-up all right. You can come in and make the tea any night, it's the red carpet for you, boy. Do you live about here as well?' she suddenly asked Jean.

'Round the next corner.'

'Never seen you, but of course I never see anything but the jiggin', if you believe my Da. Where do you work?'

'Whittingham George,' Jean said, and the name engraved itself on his brain in letters of orange fire. 'They make bolts.'

'Oh, a factory.'

'No, the factory's in Sheffield,' Jean said. 'It's just a branch office.'

'I never could stick that, an office,' Veronica prattled on. 'More interestin', in a shop. Of course it's murder on the old dogs sometimes, but you do see life.'

They had already reached the corner, and Veronica went straight on talking, 'Oh, this is your corner, well, cheerio. Nice to have made your acquaintance.'

Peter, with his teeth on edge, said, 'I'll be seeing you,' and Jean said what sounded like M before she turned away. She was quite calm, and almost friendly, he thought.

'Is that a friend of yours? She's a smashing looking girl,' Veronica said. 'Classy Chassis. She looks quite nice.'

'Oh, Christine knows her,' Peter said.

'Oh, I just wondered for a minute if you were kind of keen, trust me to barge in between youse, but that's not the one that you went out with the other night, is it? She was quite nice as well, a bit toffee-nosed, though, no offence.'

'No, no, no offence.'

'I don't think you're very interested in girls, are you, Peter?'

'Oh, I don't know.'

'Oh, I bet you're a dark horse all right. You never go to the dancin', do you?'

'No.'

'No, I canny picture you, somehow. A lot a girls would go for your type, though. The strong silent type.'

Peter hooted with laughter, and Veronica said:

'Well, you know what I mean, you haveny got the usual patter. Mind you, I bet you could talk if you were wound up. Crrk crrk.' She turned an imaginary key in Peter's back.

'I would be surprised,' he said.

'I bet you think I'm a terrible blether.'

'No, no.'

'Sure I am. You grow up among the Dougans, you got to keep talkin' or you never get a word in edgewise. Everybody shoutin' and Da barkin' like a fox terrier.'

'He's a pretty tough hombre,' Peter agreed.

'The great dictator,' Veronica remarked airily. 'It must be nice to live in a wee family like yours, no screaming matches every five minutes.'

'Oh, we have our moments,' Peter protested.

'Aw, you've got a nice family. You should hear the old lady when she gets going about the Haddows. Honest, the sun rises and sets on you and your Da. You're the greatest.'

They had reached the Dougans' gate.

'Well, your old lady's the greatest as well,' Peter said. 'She cooks your tea *every* night. God.'

'I bet that put you off cooking for life.' Veronica laughed. She showed no eagerness to go in.

'No, no,' Peter said. 'Just call on me any time you're hungry.'

'Boy, are you asking for trouble?'

'Yes, usually.'

'Oho?' Her expression became heavily speculative. 'People that asks for trouble sometimes gits it, pardner.'

'I believe you. Well, cheerio, Veronica.'

'Cheerio, Peter.' She laughed at him as if in some way she had exposed him. Peter went into the house muttering 'Whittingham George, Whittingham George,' his skull vibrating with the sound of Veronica's voice.

5

Peter and Big Joe Chadwick were in Davie McAllister's front room holding a post-mortem on Davie's birthday party. Mrs McAllister brought in a plateful of cakes that had survived the party and told them to finish them. Davie was a pampered only child, and the front room had no regular use except as his study. His father had even made him a desk to make homework easy for him. Davie usually did it in an armchair with his legs over one arm and his books on his knees. Peter was collapsed in the other armchair and Big Joe was pasted along the couch.

'I must be getting greedy,' Big Joe sighed dreamily. 'I could have gobbled up that whole roomful of women myself. If I ever have a party I'll just invite six women and nobody else.'

'And then go up with the spring blind?' Peter enquired. Big Joe stretched his beef complacently. 'Anyway, look at these sultans,' he said.

'They don't have all their wives at once,' Peter said.

'How do you know?' Joe asked truculently. 'They've got drugs to keep them keen.'

'Aphrodisiacs.'

'I wouldn't need any,' Joe grunted. 'I must have had them in my bloodstream when I was born. Did you know they used to have stud farms for slaves in ancient Rome? What a life! Imagine being a prize stallion.'

'Of course,' Peter said, 'they only lasted about six months. Then Phfft! the knacker's yard.'

'That's ridiculous!' Big Joe's manhood was affronted. 'Anyway,' he added, 'what a death.'

53

'One crowded hour of glorious life,' Davie said through a French cake.

'I bet it was lousy,' Peter said. 'Thousands of big fat middle-aged Tally dames, with smelly feet.' Davie turned on him with tight-lipped rage. 'You always have to sicken us,' he said.

'Well, do you think they looked like Alice Jackson?' Davie waggled his head and gave a mollified grunt.

'I don't think much of your Lily,' Joe said, and Peter said, 'She's not my Lily.'

'She's useless, anyway,' Joe said. 'She looks all right, but you would think she was frightened she'd crack.'

'That's right,' Peter agreed. 'Like cuddling a paper parcel stuffed wi' china cups. Alice is better. Alice is co-operative.' Davie reacted on cue.

'Don't try to give us that stuff, Haddow,' he said, furious. 'You never tried anything funny with Alice. By God, if you did I'll kill you.'

'Of course I never tried anything funny. But what are you supposed to do when you're lying at the back of the couch in the dark and she rolls on top of you and starts to bite?'

'Aye, that's right,' Joe said thoughtfully, carefully not looking at Davie. 'I nearly got a big lump out of my ear.'

'Shut up, the two of you!' Davie snarled. 'Alice isn't like that,' he mumbled pathetically.

'You mean she didny bite you?' Joe asked in overdone surprise, and as Davie went white at the nostrils again he put up his arms and cowered and said, 'Honest, she never bit me, Davie, it was him, honest.' He pointed at Peter, and Davie subsided, muttering, 'Bloody funny rats.'

'I was reading about some minister,' Peter remarked, 'dripping about teenage immorality. You notice they never tell you where to get it.'

'Oh, you can get it,' Davie said mysteriously.

'Where?'

'Cathie Martin.'

54

Peter and Big Joe groaned, and Davie blustered in self-defence, 'I never said I *liked* her.'

'I dodged her all night,' Joe complained.

'She's got square hips,' Peter said.

'Well, what about it?' Davie demanded doggedly. 'She's mustard. She lets you do anything.'

'Sounds ghawstly,' Peter said.

'Curse my horrible British luck,' said Big Joe, and when Peter wrinkled his face in protest, Joe went on, 'Well, you don't have to look at her in the dark. How far did you get, Davie?'

'You can bloody find out yourself, if you think she's so horrible.' Davie was huffy.

'You're both suffering from satyriasis,' Peter pronounced.

'Well, so are you, whatever it is,' Davie retorted irritably, 'only you kid on you're bloody superior.'

'I'm just an ordinary sex-maniac,' Peter said. 'Anyway, I thought we were going to pool the English and French. I'll scribble a translation and you can look up the hard words in jolly Macaulay. And for God's sake just look up the hard words. We all know what "the" means.'

'Aw, very funny. Just write the French so's I can read it, the last time I got *puis* as *peur*. Curly knew it was cribbed.'

'I'll print it,' said Peter, 'and include a few mistakes.'

'Never mind that!' Davie cried hotly. 'You do it right and I'll put in my own mistakes. I know the kind of mistakes I make.'

Big Joe, with the English and French homework comfortably behind him, munched a fruit-cake and closed his eyes.

'I just thought of the most horrible experience in the world,' he said dreamily. Peter and Davie carried on scribbling. 'You've married this big beautiful blonde, ooh, sensational, big bulgers, big thick luscious lips . . .'

Peter said uhuh and kept on scribbling, but Davie, who could only do one thing at a time, laid down the dictionary and exhorted Joe to hurry up.

'. . . well, you go on your honeymoon to this posh hotel suite, and she goes into the bathroom to change.'

'Hurry up!' Davie complained.

'. . . well . . .' Joe sat up to live out the exciting bit. 'Well, you tear off your clothes in two seconds, and you're dancing round the room bollock-naked – to get loosened up – and she comes to the bathroom door in a white nightie . . .' he stared at Davie to see if he had his audience, and he had. Davie waved in a fury of impatience.

'Well, she looks at you for a minute and then screams, "You dirty beast! . . ."'

Davie covered his eyes and curled up in horror, sniggering.

'No, I've got a worse one than that,' Peter said, and Davie cried, 'Oh, you've always got a worse one.'

'Okay.' Peter shrugged his shoulders and carried on scribbling, and Davie spoke to him in a low scream. 'Well, *tell* us!'

'Oh, all right. You're sitting having dinner on the terrace of this same hotel – on the Mediterranean, Perpignan or somewhere. *Filet mignon, crêpes Suzette*, champagne or Chambertin or something like that . . .'

'I don't think that's as horrible as mine,' Joe said. 'Now you tell one, Davie.'

'. . . so after waiting for Chadwick to close his illiterate trap, you notice a stupendous dame at the next table, *alone*. Low-cut gown and so on.'

'Ach, it's the same story,' Joe grumbled.

'. . . and you lift your glass and waggle it at her to drink a toast, so she does, and then she invites you to come home with her to her villa because there's nobody else at home.'

'And you wake up and it was all a horrible dream,' Davie said disgustedly.

'Shut up. So you say you'll be charmed, and you stand up to pull out her chair, and then she stands up. And suddenly you notice she's only got one leg. *In the middle.*'

Big Joe went white.

'I hate that,' he said. 'It's not horrible, it's nasty. You

must be a pervie to think up anything like that. Waugh!' Davie screwed up his face and made a little staccato whining noise. Peter complacently resumed scribbling.

'Hey, Haddow,' Davie said aggressively after a few minutes. 'What about Jeannie-Peenie? I bet you never did anything.'

'You *must* be a liar about Jeannie-Peenie,' Big Joe coaxed Peter. 'It stands to reason. How could anybody like Jeannie-Peenie be interested in a school-kid? It's not as if you were big and handsome, like me,' he added reasonably.

'How dare you mention Jeannie-Peenie's name in this foul company.'

'Aw, chuck it,' said Davie. 'So you never tried to make a date with her?'

'Tomorrow night,' Peter said coldly, and watched Davie out of the corner of his eye, without pausing over the French exercise. 'And never mind asking where, because there are Some Things . . .'

'A gentleman doesn't discuss!' they chorused. 'Rotten, lucky, pig,' Big Joe added feelingly.

There was no connexion between Jeannie-Peenie and sex, as discussed in good filthy male company. The two things were totally unrelated in Peter's mind. He took Jean to the pictures, at Anniesland, in order to avoid meeting anybody he knew. He was careful not to look like going anywhere near the back row. But when the lights went down she put her hand in his and he watched a Technicolor blur. When he felt their two hands growing damp with sweat, he took out his clean hankie and put it between them, and she gave his hand a squeeze in acknowledgement. He was careful to squeeze back only once.

His whole consciousness was concentrated on the small area of skin where his fingers touched hers. From time to time he found himself forced to take deep, long breaths, and once she looked round at him in concern. He smiled back at her.

Afterwards they went to a café, also at Anniesland, and

57

he scanned the faces fearfully for a sign of Davie or Big Joe, or anybody.

'I'll pay for the coffees,' Jean said.

'It's all right, I've paid for them.'

'Oh. Well, I'll pay for my share of the pictures.'

'All right.'

She laughed happily.

'I'm glad we didn't have to argue about it.'

'Our first argument! Dawling,' he said, 'we've just avoided our first quarrel. Anyway, I have to pay it back to Christine, so this'll make it quicker. What's wrong, are you angry because I borrowed money to take you out?'

'No, it's just that not many people would admit it straight out.'

'Huh. Money. Money's so unimportant it's no use being dishonest. When I met you coming off the bus, it wasn't an accident at all. I arranged it.'

'Oh?'

'And the other twice as well. I got the name of the place where you worked and waited till I saw you coming out and then slipped into the bus queue at your back.'

'I knew that.' She laughed again.

'Were you mad?'

'What for?'

'Well, it might have been a nuisance.'

'Yes, terrible.' She laughed again.

'I couldn't work up the nerve to ask you out. And then the last time, I was sure that Dougan dame was on to us again, I thought I would never have a chance to talk to you. I think that's everything I've got on my conscience at the moment. I have confessed all.'

'Good. Now there are no secrets between us.'

While Peter was boggling at the impossibility of ever beginning to display to Jean what she was in his eyes, Jean was alert to the point of strain. While Peter had been dreaming about her, she had not been serene and indifferent as he took it for granted she must be. Their curious conversation,

58

and their curious kiss, on the evening of the dance, had left her with a feeling of shyness and discomfort. She, too, had thought of many more interesting things she might have said to him. Peter saw her as the beautiful, the fabulous, the finished Jeannie-Peenie, but Jean's view of herself was different. She would have gladly dismissed him from her memory but for the feeling that she had performed inadequately in his presence. It would have shocked Peter to know that she was unwillingly interested in him and wary of him because of what she felt was a superior intellect.

The superior intellect was pushing grains of brown sugar about on the tablecloth and muttering eenie-meenie-manniemoe. One of his thumb-nails was dirty, he noticed, and he tucked the thumb into his palm and flushed.

'I suppose it's a bit tame for you,' he said, forcing himself to grin, 'going out with a schoolboy.'

'But I'm only nineteen,' she protested seriously.

'Huh. I'm only seventeen.'

'Well.'

'Aw, you know. You must know a lot of people, with three or four good suits, and sports cars. Grey flannel suits.'

Jean, beginning gratefully to relax, giggled and said, 'No such luck.'

'I'm glad. A girl like you has to be careful, you know. Men are beasts. They're not thinking of love and marriage when you go together in a horseless carriage.'

'Do you think we should go in case we miss the bus?' They had to take two buses to get back to Whiteknowes. Both were crowded, and they hung on straps and smiled uncomfortably at each other.

'I think I've used up all my conversation now,' Peter said, as they walked up from the bus stop.

'Don't say that, I've got none. Anyway,' she peered impishly at him, 'I don't believe you ever exhaust your conversation.'

'What is this strange power I have to sicken people with

words?' Peter cried. 'I've hardly opened my mouth all night and now you, too, Brute.'

'I'm a good listener.' She laughed and tucked her arm into his to reassure him, and he said hastily, 'You're under no obligation – to take my arm. I haven't jumped to any conclusions as a result of – as a result of the other night,' he finished miserably.

'Will I let your arm go?'

'No, no, it's all right. It's nice.'

'Well, don't get worked up about it. It never happened, we'll forget all about it. I didn't mean to embarrass you,' she added sweetly, and lifted the load of her own embarrassment clean off.

'Oh, I wasn't embarrassed, it was just that it had an inalienable effect on my corpuscles. Inalienable? Illimitable? Inexorable?'

'Tell me one thing,' he said, after a lengthy silence during which they reached Jean's gate. 'Have you got a thingmy-jig? Aw, you know. Are you *engaged*? It seems a miracle if you're not.'

'Well . . .'

'That's terrible cheek, asking a thing like that. What right have I got to start probing into your private life? Somebody should shut me up.'

'Oh, don't be daft. The answer is no. Nothing official.'

'Oh, you've got a "wee understanding"?'

'I'll clock you in a minute,' she tittered. 'Oh, it's just a steady. I don't know. He's in the army.'

'And I'm a dirty cad taking you out while he's away baring his breast to the Zulu spears.'

'Oh, Peter, you're a scream.'

'Well, I'm not a cad, deep down I'm lovable and sensitive. I'm not even taking any advantages like kissing you good night.'

'I wondered if you were.'

'Nope. It's a matter of honour.'

'Well, you know best.'

'Oh, shucks.' He put his hands on her shoulders and leaned forward and touched lips slowly and lightly.

'Oh, oh,' he whispered, 'I meant to tell you all the time I was talking to you, you've got two wee lines, vertical lines, just between your eyebrows. I think they're very nice and I'll start talking again in a minute. I'd better go away while my luck is still good.'

'All right. Good night.'

'Good night. Oh.'

Jean turned back. Peter was standing at the gate like an anxious pup.

'Is it all right with you if I see you again even although you've got a steady giving his all in defence of freedom in the Queen's uniform?'

'All right. When?'

'Next Friday!'

'Is that not too soon? You still owe Christine money.'

'It doesn't matter, honestly.'

'Well, can I pay?'

'Oh, yes, you can pay.'

'All right. Good night.'

6

Samuel met Auntie Sarah's husband, Bert Quinn, in a pub, and Bert, who had much respect for Samuel, pressed him to visit the Quinns at New Year.

'We never see much of you,' he said sentimentally. 'You know, we're related and that, but I can't mind the last time we seen you at the house. Here, I'll get it. Two glasses.'

'No, I'll get it.' Ten bob. Bert always got on to big whiskies. He had a wad of money in his hand. Samuel put his last ten-shilling note firmly on the bar. 'Ach, it's the women — Emily and Sarah don't pull.'

'Aye, Sarah's a hard case,' Bert admitted owlishly, squinting at the gantry in an effort to focus. 'But New Year's New Year. Bury the hatchet, sorta thing. I would really be right pleased to see you, I always enjoy your company. We'll get a good bucket, anyway, that keeps everything on an amical footin'.'

'Oh, we'll see. I'll look in if I'm still on my feet.'

'That's a date,' Bert said, solemnly insisting on shaking hands. 'You'll be on your feet all right, never seen you up nor down, Samuel.'

Emily was panic-stricken when Samuel reported the invitation. She twittered around looking for a way out.

'But what if people are coming to us?' she cried. 'You know Alec and Nan'll be coming. They always come. You know it just upsets me, going to Sarah's. I like my own house at New Year.'

'Well, Alec and Nan can come to Sarah's as well,' Samuel said testily. 'She canny eat you, she's your sister, for God's sake. This is the first Hogmanay I've had off for two years,

I'm entitled to get out somewhere. Why should we always be the ones that sit like stookies for other people to come and pester?'

'We can't go out and leave Julie,' Emily said desperately.

'Ach, to hell wi' Julie. Give her a gill of whisky and let her sleep it off.'

Julie began to dance up and down on the armchair, shouting, 'Hurray, hurray, I'm getting whisky!'

'You're getting a thick ear if you don't shut up,' said Samuel irritably. 'Damned kids. We're going and that's flat. We don't need to stay long if you don't like it.'

Emily went into the kitchen and filled the kettle, staring numbly at her sentence of death.

Peter had got into the habit of going for a walk at six in the evening. If Jean saw him from the bus she got off three stops early and they walked the rest of the way together, but separated before they came too near home. Without discussing the point, they adopted an attitude of discretion.

'The folks know about you, of course,' Jean said, and Peter looked startled. 'It's all right,' she laughed. 'They joke about it. My mother thinks it's sweet.' She didn't add that her mother endlessly sympathized with her about 'that child's schoolboy crush on you'.

'Oh. Well, that's nice,' Peter said.

'Yes,' Jean said thoughtfully. 'She keeps on saying it's sweet.'

Peter caught an overtone that perturbed him, but had no time to think about it.

'I got this for you,' he said awkwardly. 'For Christmas.'

'Oh, Peter!' Moisture welled treacherously in Jean's eyes.

'It's just a bottle of scent,' he said contemptuously, deliberately choosing the word scent instead of perfume, in order to belittle the thing as much as possible. Jean blew out a breath of pleasure.

'Oh, you're so nice. I haven't got *anything* for you, yet.'

'Don't! You don't need to get anything; I don't want

63

you to get anything! I wish I could get you thousands of things.'

'I don't want thousands of things. I've got enough.' She held the little package to her. Peter coughed.

'I was just thinking,' he began. 'What do you do at New Year? I can't imagine what we could do,' he went on morosely, 'but I just thought, if, you know, you were going out anywhere, not with your family, I mean, I might see you. Just for a wee while.'

'Oh, it's no use! We always go to the Hornes, or they come to us. We've been doing it for oh, centuries. I think the Hornes expect Archie on leave, as well.'

'And Archie is . . .?'

'Uhuh.'

'Well, that's fine,' Peter said brightly. 'Don't start apologizing. I haven't got any delusions of grandeur, you know. Come on, laugh and be happy, honestly.'

'All right.' She bared her teeth.

'Ah, me,' he said soulfully, 'I know my fate. To step gracefully into the background with a brave smile and die the Roman way. Blast this sword, it gets stuck in my toga every time I commit suicide. They don't put the stuff in these togas nowadays.'

'Don't you dare.'

'I'm not going to commit suicide, don't be daft. I've got too many exams to pass,' he added ruefully.

'I wish I *could* see you at New Year.'

'Ach, that would be no fun for Archie. No, forget it, honestly, Jean. After all, our relationship is strictly Platonic, we don't make any emotional claims on each other.' He felt that had a good sound. So did Jean, though she didn't get it.

'No.'

'Well,' Peter said, 'I'll see you *some* time.'

'All right. And thanks for the wonderful present, Peter.'

'How do you know it's wonderful? You haven't even smelled it yet.'

'I don't care, it's wonderful.'

Peter went home, determinedly not hating Archie Horne.

Samuel came home at about seven o'clock on New Year's Eve, pleasantly launched on the coming celebration by a few drinks with his mates at the gasworks.

'Sure I've to get staying up all night, Dad!' Julie shrieked at him as soon as he arrived.

'Certainly, certainly, hen, anything you say.'

'Oh, for heaven's sake,' Christine snapped, and Julie put out her tongue at her.

'I've just told her she's going straight to bed at nine o'clock,' Emily complained. 'Growing children need their sleep.'

'Ach, she's got no school, she'll make up her sleep. Let the wean hear the bells.'

'And what are the rest of you up to, if it's not an impertinence to inquire?' Samuel said genially. Peter shrugged his shoulders.

'Somebody'll have to stay here with Julie,' Emily insisted, and Christine said, 'I'm jack-easy.'

'Well, in that case,' said Emily, 'Peter can come to Sarah's with us – if we ever get to Sarah's,' she added, sniffing querulously at Samuel's breath. 'He can keep an eye on you.'

'The day I need Peter to keep an eye on me you can screw the lid down on me. Come on, bring on the steak, eggs and chips, I'll need *something* in my stomach.'

As the evening wore on, with the unnatural waiting quietness of Hogmanay, Samuel grew restless. He started jumping from his chair and pacing the room, clapping his hands together and rubbing them. Peter gathered his maths books and started reading. Christine dragged out a wool rug that had been in the making for eighteen months and put it over her knees.

'Come on, come on,' Samuel complained. 'By God, it's a long shift till midnight. Is that clock stopped?' He picked it up and shook it brutally, and Emily irritably refused to notice.

'Well!' Samuel clapped his hands together yet again. 'This is the fine-lookin' funeral. I don't know about anybody else,' he muttered, 'but I'm for a wee half. What's a funeral if you don't have a wee half?'

'Leave that bottle alone,' Emily said timidly. 'It's bad luck to open it before the bells.'

'Bad luck, hell, it's evaporating for all it's fit.' He uncorked the whisky and shot a good slug into a glass. 'Come on, Emily, you look as if you could use a half.'

'Not before the bells. And you know I hate the taste of it.'

'All right, all right, I'll put sugar in it and make a wee toddy. You're not gonny stand and watch a man drinkin' alone,' he said bleakly. 'A man drinkin' alone is the saddest thing known.'

'Strong drink is raging,' Emily said primly.

'We'll soon put a stop to that,' Samuel said, downing a mouthful. 'Let it rage where nobody can see it.'

The sound level was rising in the Dougans's as midnight approached. Samuel went to the window and stared out.

'You better switch on the telly,' he said. 'We'll never hear any bells above that racket. Come on, get something in the glasses. I suppose you want a half?' he accused Peter, who looked doubtful and said nothing. 'I don't recommend it, but you might as well have a wee taste. Just watch it, that's all, just watch it. Do you hear me?'

'Aye, okay, I'll watch it,' Peter answered.

'All right, all right, don't get shirty. You wouldny get served in a pub till you're eighteen.'

'All right, lemonade'll do.'

'Aw, have a drink and we'll not argue about it. I don't want any arguments at the New Year, let that be understood.'

'All right,' Emily interrupted. 'It's nearly time.'

They stood self-consciously with glasses in their hands. At the first stroke of midnight, Emily sank her drink in one gulp and cried, 'A Happy New . . .' and choked as the

66

whisky reached her throat. Samuel clapped her back wearily, and she spluttered and said, 'A Happy New Year, Samuel,' and burst into tears. Samuel patted her affectionately on the shoulder and said cheerfully, 'That's the stuff, have a good greet as usual. Ah, it's a sad time all the same, the New Year. Ah to hell wi' it. Good New Year, son. Good New Year, Christine.'

'I want whisky, I want whisky!' Julie piped.

'All right, *have* whisky,' said Samuel, and held his glass to her lips. Julie took a minute sip and then gasped, with her face contorted in horror. 'It's lovely! I drank whisky, tralala. Lookit me, I'm drunk.'

Emily dabbed impatiently at her eyes and tried to shake off her facile Hogmanay melancholy before her married son Alec should arrive, with his wife Nan, to first-foot the family home. But in a few minutes there was a confused hammering at the back door, and Samuel opened it to find a mob of Dougans brandishing bottles and screaming New Year greetings.

'Oh, don't let a woman in!' Emily twittered. There was a noisy discussion on the back doorstep before Joe Dougan detached himself from the squirm of bodies and stepped over the threshold.

'Aye, a Good New Year, Mr Hadda,' he bellowed. 'Sa great night for it. Here, just a minute, have some a mine.' He was swaying gently and pouring whisky over his wrist in the direction of a glass in his hand. Dougans spilled into the living-room, out-screaming one another in goodwill. Soon Peter found himself shaking hands and screaming back, and discovered that his glass was brimming over with liquid, and Veronica Dougan was standing with him, laughing inanely and yelling, 'A Happy New Year!' He held out his hand automatically, and she knocked it aside shouting, 'Don't start goin' formal on us!' and wrapped her arms round his neck and kissed him with terrible vigour.

'Come on,' she shouted in the din. 'It's New Year, anythin' goes!' and came at him again. Holding his glass in outstretched hand, Peter squeezed her with the other arm. 'Oh, we'll get you trained yet, Peter,' she bawled in his ear.

'Oh, here, this is my fiancé,' she added wildly, clutching by the hand a tall young man, so fair that he appeared to have no eyebrows above his pink-rimmed blue eyes. 'Johnny, this is Peter,' she screamed at him. 'Wish him a Happy New Year.'

Johnny meekly took Peter's hand and muttered something to him. He had the manner of a man recently clubbed senseless and hoping to escape another attack by being invisible. Beyond him, Peter noticed Joe Dougan purposefully approaching Christine, and Christine wearing an expression that dared him to lay a finger on her. Then the screaming suddenly stopped dead, and in the silence Mr Dougan's voice quietly said, 'That's right.' Mrs Dougan, her fat face fiery red and shining with perspiration, cried, 'Aye, that's better. Just before you all drive yourself dementit, I want to give Mr Haddow this wee minding for all the kindness he's did for me.' She brandished a half-bottle of whisky, and Samuel took it with reluctant delight. 'An' here's something for Peter as well,' Mrs Dougan went on aggressively. 'You've been that good to me, Peter son, and just shut up and say nothing about it.' She subsided into a mixture of laughter and sniffles. Peter was left holding a bulky rectangular package, which he tore open to expose a book about three inches thick, bound in imitation leather. The Dougans gasped in admiration. On the spine, in gilt lettering, he read, *Every Boy's Treasure House of Knowledge*.

'It's tremendous,' he stammered to Mrs Dougan, unbearably touched. The book, he could tell at a glance, was aimed at an average-to-dim child of ten, and the absurdity of it somehow moved him even more. To his horror he felt tears springing to his eyes. Veronica glanced quickly at him and patted him on the arm and shouted, 'Come on, open yours and see what's in it, Mr Haddow!' Screaming was resumed.

Peter's brother, Alec, and his wife, Nan, arrived in the middle of the Dougans, and it was half an hour before the Dougans managed to organize themselves into retreat, leaving a thick exhausted quietness behind them. Alec stood at the fireplace and chanted, 'There'll always be a Dougan . . .'

'I haven't even had a chance to kiss my father-in-law,' Nan protested with forcible prettiness, '*and* my junior boyfriend.' Peter yielded as gallantly as he could manage to her brisk embrace. 'My, my,' she said, 'I'll have to start carrying a ladder about if you don't stop growing, Peter.' Peter forced a smile. 'You must be nearly as tall as Alec,' she said in excessive surprise. 'Come on, back to back and we'll see.' Peter allowed himself to be dragged beside Alec, and slouched against him. 'No-o,' Nan said judicially, 'there's just a wee half-inch in it yet.'

Alec prodded him in the arm. 'Muscles as well,' he said affectionately.

'I don't know about muscles, except maybe in his tongue,' Samuel said. 'He's got twice as much cheek as you, I'll say that for him.'

'You're a drunken old blether,' Alec said easily. 'You were damn glad to get rid of me.' Nan tutted sharply at the bad word. Samuel clapped Alec on the arm.

'That's my boy,' he said. 'Oh, you've got my card marked all right. Come on, have a half. Ah, you were a good boy – both good boys,' he added. 'Come on, you can all come to your Auntie Sarah's.'

Nan started to stammer excuses about having to get back for the baby-sitter, but Alec interrupted amiably:

'I would rather shove my head in the gas oven. What's up, have you had a big reconciliation with my wee fat horrible auntie?'

'Ach, what's the odds,' Samuel said, 'it's New Year. Now don't you start again, Emily – I promised we would go, and we're going.'

'Well,' Alec said comfortably, 'I'll just toast for a while

69

here and then we'll get home. Does Auntie Sarah still spit blood every time she thinks about the time you threw her out when she wanted a brawl about you having a Corporation house, Dad?'

'Now that happened before you were born, so you don't know anything about it,' Emily cried excitedly, and Alec smiled sleepily and nodded his head.

'Aye, that was a humdinger,' Samuel sighed. He was sitting at the table, comfortably leaning on his elbows. 'Do you mind the time the Dougans wanted to get the polis to Peter for breaking Joe Dougan's leg? Can you imagine the Dougans? The *Dougans* getting the polis?'

'It was me that broke Joe's leg,' Alec corrected him, without heat. 'Well,' Samuel said irritably, 'it was some tomfoolery of Peter's that caused it.'

The memory rose up in Peter's mind with piercing sharpness. He had been eight at the time, and Alec would be sixteen. He had memories of long days spent trailing after Alec, who had suffered him and hardly ever chased him away. Alec always had exciting things to do. He had made a rope-ladder, and one night he took it down to Conyer Street to climb the tenement wash-houses with it. There was a crowd all frantic to try the ladder, and Joe Dougan, who was the same age as Alec, was openly disgusted because Alec insisted that Peter should have as many shots as everybody else, although he was only one of the kids.

Alec insisted calmly that wee Peter was better at climbing the ladder than Joe Dougan himself, and Joe, in a melodramatic frenzy, said that he could climb the ladder to the top of the wash-house without using his hands. He got two of the crowd to hold the bottom of the ladder out from the wall so that he could balance, and after getting up five rungs, he missed a rung with his foot and swung downwards with his other foot caught in the rope and broke his arm against the wash-house wall. It was Joe Dougan's famous disaster.

70

Later in the evening, Mrs Dougan banged thunderously on the front door, and the old man went out himself to talk to her. Peter never knew what Samuel said. He and Alec had stood in the living-room straining their ears, but they could hear only Mrs Dougan's voice shouting about the polis and her poor boy. When Samuel finally shut the front door and came into the living-room he was trembling. Without a word he slapped Alec across one cheek. The noise of it was deafening, and Emily jumped.

'Where is it?' Samuel demanded. Alec went to the back bedroom without a word and came back with the ladder. The old man took it without a word and started stuffing it into the fire.

The difficulty was that there wasn't much of a fire in the grate, and there was a lot of rope-ladder. It kept spilling out on to the hearth. Nobody said anything. Emily looked from face to face and her mouth wrinkled in apprehension and confusion. Then, Peter remembered, he had seen the old man shivering; then he realized it was laughter. Without turning his head from the fire, Samuel said:

'Well, I'll say this – you've invented a dampt fireproof rope-ladder.'

Alec, with one cheek white and the other flaming red, smiled tremulously. Emily, sizing up the situation with her usual inaccuracy, said:

'I'll go into the kitchen and get a knife to cut it up.'

Samuel ignored her. He turned to Alec with the indestructible rope-ladder and told him to get it out of the road.

'Maybe that'll teach you sense,' he mumbled, avoiding Alec's face. 'And remember that – every Dougan alive is a born idiot. D-O-U-G-A-N spells eedjit. They could commit suicide wi' – wi' a feather duster, and you would get the blame.'

'But what if they get the polis, Samuel?' Emily asked tearfully.

'The polis? The Dougans? The Dougans *voluntarily* getting the polis? There'll be ten blue moons in the sky.'

There was a lifelong coolness between the Dougans and the Haddows after that for nearly three weeks, and then Joe had to come in and show off his plaster cast to Alec, and Emily gave him chocolate biscuits to ease the pain.

'Some tomfoolery of Peter's,' Samuel insisted, wrinkling his brows to reassure himself of his recollection.

'Peter was only an infant,' Alec murmured wearily. 'I was the villain.'

'I don't remember it that way,' Samuel muttered doubtfully. Peter suddenly felt sick and exhausted.

'I'll just go to bed,' he said. 'I'm tired.'

'Oh, don't do that, son,' Emily pleaded. 'If we've *got* to go to Sarah's I'll feel better if you come.'

'And don't forget to come and see us before the holidays are finished,' Nan accused him. 'Or I'll be wondering if you're unfaithful to me. You've never bathed the baby yet.'

'Oh, that'll be great,' Peter laughed, and muttered, 'Well, nobody can say I'm not *wanted*.'

Sarah and Bert lived in a flat, two storeys up, in Maryhill Road. Its outside door was flushed with hardboard and grained to resemble limed oak, and had an outside chromium letter-box and an illuminated bell-push that actuated a vast set of cathedral chimes somewhere inside. Bert came to the door with a glass in his hand. His tubby face was slightly slack and his eyes were bloodshot. He had loosened his collar-stud and his collar stood out at both sides with the tie hanging from the ends.

'A Goonoo Year, boy!' he cried. 'Trust Samuel, good ol' sober Samuel. Goonoo year, Emily. My God, is that your boy? He's a hell of a size. Naw, it's just my knees that are foldin' up again. Come in, come in, Sarah'll be delighted.'

There were several people in the kitchen, and a babble of voices, but Peter saw his Aunt Sarah at once. She stopped in mid-sentence as the Haddows appeared, and hoisted her plump little body upright with a smile; an odd little smile, thin in the lips and seeming to contain pleasure and, obscurely, triumph as well. She hypnotized Peter. She flounced, there was no other word for it.

'Well, if it's not the bold Samuel!' (As she might have said 'So they paroled you after all!') 'Not to mention my long-lost sister. Well, welcome to the humble abode, after all these years!'

It was not exactly a welcome, but Samuel smiled blandly and said, 'I've never seen you looking so well, Sarah.' She was momentarily taken aback, and with an obvious effort she advanced and put her cheek to Samuel's and then to Emily's.

'Well,' she said, with a sharp waggle of her head, 'you're more than welcome, and that's not a word of a lie. May God strike me down dead on this spot if it's a lie.'

There was a bewildering sequence of introductions, and Peter sat down jammed beside his Cousin Joseph and a pale girl with a drooping chin and a startling size of eye-make-up in black and green.

'This is the girl friend, Margaret,' Joseph mumbled. 'My Cousin Peter. He's still at school, aren't you, Peter?'

'Uhuh.'

'Donno how you stick it.'

'Oh, it's all right.' There was nothing, absolutely nothing, that Peter could think of to extend the conversation.

'The auld boy's got a right bucket, int he?' Joseph muttered. 'There'll be a fight, any minute.'

It didn't seem likely, although the noise of voices was deafening. Most of the other people in the kitchen were towards middle age. They seemed to be discussing at the moment the terrible price of getting things done in the house, and Auntie Sarah was saying:

'Well, I know what it cost me to get this new interior fitted *and* I got it wholesale. They would take the bread out of orphans' mouths, may God strike me dead if I'm telling a lie. Of course, you've never seen our new interior, Emily,' she added with cloying sweetness. 'We may live up a tenement close, but I like a nice house.' She gestured towards the fireplace, a splendid mass of tiles in four colours forming little shelves at several levels.

'It's nice,' Emily said timidly, and Sarah nodded in grim satisfaction.

'Come on, somebody give us a tune on the piano,' she said. Nobody moved, but heads turned towards the baby grand that had been fitted tightly into what was once a bed recess.

'Never mind the piano, Maw,' Joseph said, 'put on some records.'

'I told you that hi-fi would not be played tonight,' his mother snapped at him. 'We'll never hear ourselves having a conversation with that thing blaring.' Peter's head swung towards the hi-fi, an enormous machine with splayed legs, struggling for space along one wall in competition with a walnut cocktail cabinet, open and illuminated from inside. Fifty or sixty cans of beer were stacked on the sink draining-board in addition to the selection of hard liquor in the cabinet. Everything looked smooth and new. The four walls of the tiny kitchen were each done in a different wallpaper. A two-foot plaster Madonna stood on the lid of the grand piano.

'Well, is nobody going to give us a song?' Sarah demanded fiercely. Bert put down his glass and cried, 'I know who'll give us a song!' He lurched from the kitchen and returned in a few seconds carrying his six-year-old daughter, Teresa, in his arms. She was wearing a night-gown and rubbing her eyes.

'You put that poor wean back in its bed!' Sarah barked, and Teresa began to whine. 'There you are!' Sarah went on, 'Oh, you're the smartie, you give a damn for no man but yourself, that's your reward.'

'I want to sing!' Teresa wailed, exciting a chorus of laughter and admiration from the guests, apart from Samuel and Emily. Bert stood the little girl tenderly on the kitchen table, and without a moment's hesitation she started to pipe the Bach-Gounod 'Ave Maria'. A deathly silence fell on the kitchen. Sarah closed her eyes and set her face in a mould of reverent ecstasy. Teresa had a high, shrill little voice, and she had acquired a number of mature techniques. She used a violent tremolo on long notes, and where the melody rose, she tilted her head back, closed her eyes and held her fists near her shoulders, somewhat like Al Jolson, and jerked her torso forward to underline the fervour of the music. Before he could prevent it, some dark chamber in Peter's mind threw up before his eyes the words, 'Hail Mary, Mammy of God', and he closed his teeth tightly on his lower lip and lowered his lids to prevent his eyes from shooting straight out.

Teresa's protracted Amen was greeted with stunned silence, and then a long exhalation of held breaths. Auntie Sarah put a hankie to the corner of her eye and shook her head. Beautiful, beautiful, said two other women, conscious of a deep spiritual experience.

'That's my wee darlin',' Uncle Bert cried, lifting Teresa from the table and hugging her. 'Naw, it's all right, don't bother,' he added, as one of the women pushed a half-crown into Teresa's willing little hand. Soon several other people were groping for half-crowns and pressing them on Teresa, who smiled shyly and clutched them tight.

'Youse shouldn't spoil the wean like that,' Sarah said complacently.

'Oh, she sings beautifully, Sarah,' said a thin sad woman drinking port. 'You should get her trained, a voice like that is a Gift.'

'Aye,' said Sarah aggressively, 'God has been good to our wee Teresa. Here, seein' you're up, hen, you can give us a song on the piano. She canny really play, but she's got a wonderful ear.'

Teresa slid out of her father's arms and stood in front of the piano, first piling her half-crowns at the bass end of the keyboard for safety. Then she started to sing 'Oh, Johnny'. As she sang, she flailed her two little hands up and down, letting them strike where they fell. This number

75

she sang with a little squeak at the end of each line. Influenced by the surprising sounds from the piano, her voice leapt nimbly from key to key, and finished on a disappointingly low note which made it difficult for her to give it the big punch. Still, she finished to applause and enthusiastic shouts, and it was only a belated caution, or perhaps the dawning suspicion that they were being taken for suckers, that prevented the guests from showering further half-crowns on her.

When Bert carried her out of the room, she smiled gently at everybody, but he didn't return at once, and Teresa's voice could be heard from the bedroom shrieking that she wanted to sing more; and Bert's voice bawling threats at her before he reappeared, to sit down heavily and join in an argument that had started between Samuel and a small man with red hair, about the force of gravity.

'Now just a minute,' the red-haired man was saying. 'Was I not at sea for thirteen year? Never mind what happens in a basin, a basin's nothing a do wi' it, I'm talking about the middle of the Atlantic Ocean between here and Li'l Ole Noo Yoick, where I have been personal, dozens a times. Now we'll say it's five mile deep, will you agree wi' that?'

'All right.'

'Right, well, now we're *gettin'* somewhere, if you agree wi' that. Now if a ship sinks it goes down, you agree wi' that?'

'If it makes you happy.'

The red-haired man could see he had met a right stumer in Samuel, but he plodded patiently on. 'All right, well when it gets down two and a half mile, what happens, do you think?'

'It gets wet?' Samuel suggested hopefully.

'That's irreverent to the argument,' the red-haired man dismissed Samuel's flippancy. 'What I'm sayin' is this – two and a half mile deep, the pressure's the same up the way and down the way, right? Come on, anybody can see that.'

'That's very interestin',' Samuel said, with an air of awe that Peter felt was dangerously overdone, and Bert chimed in, 'Now you got to admit Hughie's right, Samuel, I would never of thought of that.'

'All right, well!' Hughie cried in triumph. 'The pressure's the same up the way and down the way, the ship canny move – it's stuck right in the middle.' Hughie stamped his fist on the table with grave finality. Peter, fairly itching to demolish Hughie, saw his father covering his face with one hand and winking at him, and decided to nod solemnly at Hughie and keep his mouth shut. But Bert cried to him, 'Is that no' right, Peter? Come on, you're educated, you can prove it.'

Auntie Sarah, who had been growing restless at the sight of her party degenerating into a stag argument, and was calling for more music, jumped on Bert's respectful address to Peter.

'What does Peter know about anything, he's just a kid!' She tightened her lips and made the word excessively insulting. 'Hughie's a practical man.'

'That's right,' Peter said, startled and discomfited by the spontaneous hatred in Sarah's voice. 'I've never been in a boat that sank in the middle of the Atlantic.'

'There you are,' said Hughie.

'Well, is naebody gonny sing?' Sarah demanded malevolently. 'Come on, get up you, Joseph, you've been sittin' there like a dummy.'

'Ach, I don't feel like it, Maw,' Joseph grumbled.

'You'll bloody well sing an' enjoy yourself or I'll wrap this bottle round your skull!' Sarah shouted. 'What kind of New Year celebration is this supposed to be?'

'All *right*, Maw,' Joseph said, and got to his feet, looking aggrieved and unenthusiastic. 'What'll I sing?' Everybody shouted suggestions, but Joseph, whose ear was carefully attuned to his mother's orders, finally waved his arms peevishly to silence the crowd, shouted, 'There was . . .' and muttered, 'Too high,' and started again on 'The Wild

Colonial Boy'. He was still too high, and the veins stood out on his neck as he strained for the high notes. He sang with his eyes fixed rigidly on the top of the opposite wall, and sat down with his face purple and felt his throat in deep embarrassment. There was a scatter of handclapping and comments, but Sarah had her eyes fixed on Samuel.

'I notice you didn't seem to like the song,' she spat.

'Sure, sure,' Samuel said equably. 'Znothin' wrong wi' the song,' and Bert said, 'Sure he liked it, Sarah. Come on, give us your glass.'

Sarah didn't even condescend to notice Bert. Her lips were pursed and she planted her fists on her fat hips. 'Just get this straight,' she gritted, 'this is a good Catholic house an' if we want to sing good Catholic songs we'll bloody well sing good Catholic songs, we don't need your high an' mighty permission.'

'Ts ts,' Bert pleaded. 'Nobody's arguin', Sarah.'

Sarah lurched against the cocktail cabinet and painfully refocused on Bert.

'Who the hell asked you for your opinion?' she demanded. 'I know what Mr High and Mighty thinks of me – and my own sister as well, my own flesh and blood, just because I married a Catholic and turned. An' a damnt good Catholic,' she added sentimentally. 'You shut your flamin' mouth, Bert, and don't interfere! Mr High and Mighty Haddow in his High and Mighty Corporation house.'

The guests stared straight ahead, torn by the strain of trying not to hear anything and looking sympathetic and neutral at the same time, and Samuel murmured soothingly:

'Aye, it's a shame, Sarah.' Samuel was having the time of his life, but Emily had clutched his arm and was staring at Sarah in twittering terror.

'Don't come your funny man wi' me!' Sarah barked. 'Oh, I know, I know, Catholics never prosper in this town.'

Samuel nodded with the judicial heaviness of a stone-deaf High Court judge, and Emily said nervously, 'Well, it's awful late, it's really time we were getting home. Thanks very much for the party, Sarah.' She was working on the principle that if you ignore anything it will go away.

'Oh you can't wait to shake the dust of my house off your feet!' Sarah attacked. But Bert had rammed a full glass into Sarah's hand and was crying, 'It's the New Year, for God's sake, let bygones be bygones. What's the use a bringin' up religion?' he added reasonably.

'That's right,' Emily quavered, 'everybody's entitled to their own opinion.'

'Well, by God, I'm no' ashamed of mine,' Sarah yelled, but into her glass, and the strain began to slacken. It tightened again unexpectedly when red-haired Hughie, who had been tactfully sitting silent and frozen, said thoughtfully:

'Be fair, all the same. Catholics do all right in this town. It's a scientific fact the place is rotten wi' them!'

'And what do you mean by that, you wee Orange get?' Sarah demanded.

'No offence, Sarah,' Hughie explained. 'You gotty be tolerant about people's religions, but it stands to reason the Catholics are swampin' this city. Look at their big families, it's all organized so's there'll be more Catholics than anything else in a few year. I mean, you gotty be tolerant, but you gotty face facts.'

There was a horrifying silence as Sarah threw her glass into the fire. Joseph looked at Peter and they both raised their shoulders in silence.

'Are you gonny listen to that wee Orange guttersnipe insulting your wife in her own house?' Sarah asked Bert, who mumbled, 'Naebody's insulting you, Sarah. Come on, forget it.'

'Here, who are you callin' an Orange guttersnipe?' Hughie asked shrilly. 'Just nark it, see?'

'Aw, come on, jag it in,' Bert pleaded. Hughie threw off Bert's amiable hand and said in a thin, ugly voice:

'Get the paws off, you! I don't stand for that from no Fenian. Don't think I'm frightened to get the jackets off.'

'Och, shut your face,' said Bert, giving way at last to

irritation. 'You want the jackets off, you can have the jackets off.'

Bert and Hughie stared muzzily at each other and ceremonially peeled off their jackets. Bert was wearing a white shirt underneath. Hughie was wearing a vest, and under that a Fair Isle pullover. He began to unbutton the vest with dignified deliberation, while the guests chorused protests and pleas for peace. None of these registered on Bert or Hughie. Samuel looked at the two of them with bright interest and said nothing. Emily caught her breath and gasped, and if she had been wearing an apron, she would have flung it over her face and wailed. Finally, Hughie hung his vest carefully on the back of a chair and he and Bert jostled their way out of the kitchen, throwing off restraining hands. Samuel immediately joined them, turning at the door to say:

'They're too drunk to do any damage, so the rest of you stay where you are and keep out of trouble.' Sarah immediately rushed to the kitchen window, threw it open so that she could lean out and watch the fight, and others joined her until there was a mass of bodies jammed over the sill.

Emily sat snivelling quietly. Peter and Joseph and Joseph's girl friend looked at one another in embarrassment, and there was a sudden noise outside on the stairs, and a high-pitched yell.

'If he's harmed a hair of my man's head I'll swing for him!' Sarah gasped, trying to drag herself from the crush at the window. Before she could get to the door, it opened. Bert and Samuel came in, carrying the limp form of Hughie, and Hughie's wife, the thin sad woman who drank port, gave a shriek and theatrically fainted.

Bert sounded humble and chastened.

'He fell down the stairs,' he said. 'I never laid a finger on him. He'll be all right.' He and Samuel laid the senseless Hughie on the floor by the table, and Sarah, impatiently pushing Hughie's wife aside with her foot, flung herself at Hughie's body.

'May the saints forgive me for what I done to you this night, Hughie!' she cried. 'Quick, somebody, get brandy, somebody.'

'Oh, Jesus,' said Bert. '*Brandy!*'

* * *

Peter and his parents had to walk home. Emily swung between a state of dumb shock and an even more tiresome spate of tearful comments on how she had foreseen trouble all along. Samuel walked fairly straight and almost soberly, but he had the palpable mellowness of a man who had drunk sufficient.

'I'll take your arm, Peter,' he said, 'just to keep me on the pavement.'

'You're not drunk, Samuel, don't talk like that,' Emily complained. 'You were the only man that wasn't drunk there. At least you never lost your temper.'

'I haveny got a temper to lose,' her husband said, a little thickly. 'The Haddows always keep the head. Zat right, Peter?'

'Sure thing.'

'This fresh air's a sod, though,' Samuel said, stumbling. 'Straight to the old scratcher.' By the time they had reached home, he was hanging heavily on Peter's arm and lurching in all directions. Peter led him straight to his bed and started unlacing his shoes.

'I'm drunk!' Samuel said in surprise.

'You're all right.'

'Sa terrible thing, seeing your own father drunk.'

'No, it's all right.'

'You despise me,' Samuel said angrily to the ceiling.

'I'm just helping you,' Peter soothed him.

'Ah, you're all right, Peter, you're all right. Don't pay any attention to me, I might shout the odds sometimes but you're all right.'

Christine was in the living-room. She had two chairs

81

pulled close together. She sat in one of them with her wool rug over her knees. In the other, with the other end of the rug on his knees, was Davie McAllister.

'You did the right thing, Christine,' Emily was saying plaintively. 'It would be better if we had all stayed at home.'

'A Happy New Year,' Davie said sheepishly.

'I find this cosy domestic picture unutterably sickly,' Peter said. 'You should have come to Auntie Sarah's. Three songs, three arguments, one fight and a smashing nose-dive. It was the mostest I've ever mostested. Zowie splat bam kerrunch! Have you two been having a wee session on the quiet?'

Davie blushed deep red and Christine withered Peter with one of her withering glances. Emily was teetering in and out of the kitchen and washing cups.

'Was there anybody here?' she cried.

'No, nobody,' said Christine. 'Oh, Jean Pynne came in for a few minutes, with her boy friend. Quite nice.'

Davie looked at Peter in agonized sympathy.

'You sit down, Mum, I'll make some tea,' Peter said. He stood in the kitchen watching the kettle until the colour left his face. His misery was so sharp it was almost thrilling.

7

As the month of the Highers approached, Peter dutifully buried himself in work. He had never doubted that he would pass somehow, and the social code of the gang had always attached its worst stigma to anybody who was suspected of doing anything that looked like voluntary study beyond the line of duty. But the code had altered abruptly. It was practically *de rigueur* to be buried alone in books every evening in the week, and the discussions at school widened from gossip and sex to include methods of study. Wee Jimmy Webster claimed that his uncle had studied Pelmanism and that you couldn't fail an exam by this method, but he got vague when asked what the method was, and was properly sneered to silence, an habitual fate for Jimmy Webster.

Peter suggested seriously that the best way to do revision was propped against the wall, on his head, so that the brain got extra supplies of blood, and was delighted when he was shown into Davie McAllister's front room one night by Mrs McAllister, to find Davie standing on his head on a cushion and trying to read history. Peter's bedroom had never been equipped for anything but sleeping, but he self-consciously insisted on having the old cane armchair put into it so that he could work in peace. Winter was an unfortunate time of the year for this. His bedroom was always freezing, and he sat shrouded in blankets, with a tiny electric radiator which he kept moving from his feet to a position behind the chair, and then on to the chest of drawers to heat his head. He devised a technique of holding books through blankets. Occasionally he suspected that the whole thing was a charade, but there was no point in not

83

doing it, because everybody else was doing it, and there was nobody to talk to. Davie was so stubborn about the new fashion that he savagely refused to come out, or to let Peter into his house, during the hours decreed for solitary confinement.

The custom was to study until nine o'clock and then meet at the corner of Hirta Street to have a walk and pump fresh air into the tired brains, and the conversation among the members of the crowd who turned up for these late strolls tended to be sententious and grave, for anything up to ten or fifteen minutes. Light relief included Jimmy Webster's detailed schemes for torturing Wee Aikie, the maths teacher, to death. Jimmy spent a lot of thought on this, and showed a patient talent for variations on a simple theme of obscene agony. It was one of his ways of getting his share of the conversation. Most of the time, no matter how hard he tried, he had an irritating effect on everybody, and although Joe Chadwick was the only one who habitually told him to shut up, everybody else felt like it. The gang started appointing new meeting-places in the hope of dodging him, but he had the other talent of the terrier for nosing out conspiracy and he nearly always caught up with them.

Peter found Jimmy Webster as irritating as everybody else did, and the fact interested him, because he noticed that other people could say things and command respect which in Jimmy's mouth always provoked impatience and nausea. Peter wondered how he himself would feel if he thought the gang was corporately scheming to avoid him, and decided that if this ever happened, he would stay alone. He found that he could enjoy the melancholy bitterness of being alone and feeling noble and sorry for himself.

Davie McAllister suggested to him one evening that it might be nice to have a couple of evenings in a week in joint revision.

'Okay,' Peter said. 'Your front room must be warmer than my refrigerator. But you're bonkers if you think it'll do you any good cribbing my revision – you'll be on your own at the Highers.'

'All right,' Davie said hastily. 'One night at my house and the other at yours.'

'Don't be daft, Davie, a night in my house is like six weeks in an igloo with a hole in it. You can hear the ice cracking inside your skull.'

'We'll just forget the whole thing, then,' Davie said. 'You're always the bloody same, everything has to suit you.'

'All right, all right,' Peter pacified him. 'You can come and freeze if you like. God,' he added absently, 'the trouble you go to just to gape for five minutes at a dumb dame like Christine.'

'You shut up about Christine!'

'Are you referring to my sister?' Peter demanded icily, and Davie fell into pleading.

'Aw, chuck making a fool of me, Peter. Christine's . . . nice, even if you don't like her.'

'Have you spurned Alice Jackson?'

'No, it's got nothing to do with Alice. Christine's different.'

'She sure is – Christine natters at you about her boy friends and you think she's being nice to you. For God's sake, she's just using you as a pet dog.'

'I don't care,' Davie muttered defiantly. 'I like it. You can like a girl without wanting to . . . you know.'

'Okay, be a Pomeranian if you like,' Peter said and on a perverse impulse added, 'Are you sure you've never had a wee session with Christine? You looked awfully guilty on New Year's night when we discovered you holding feet under the wool rug.'

'Now shut up! Shut up, I'm warning you, Haddow.'

'Well, if you think she's nice, you mean to say you've never thought of cuddling her?'

'I don't understand you, Haddow. She's your *sister*!'

'Only to me, though. Come on, Davie, admit it, you sit

there listening to her ghastly patter and look sympathetic, but your tiny mind is pulsating with lust, isn't it?'

'You know, Haddow, you don't understand your sister at all.'

'Biology, biology, my boy,' Peter said, in a fair impersonation of Gutty Greer. 'The mm endocrine glands, mm.'

'Huh. You would like it if I made a pass at your sister.'

'I would love it. Anything for a bit of bloodshed.'

'Would she clobber me, right enough? Aw, shut up. I've got too much *respect* for Christine to try anything.'

'Spoken like a true clean-cut poodle,' Peter cried. Davie ruminated for a few minutes, and then coughed and asked:

'Anything doing about . . . Jeannie-Peenie?'

'There never *was* anything,' Peter snapped. 'Forget it.'

'Okay.' It never occurred to Davie to upbraid Peter as he would have done a few weeks ago. He had an innate respect for tragedy. He joined Peter timidly in a lengthy silence, which Peter finally broke.

'Women, my boy, are a dead loss.' It sounded adolescent and phoney as he said it; not because it wasn't true, but because it didn't have the round tone of finality it had had in his head before he said it. He could tell that it had embarrassed Davie, too, and he decided to laugh.

'Where did it get me, being a dirty old man?' he giggled. 'Now I'm approaching the end, I think I'll jag the whole thing in and shut myself up in a convent.'

'You mean a monastery, you idiot.'

'What the hell could I do in a monastery? What do you take me for, some kind of a monaster?'

There was comfort to be found in assuring himself that he was a sour, cynical misogynist for life. Sometimes he exuded cynicism so palpably that he suspected even Alice Jackson was intrigued, and had started to aim her leg shows in the maths class at him instead of at Davie. There was comfort in this suspicion, too. He felt that a new aura surrounded him, when he remembered to remember what he was. Now and then he practised a world-weary sneer in the mirror. Even Honey Parish noticed it. He was sure there was a new quality of speculation in the way she sometimes looked at him when he passed her in the corridors.

He declined to join in the small stir of anticipation when it was discovered one day that Curly McCrae, the French teacher, was off with a cold, and that Honey was taking the class instead. The rest of the gang straightened up and flexed their muscles when she came, and there was a suspicion of a mass sigh as she sat down on a corner of the table at the front of the class, but Peter held himself coldly aloof and tried a modified version of his sneer.

'Are you ill, Haddow?' Honey asked irritably.

'No, miss.'

'Well, try not to look sick, you're bad enough when you're cheerful.' Peter quietly seethed, and turned his sneer, the full-scale version, on Tom Arthur, who was laughing with spurious loudness. It was a bad start for Honey. She felt quite unwell herself, and the sudden order to take extra classes in Curly's absence had evoked a sense of grievance that would never have occurred to her at other times, but had been quietly festering all afternoon. Wrapped in her own resentment, and angry at herself for feeling resentment, she perceived only dimly that it was going to be one of those troublesome periods. When she asked the class which chapter they had been studying, there was a confused yell of answers, nearly all different. The noise went through her head like a drill, and she yelled back.

Suicide, she thought desperately, it only encourages them. She picked on one of the girls, who told her dutifully that the class was revising irregular verbs.

'All right,' Honey said quietly to the same girl, 'conjugate the verb to come.'

'Kid stuff,' somebody muttered on the boys' side, and she steeled herself to ignore it.

'You,' she said, pointing to Joe Chadwick. 'The imperfect tense of *boire*.' Big Joe slouched upright.

'I don't know it . . . miss.'

'Why not?'

'I've been revising different ones from that. I could give you *voir*, if you like.'

'Sit down!' Honey stamped her foot, and regretted it, for the jolt shook her body and her eyes swam. She hated the class with a bleak, murderous hate. She concentrated on the girls. Thank heaven for little girls, she thought, without much fervour. It was just a question of getting through the forty minutes, minute by minute. It never lasted for ever.

But it had a good try. Ignoring the boys altogether was not going to work. Left alone, they seemed to simmer just beyond the range of her vision, cooking up nastiness and hostility. And how long could you ask questions on irregular verbs? *Venir, voir, boire . . . venir, voir, boire . . .* What were the others? She picked up the French grammar and somehow felt that to consult it would be an admission of failure that would finish her. Oh, *être*.

'The past definitive of the verb to be. Haddow.'

'*Je fus, tu fut, il fut . . .*'

'. . . and take that sneer off your face.' This was unwise, the only thing was to pretend not to see the monsters' stupidities. 'Go on, hurry up,' she said impatiently.

Peter continued with his own sense of grievance audibly prickling. Brief authority, he was thinking, women, the dignity of man, bitches. He was surprised at how much he could dislike anybody like Honey and still look at her and find her beautiful.

'Mr McCrae usually gives us conversation when he runs out of irregular verbs, miss,' Joe Chadwick suggested innocently. He was so big and beefy that Honey shrank from a head-on clash.

'I can imagine,' she said grimly, 'what fun that must be.'

'It's very educational, miss,' Joe insisted, with a babyish earnestness that terrified Honey. 'All right!' she snapped. '*Vous pourrez dire quelque chose de très drôle, j'en suis sûr.*'

'*Puis-je dire* anything *du tout, mademoiselle?*' Joe asked oafishly, and Honey, with dread rising in her, said '*N'importe. Dépêche-toi.*'

'*Eh bien,*' Joe mouthed with painful care. '*Avez-vous un garçon ami?*' There was a hoot of laughter from the boys.

'I expect that kind of question from first-year infants,' Honey said savagely. 'In fact, I've had it from first-year infants.'

Big Joe looked innocent and hurt.

'*Il faut parler français, mademoiselle,*' he said.

'*Soit. Je reponds, Merci, non – je préfére la solitude.*'

'*Ici, ici,*' Peter muttered, and she swung on him in vexation.

'*Pardon?*' she asked, with dangerous calmness.

'*Ici, ici, mademoiselle*. It means here, here.'

'If you try to be funny again,' Honey said grimly, 'you'll be in trouble.' Stupid, stupid, it was a harmless thing to say, I'll probably laugh at it some other time. But that Haddow brat is the last straw.

She sat down decisively on the corner of the table and took a grip of herself.

'*Parlons d'autres choses,*' she commanded. Her gown slipped aside, and revealed her long nylon shins, and there was an unsubdued wolf whistle from the rear corner of the class. Honey stood up.

'Come out here,' she said quietly. 'You.'

Jimmy Webster, shrugging his shoulders as if bewildered, went out to the front of the class.

'I would like an explanation of that,' Honey said. Jimmy shrugged his shoulders and continued to look innocent. He was buoyed on the tangible atmosphere of hysteria that his whistle had created, and a snigger broke from him.

'Hold out your hand,' Honey shouted. 'Both hands.' She rummaged noisily in McCrae's desk and pulled out his belt. Jimmy Webster was standing with both hands stretched out at his sides, goading her further.

'In front of you,' Honey said. Blinking horribly to indicate

89

puzzlement, Jimmy Webster slowly swung his hands together before him, and she aimed savagely at them. As the leather strap struck, there was a perfectly synchronized, quiet shout 'Oo!' from the class. Jimmy Webster gave her a bright smile of encouragement.

'Oo!'

'Oo!'

The shout was growing louder each time, and each time Jimmy Webster made an exaggerated face as the belt swung, and then a bright smile. All control snapped in Honey. She swung again and again, saw the smile vanish from his face, and heard the horrid little shout tail away.

She had a mad desire to laugh. Jimmy Webster's face had suddenly grown blotchy and tears were rolling down his cheeks. She had lost count. She opened the desk and threw the belt back inside, made to slam the desk shut, but instead, left the lid up and stood behind the desk. Jimmy Webster was still standing stupidly in front of the class.

'Go to your seat,' she shouted. He walked back to the rear of the class with his hands hanging by his sides and as he sat down Honey heard a small sob that pierced her head like a scream. Standing behind the desk, with one hand holding up the lid that hid her from the class, she trembled in a panic urge to flee, to shriek, to be dead and out of sight. She put the lid down slowly and said:

'Open your books and write down the principal irregular verbs. We . . .' but decided to say nothing more. The silence was deep enough for her to hear a muffled catching of breath that repeated itself over and over from one of the back seats. The girls were bent over their books. On the boys' side, she saw, mistily, faces staring at her, whose lack of expression was in itself baleful and bitter. The muscles of her face had abandoned contact with her will. She didn't know whether she was scowling or smiling. For a moment, Peter's face rose out of the others; the sneer gone and the brow drawn down, the lips drawn back. He looked like a caricature of The Enemy.

Peter was too unconscious of his expression. He was staring at Honey in unendurable horror and pity and love both for her and for Jimmy Webster, and guilt that he couldn't fathom.

The period bell rang, too late. Honey left the classroom without looking back and ran upstairs to the staff-room. The noise that exploded as soon as she was gone was angry and bewildered. Jimmy Webster, surrounded for once by friends, threw them off ferociously and jostled his way through them to Gutty Greer's room next door for the last period.

Gutty scanned the class with his vague, reptilian eyes and ambled down one of the aisles.

'Make y'self useful, Webster,' he mumbled. 'While we mm take Mr Shakespeare's name in vain, you can nip out and get me a box of matches. Don't tell anybody, child labour's hm illegal. Don't dawdle, boy. Take your time. You Rule, boy,' he continued menacingly, 'what is the hm element common to all the um tragedies of the man who mm claimed to be William Shakespeare?'

At four o'clock the boys in the class broke into knots and tried to exorcize their feelings in arguments about the exact count executed on Jimmy Webster. He hadn't reappeared in Gutty's class and Gutty hadn't mentioned his absence. Davie McAllister was particularly overwrought, but in the middle of his third wave of obscenity, he suddenly said to Peter:

'Hey, I've been trying to get you since two o'clock. I saw Jeannie-Peenie at dinner-time.'

'So what?'

'Don't be a mug! I mean I met her, she was speaking to me.'

'Oh, great day in de mawnin',' Peter said limply.

'She was asking for you. She stopped me and asked me if there was anything wrong with you.'

'Did she?' Peter was wary, and affecting more wariness than he felt.

'For God's sake what's up with you?' Davie demanded. 'She asked me if there was anything wrong with you.'

'You said that already,' Peter said, snapping his fingers. 'Come on, money, money. Gimme money.'

'Away and take a flyin' kick at yourself. Did you hear me?'

'Money, money! It takes fourpence to telephone, have you never heard?'

'Oh. Fourpence. I've only got a tanner.'

Peter continued to snap his fingers.

'Come on, give, give. You'll get it back.'

'Never mind, you can keep it. Hey, it's your house tonight, isn't it?'

'Sure, boy, sure. Roger. You're a good kid, a good kid, know that, boy, eh? Eh, boy?'

'Aw, shut up the Steiger stuff or she'll never know you on the phone. Can I come and listen?'

'Later, boy, later, not now, I'm busy, can't you for Chrissake see I'm busy, boy?'

Between the bus stop and Jeannie's house, Peter had briefly assured her that there was nothing wrong with him and instead of making some tortured explanation of Archie Horne, Jean found herself listening to an agonizing recital of the scene in the French class. She shut her eyes and shook her head.

'It's horrible,' she said.

'I shouldn't have told you.'

'Yes, yes, Peter! If it had happened to me I would want to tell you. There's nobody else I could tell.'

'Not even Archie?' He couldn't prevent himself.

'He's away, anyway. No, not even Archie, anyway. I've kept looking for you from the bus.'

'Ach, you know, the Highers. I've been busy.'

'I know.'

'I haven't been busy. I've been miserable.'

'Oh, me too, me too. I wanted to talk to you . . . just talk . . .'

92

'Listen, you mean.'

'Yes, listen.'

'I wanted to cry on your shoulder. Especially today.'

'Oh – oh, I wish you could. I wish there was nobody for miles around. There's always too many people.'

'Can you bring your shoulder on Friday?'

'Yes, Peter. Do you have to take so long to ask me? You probably won't feel like crying on Friday.'

'Oh, I will, I can do it all the time.'

'Don't do it when I'm not there. Please, Peter.' There was a premonition of tears in her own eyes.

When Davie arrived at Peter's to steep in maths, Peter told him that his father was working late and his mother was out visiting.

'I'll swot for you in the refrigerator for an hour,' he said expansively. 'You can sit in the living-room and watch Christine drying her hair. It's a macabre spectacle. You've only got Julie to worry about and if you give her a tanner she'll stay in the kitchen and make her death-mask. She's been working on it for a week.'

'Are you sure it's all right?'

'Sure, away and wag your tail, poodle.'

'I'll kill you, Haddow, I'm telling you, I'll kill you.'

8

Julie had boiled a sheep's head till the skull was clean and bleached, and she was trying to coat it in luminous paint. Samuel was staring at it, with outraged astonishment surging inside him.

'Get that filthy thing out of the house,' he demanded in a high-pitched voice. 'What is this supposed to be, a cemetery? It'll stink us out.'

'There's nothing left on it to stink,' Julie said. 'It's an emblem for my gang.'

'I don't know what the hell kids are coming to. Who said you could bring that into the house?'

'Mum.'

There was little point in arguing the toss. She was probably lying, but Emily wasn't there to deny it, and there was a core of patient stubbornness in ten-year-old Julie that would always win in the end. She was beyond his comprehension.

'Have you got no dolls to play with? What do you want with that filthy thing?'

'It's an emblem, I told you.'

'And what do you do with it?'

'You don't *do* anything with an emblem,' Julie said, patiently humouring him. 'You just have it. Every gang has to have an emblem. This paint's a swindle,' she suddenly whined. 'Peter, it'll not go on.'

'It's trash,' Peter said briefly. 'It's only a water-colour, it'll never do for bone. It's poisonous as well. Phosphorus.'

'Who the hell sells poison to kids?' Samuel shouted. 'Is it poison right enough?'

'Aye, but only if you drink it,' Peter explained. 'So is

enamel. He, try coating the skull with plaster. The paint might take on that.'

'You shut up, she can think up enough idiotic tricks on her own. Get that thing out of my sight or it'll go in the fire.'

Breathing through her nose at the stupidity of parents, Julie picked up the skull and the saucer of paint and stamped into her bedroom. Peter wandered after her.

'You could stick bits of paper on it and then paint the paper,' he suggested. 'Does it shine good?'

'Super.' Julie switched the light off and a dim purple glow was visible in the saucer. 'You're supposed to keep it in the sunshine for a while, that makes it shine better. What's the use of sticking paper on top of it? Then it would just be a paper skull.'

'Well, just stick it here and there. What *are* you going to do with it, anyway?'

'It's an emblem,' she muttered huffily. 'I'll scare Sadie Martin to death, anyway.'

'You'd better not scare anybody else to death, or you'll be bang in trouble,' Peter warned her half-heartedly. 'If you were thinking of walking about with it on the waste ground, for instance, with a black cloth over your head.'

'What would the black cloth be for?'

'It would make you invisible, stupid. Then nobody would see anything except a luminous skull floating above the ground.'

'Super. Do you think Christine's got an old black shirt, or anything?'

'If she has, she'll have your own skull on the end of a pole if you touch it. In fact she'll do a wulkie if she finds it in her bedroom. You'll have to hide it. Christine *will* fling it in the fire.'

'Yes, she's rottener than the old man. Where will I get glue if I'm going to stick paper on it?'

Every project of Julie's demanded lists of things and materials that Julie never had. Peter went to his room to rummage for a tube of glue that had once been there. He was patiently sticking little bits of paper on the sheep's skull when he realized that time must have been passing. When he dashed to look at the alarm-clock in the living-room he found that it was already after seven. He was due to meet Jean at seven.

'I can finish it myself,' Julie said contemptuously. 'It looks stupid with bits of paper all over it.'

'So would you if somebody boiled your head,' Peter crushed her. Jean was standing at the corner and smiling as he arrived.

'It's *terrible*,' he said. 'Twenty minutes late. How dare you?'

'You just don't have any respect for me,' Jean said, and took his hand. 'What do you want to do?'

Peter affected to think deeply, feeling awkward and gloomy. He had been counting on Christine's arriving home before he left because, although he still owed her five shillings, he needed another loan to see him through the evening, and he knew she would have plenty. He had no objection to Jean's paying him into the pictures, but he found himself unable to break this news with the devil-may-care casualness that he wanted. He cursed Christine.

'I thought that maybe . . .' Jean said. '. . . Maybe you wouldn't want to, though. If we got out early would you like to come home for a cup of tea? But the pictures get out too late, we'd miss the big picture.'

Peter was suddenly confused and apprehensive and excited.

'Are you sure it's all right?'

'Yes, of course.'

'All right, if it's all right. We could just go for a walk, then.'

'All right,' Jean said doubtfully.

'I wish it was dark.' Peter felt unsure of himself. 'It's dark across the waste ground. I bet you would hate that.'

She took his arm and laughed into his eyes.

'It must be frightening.' They walked along the path across the waste ground, out of the light from the street lamps.

'Mm. This is the only dark place for *miles*.'

'We're practically at the other side, that's the snag. What do we do then? It's all a conspiracy to get us into the light again.'

'We could walk back again,' said Jean.

'Just think of the amount of energy we could save if we just stopped in the middle.' Peter's heart was hammering in his chest and sounding in his ears.

'All right, if you like.' Jean stopped, uncertainly.

'I couldn't even see your face if I wanted to kiss you good night,' Peter said. His voice came out cracked, and before he could turn to face her he heard footsteps ringing on the tar macadam. 'Oh, great,' he said. 'There's a whole army using the path for maze-marching.'

'Come on.' Jean took his hand and started running away from the path. Peter plunged after her, breathless across the uneven grass.

'I think you're a disgrace to your sex,' he whispered. 'Dragging innocent schoolboys into bits of waste ground in the dark.' He stood uneasily beside her. 'We could sit down, but the grass must be soaking.'

'I've got a plastic mac.'

He could hear the plastic rustling.

'Will it not tear?'

'Shut up and sit down.' Her voice came from low down and he strained his eyes to see her. 'Down here,' she said. 'You can see better if you shut your eyes.'

'That sounds logical.' He sat beside her and clasped his hands round his knees. 'I've never kissed you at all, except twice at your gate and twice in the pictures.'

'Eleven times in the pictures.'

'It only counts as twice. I must have supernatural powers of self-control.'

'Yes.'

97

Without moving his hands, he turned his body uncomfortably and twisted towards her till their lips touched momentarily.

'That's the first time I've ever kissed you alone, in the dark.'

'Yes.' Jean sighed happily and sat waiting, without impatience. Peter lay back until he felt his head touching the grass. The waste ground was hardly much more than an acre of grass that had been left uneven and scarred from the places where brick air-raid shelters had been built on it during the war.

'This should be in the sunlight,' he said. 'On a cliff somewhere. You can hear the sea bashing on the shore. I've got an open-necked shirt on and I'm chewing a long bit of grass and looking at wee white clouds scudding across the sky. There's always a lot of wee white clouds scudding across the sky at the time.'

'I like it just as nice in the dark.' She giggled. 'With the lamp-posts scudding across the street.'

'Mm. No, it's always sunlight in these pictures. It's so nice that I can look up and see you turning round and smiling down at me. The girl always does that as well.'

'Well, can't you see me?'

'I can see the light reflecting on a wee shiny bit in the corner of your left eye. And one of your teeth.'

'And then the girl bends down.' She bent and kissed him, and relaxed against him as he put his arms round her. They held each other closely until Jean rolled off and lay on her back. Peter raised himself on one elbow and looked down at her face, faintly visible in the darkness, and kissed her gently again and again.

'I'm supposed to feel passionate and fierce,' he said.

'Are you?'

'I don't think so. I just feel . . . pleased with myself.' He felt her cheek lightly with his fingers, then laid his hand gently on her cheek so that his fingertips were tickling

98

her ear. 'I don't really know *anything* about sex,' he admitted ruefully.

'Tickle my ear again.'

'I must be immature.'

'No, you're not. You're far brainier than me.'

'That's got nothing to do with it,' he corrected her plaintively. 'I just know a lot of facts. A child can do that.'

'I don't know *anything*. I'm the most ignorant person you ever met.'

'Oh, Jean, you're so beautiful and wonderful. It doesn't seem possible that this is happening to me.'

'It is, honest.' She took his hand and began to kiss the fingertips gently, one after the other. Peter lifted the hand away and kissed her in long-drawn warmth. 'Not true, not true,' he muttered.

'True, true.' She strained up to kiss him again. 'See?'

'It's funny that I don't feel fierce. People are supposed to.'

'Maybe it's too cold.'

'I think you're a very wicked girl.'

'Am I? Why?'

'Don't listen to me. I can't see the two wee lines between your eyebrows. Did I tell you I thought they were marvellous?'

'They're just lines. Bad temper, probably. Peter?'

'Um.'

'Will you tell me all about sex? Maybe not now, if you like. Some time. Honestly, you would never believe how ignorant I am.'

'That's silly. You must know the basic facts.'

'Oh, I know. But I don't *know* if I know. People never talk about it sensibly. I've always wanted to get a book about it, but I would be afraid to get one. Anyway, my mother would throw a pink fit if she found it.'

'Parents are incomprehensible. You would think it was the nineteenth century. A hundred years ago they used

99

to put frilly covers on piano legs because they thought legs were rude.'

'They didn't!'

'Oh, laugh again!'

'I *can't* laugh. Only by accident.'

'Of course you can. Laugh, instantly! See, you're laughing.'

'Oh, I love the way you can make me laugh.'

'I love the way you can make me make you laugh. Would you kiss my nose?'

'Yes.'

'I bet you wouldn't bite my ear.'

'It would hurt!'

'You don't need to bite right through it. It's just an experiment. I keep reading about people biting each other. Frankly, I don't get it.'

'All right, but tell me if it hurts.'

'No, it doesn't hurt. It's quite nice.'

'Very nice?'

'No, just quite nice. Is it nice when I bite yours?'

'It's all *right*.'

'Maybe it's an acquired taste. Would you not feel embarrassed if I started to tell you about sex?'

'No, not if it was you. I know you wouldn't be laughing at me.'

Peter was filled with quiet, calm pride, at the discovery that he could contemplate talking about sex to Jean without inhibition and without any urge to exploit it.

'Well,' he said. 'No, just a minute. I'll lean on my elbows. I don't want to touch you while I'm talking.'

'All right.'

'Would you rather I talked or kissed you?'

'It doesn't matter. I mean, I like it whatever you do. I never get tired of listening to you.'

'You're mad, girl, mad. Still, all right. Well, men and women are a different shape. Right?'

'Yes.'

'No, don't touch me. Try to curb your insensate lust,

woman, you'll have your opportunity after the lecture.'

'All right, I didn't mean any harm.'

'Right. Blast, we'd better start at the beginning.'

'The birds. And the bees.'

'No, no, just the perpetuation of the species. It all begins with the reproductive process and the perpetuation of the species, which is a damn dull idea when you think of it.'

'Ye-es.'

'Well, it's all worked by evolving a human race divided into two types. Each type is highly specialized for different jobs, and they have a different shape so that they're built for their job.'

'Yes. Funny, it sounds so natural, that way. What's all the fuss about, that puzzles me. I mean, I know what it's about, but why?'

'Well . . .' Peter cupped his hands under his chin and stared across the waste ground; and talked and talked. Jean lay on her back and nodded her head in the darkness, warmed and flattered by the feeling that she, too, was candid and reasonable and un-silly about what were – after all what were they? Simply scientific facts. It was infuriating to think of how childish people could be about them.

'There, you know everything in the world,' Peter said.

'Hee hee.'

'What's funny?'

'I was wondering if that's what happens in these pictures – you know, on the top of the cliff, when it slowly fades out. Does the girl look down at the man and say, "Tell me all about sex," and the man says, "Well, we'll start with the perpetuation of the species"?'

'No, no. The girl kisses him, like this. And then she says, "What are you thinking?"'

'What a question.'

'It's a perfectly sensible question.'

'And does he say, "I'm thinking about the perpetuation of the species"?'

101

'Don't be silly.' She took his hair in both her hands and shook his head, and then kissed him. 'What are you thinking anyway?'

'It's impossible! I'm thinking about three thousand four-hundred and eighty-two things at once.'

'I'm not.'

'Yes, you are. I'm thinking that the street lamps are shining over there, and what's the time? And this plastic mac feels shiny, and the colour of your hair, and the first time I took you home, and how nice it is to be here with you, and the rough nail on my pinkie, and the soft bit on your cheek, and I can't see any stars, and the dark colour of your eyebrows – how do eyebrows get that shape? It's sensational. I'm even thinking about other things I don't even understand. Things keep reminding me of some feeling. Maybe it was a feeling I had in a dream and I've forgotten it, but I can feel it away at the back of my mind.'

'Is it a nice feeling?'

'I don't know, there are a lot of them. Do you know what it's like? You know when you watch a play on television, and somebody comes into the house halfway through it and asks what it's about? It takes twenty minutes or half an hour to explain what happened before they came in, and yet you know it all *in an instant*. It's all in your head . . . you know . . . the whole story, even if it took an hour to watch, you know it all, phfft.'

'Yes! That's funny.'

'Well, if you ask me what I'm thinking, it's like that. By the time I explained a quarter of the things I'm thinking, it would be twenty minutes later and I would have thought of a million other things.'

'Oh, it's horrible! You could never catch up!'

'There, there. You don't need to ask me. We can just do this. Then you get it all through my lips by electricity.'

'I haven't quite got it.'

'All right, we'll try again.'

'Maybe the electricity takes a long time to get through.'

'Oh, Jean, don't let me talk ever again. Just let me kiss you.'

'Mm.'

Jean wore a wrist-watch, but neither of them carried matches, and they had to get up and walk towards the lamplight to find the time. It was just after nine o'clock. Jean started to pull a comb through her hair in quick, decisive strokes.

'There isn't any grass at the back, is there?' she giggled.

'No. Do you just have to do that – comb it like that?'

'Yes.'

'You don't go to bed with curlers in it, do you?'

'No!'

'If you had, I would have emigrated, honestly.'

'Well, I don't, so you'd better stay here.'

'What is this all about? Is the family going to inspect me under a wee microscope?'

'Don't be foolish, I would take any of my friends home.'

The statement gave a small jolt to Peter's euphoria, and the name of Archie Horne, which had lain forgotten under his consciousness all evening, shot into his mind and hovered on his tongue, but he left it unuttered. He felt diminished, too, by the reflection that apart from Archie there seemed to be many friends who had risen to the privileged status of being taken home by Jean. Even if they had all been girl friends he couldn't help resenting their prior arrival and their longer acquaintance. At the same time, he was impressed by the effect created by Jean's words, of a well-regulated household where people's friends could simply be brought. He would never have felt so sanguine about taking friends to his own home, except perhaps Davie. But then Davie didn't matter, he argued to himself. He took it for granted that Jean's home *would* be well-regulated and predictable, like one of the smooth, coloured, happy-smiles homes in a magazine advertisement for linoleum. Jean clearly belonged in such a stable, un-hysterical setting. He found himself growing unnecessarily nervous and apprehensive as they arrived at her house.

'You're sure it's all right? Do they not just want to have a good look at me before they tell me never to darken their door-mat again?'

'Idiot, idiot.' She kissed him swiftly, and then with a gasp she pulled a hankie from her bag and scrubbed his lips with it. Peter stood to permit this with an idiotic smirk.

'It's me,' she called, as they entered the little hall. A door opened in the darkness and her mother looked around it.

'Oh, that's nice, Jean.'

'Help,' Jean muttered, 'did you see that? The minister's here.'

'What is this, a shotgun wedding?' Peter whispered the words, but a nervous giggle broke through the middle of them. The living-room door was still open.

'Oh, God, did she hear me?' he whispered.

'No, she couldn't have.'

But he was convinced that her mother had heard him, and that this would be classified as an appalling, cheap, nasty joke and instantly condemn him for all time.

'What's all the whispering?'

'We're just hanging up our coats, Mother.'

Mrs Pynne received him with a pretty, enthusiastic smile. She was rather a pretty woman, with a neat figure, in her forties, somewhat shorter than Jean. She dressed nicely. She was wearing a plain woollen dress in some middle shade of green, with one bulky topaz brooch at the throat; and very smart green shoes.

Her husband, who looked fairly tall sitting in an armchair, was running to tubbiness. He had a good-natured, slightly pug face, and instead of rising when he was introduced to Peter, he merely stirred a few inches in his chair and said ahum with an amiable casualness which Peter found more comforting than Mrs Pynne's conscious emanation of welcome. The minister was indeed there, sitting on the sofa with a napkin over his knee, and he half-rose to shake Peter's hand.

'Now there's no need to be nervous, anyone,' Mrs Pynne said. 'Mr Garside isn't going to ask why he hasn't seen anyone at church recently.'

'I wouldn't dare,' said Garside. 'They might tell me.' Peter controlled his automatic impulse to disapprove of the minister. He had a festering contempt for people who fell into his category of Muscular Christians, in which he had already placed this specimen before even meeting him, after hearing him discussed by the revolting Stoolie Rule at the badminton club. Garside, he noticed, had the cunning not to look like a beefy-slap-on-the-back-boy's crusader. He was stocky and thick in the bone, and although his face looked youthful and healthy, his eyes were sunk deep in the sockets. His voice was deep, but offhand, with no trace of clerical boom, and two fingers of his right hand were deeply stained with nicotine.

Peter found himself sitting beside the minister, with a perilously fine china cup and saucer in his hand. He took it for granted that he would either spill the tea or crunch the saucer to powder, and he concentrated on avoiding these disasters. He was almost grateful for Garside's presence because it clearly averted any danger of Peter's having to make conversation as well as wrestle with the most breakable crockery he had ever handled. All the furniture in the Pynnes' living-room was rather less battered and discouraged than the furniture at the Haddows. The wallpaper was fresh and bright. Nothing looked too new, but it all looked young and cared-for. A linoleum advertiser could very nearly have shot it as it was, merely by lifting the carpet and putting down linoleum. Is this your home? he thought. It may look secure, but are you really protecting them? No, that was insurance, not linoleum. Are you really protecting your daughter? What would you scream, he thought, looking respectfully at Mrs Pynne, if your daughter told you I had just been teaching her about the forbidden secrets of birth control? The secret knowledge was a comforting possession which he wrapped round

105

himself, against his sense of being among strange people, in a strange place where he didn't know the rules.

'. . . like to see plenty of young people about the house,' Mrs Pynne was saying.

'You're probably more successful at attracting them than I am.' Garside smiled comfortably. He had a pleasant manner of saying banal things with a sense of relaxation, and Peter momentarily envied him. Mrs Pynne rewarded the minister with a deprecating smile and said to Peter:

'Of course, you must be the youngest of Jean's army of pals.' The word pals jarred uncomfortably. 'What is it you are, Peter? Sixteen?'

'Seventeen.' His smile felt toothy and gauche.

'Oh dear, it seems almost impossible to remember. How are you getting on at school, Peter?' Peter had no doubt of it now, he was being stood in short trousers, with his head barely reaching the arm of the chair, and catechized as a rather drab infant non-prodigy. He shrugged his shoulders wryly and the china cup teetered horribly in the saucer for a moment before he caught it. 'He's sitting for his Highers this year,' Mrs Pynne explained to the minister, who turned to Peter with an eyebrow raised in interest. 'How will you do?' he asked.

'I'll pass,' Peter said. He had meant to make the words indicate a bare pass, with luck, but remembered that it was dangerous to shrug his shoulders, and the words sounded sharp and aggressive.

'Oh, well!' Mrs Pynne said, amused. 'That's one thing you must say for young people today – they're not lacking in confidence.'

'I didn't mean that,' Peter explained earnestly. 'You know . . . the Highers are quite fair, according to everybody, so I should scrape through all right if I don't get nervous.'

'I can't imagine it,' Mrs Pynne said, 'though I must say I think life is so much more complicated for young people now than it was in my youth. Goodness, how many centuries ago.' She sighed prettily, and Peter's mind leapt to

106

produce a gallant retort, but he prevented himself in time from making it, because he had almost said, 'Oh, not more than two centuries at the most.' That would really have made me the all-time favourite . . . Garside in any case had already said:

'Away you go, you're not even old enough to remember boogie-woogie. That's what dates me. I was even a Benny Goodman fan.'

'So am I!' Peter cried. Although he didn't quite see how, he realized that it was the wrong thing to say, for Mrs Pynne. Or perhaps he had said it too soon, without giving time for the minister's compliment to die away. He closed his mouth and swore to leave it closed permanently. The china was still in his hand, Jean was sitting on the arm of the sofa, so that he couldn't even see her without obviously turning round to stare at her, and he settled himself to endure the time ahead of him and speak only when he was spoken to.

Garside appeared not to have noticed any discomfort. He chattered easily, saying little with soothing conviction, while Mrs Pynne listened with relaxed pleasure and Mr Pynne smiled and said nothing. For an instant Peter thought he felt Jean's finger pressing into his back to remind him that she was with him, but it turned out, after several minutes of suspense, to be the piping on one of the box cushions on the sofa. Then he realized that Mrs Pynne had introduced a new topic.

'. . . the Fitzhughs – perhaps you don't know them, Mr Garside.'

'No-o.'

'Och, you must have heard about them. He got nine months for being mixed up in a robbery.'

'For resetting, actually,' Peter offered humbly.

'Well, they say it's worse to receive stolen goods than it is to steal them, I believe.'

'There's something in that,' Garside said, not too comfortably. Peter knew the Fitzhughs by sight. Johnny Fitzhugh had a betting shop somewhere in the South Side. It had been a glorious scandal when somebody broke into his house while he was away for the week-end, and the police who were called by neighbours found boxes of stolen cigarettes stowed in the bedroom. Johnny drove a cream Velox with ocelot upholstery, and his wife was blonde and smooth. Peter liked her. One day he had carried a bag of shopping for her, and she had given him a big warm smile when he refused to take half a crown for his trouble. She had said that she would invite him in for a drink, but that she never entertained men while her husband was away on holiday, and some quality of cheerful honesty in her had warmed his heart.

'But *that's* not the real story,' Mrs Pynne was going on. 'Honestly, the longer I live the more people *astonish* me. He got out this week, and I wish you had *seen* the fuss.'

'Oh?' It was all clearly new to Garside, and he was waiting for more before he reacted.

'Well, honestly, you would expect people to have the sense to keep quiet after all – not call attention to themselves, I mean. Personally, I would have died of shame.'

'It can't be easy to keep a thing like that quiet,' Garside said soothingly.

'No, but you know what I mean. Do you think he had the plain common sense to go home quietly and hope everybody would forget it? It was like a *birthday* party! You should have seen the cars rolling up – friends, relatives, everybody. The noise must have been tremendous.'

'Well,' Garside said, with his bedside manner and a little touch of humour, 'I don't suppose the man's had many jollifications in Barlinnie.'

'Well, that's hardly what Barlinnie's for,' Mrs Pynne said gravely. 'But what tickles me is that he arrived home in his car with a huge big rocking-horse for their little boy and armfuls of presents – as if he had been away on a trip, or something. I would have thought his family would have died of shame.'

'I don't know.' Peter was angry to find his face colouring, and he knew he should say nothing, and he went on, 'If I was in prison for nine months, I would like to have a party when I came out. I think it would be quite nice if my wife didn't feel ashamed of me, even if I had been in prison. After all,' he mumbled defensively, 'I would have served my debt to society.'

'Oh, it's well seen you're young, Peter,' Mrs Pynne said, quite kindly. 'When you're older you'll see things differently.'

'I can't believe it,' Peter said apologetically, wishing he would shut up. 'I mean, if that was true, everybody of thirty and everybody of forty and everybody of fifty would all agree about everything.'

'Oh, you young boys are too deep for me,' Mrs Pynne laughed merrily. Mr Pynne looked at him quizzically. He looked friendly, but it was impossible to say because he had hardly opened his mouth since Peter came in.

'Ah, well,' Garside said, rising and stretching. 'I've been spoiling myself, as usual. I'd better get back to the treadmill.'

Among the polite protests, Peter sensed that he was to go too. He walked down the garden path with the minister and turned with him to wave good night to Mrs Pynne and Jean. It was barely ten o'clock.

'Can I give you a lift?' Garside asked him.

'No, thanks. I live just down the street.'

'And you're not anxious to ride with a parson.' Garside's calm, confident amusement nettled Peter.

'You should have defended the Fitzhughs,' he said. 'That's your job. Charity.'

'Aye, aye. And a fat lot of good it would do.' Garside shot him a sidelong glance of sympathy. 'When you don't approve of people, hearing them defended can make you like them even less. You're an agnostic, for instance.'

'I never said I was.'

'No.' The minister sighed heavily and then laughed. 'I

always get suspicious when I catch anybody talking like a Christian. We must have an argument some time, I haven't had a good one for years.'

'Any time you like.'

'All right, all right, don't start battering me senseless.'

'All right,' Peter laughed.

'Good night.'

Peter felt that in some way Garside had put him at a disadvantage. He wouldn't have talked like that to somebody his own age. Bloody pat-on-the-shoulder good chap, he thought viciously. It was even more irritating because he felt he quite liked the minister. Mrs Pynne was a different story.

He wanted nothing so much as to get through to Mrs Pynne, to be in with Mrs Pynne, with her pretty face and her self-possession. The world could be divided into people who were in with Mrs Pynne and people who weren't, and the important thing was to be in. He hadn't broken any saucers after all, or spilled any tea. She thought he was young, but there was no harm in that, if he had enough chances to demonstrate his profundity, his grasp of affairs, his maturity, before her. He lay in bed rescuing Mrs Pynne from burning buildings and pulling her out of whirlpools with his last dying breath, and watching the stricken admiration on her nice, pretty face as he closed his eyes with a saintly smile and expired in agony.

9

Mr Charles, the gym teacher, was a young man of heroic construction and daunting energy who had the problems of teaching and living neatly in his sinewy hand, together with a small rubber ball which he always carried in his jacket pocket and kneaded with his fingers to keep his wrist muscles in trim. He was a recent recruit to the staff, and he enjoyed the knowledge that he had brought a breath of healthy, unacademic vitality to the staff-room. He had a reverence for academic training, but as he kept telling his senior colleagues, the brain couldn't exist if there wasn't a healthy body round it, and a lot of the intellectual problems that seemed obscure were mostly the result of sluggish livers. It pleased him to see that he commanded a respectful audience in the staff-room. When he came in, the others tended to fall silent.

Charles understood boys. It was only natural, since he was young and un-stuffy and pretty much the kind of man most healthy boys wanted to be. He treated them as equals and never stooped to favouritism. He knew that boys had a deep-rooted sense of justice. Davie McAllister, whose hands and feet led independent, mutinous lives from the rest of his body, hated Charles with ecstatic fervour. Peter found him an unvarying delight. Charles went by the name of Kong among the boys. On his arrival, Peter had quickly tried to fasten the name Skinny on him, to match the splendid width of Charles's shoulders. But by an un-detectable process, he was briefly labelled King Charles and then King Kong Charles, and then just Kong. It was the third nickname Peter had tried to invent, and the third that had failed to stick. Nobody knew who had invented Kong.

111

The Highers were now only weeks away, and the atmosphere of school had changed entirely. Peter's class found itself remote and unconnected from the rest of the school, an *élite* species destined for ordeal. Teachers who had driven them peevishly for years became chummy and confidential, suddenly on their side, instead of the enemy's. Even Aitkenhead, the waspish maths teacher, started to dredge up his old mnemonics and tricks for passing exams without being strictly qualified. They plodded their way through old examination papers and calculated the chances of old favourite questions recurring.

This was always an unsettling time for Kong because there were no examination passes for gymnastics, and he was cheated of a chance to join in the big climax. In January and February he always stepped up his crusade for good muscular co-ordination as the prime contribution to success in life, or exams, or anything. The boy who could do handsprings or a clean vault over the buck was the boy least likely to lose his head over a Latin paper, Charles pointed out with increasing frequency and increasing force, to increasingly thoughtful silences in the staff-room.

Kong was aware that he couldn't put the point too strongly. There were always some teachers of the fossil type who might easily suggest that gym periods should be abandoned altogether before the Highers, and devoted to revision of exam work instead. Old Gutty Greer, who had two Honours degrees and never took any exercise more violent than poker (which he played with the unhealthy skill of a Buddha with X-ray eyes) had actually suggested aloud that the gym periods should be given over to lying in warm baths and watching cock-fights.

'Soothe the um body and hm stimulate the aggressive mental reactions,' he muttered, so ponderously that Kong was convinced that Gutty wasn't joking at all. There was something distinctly un-clean-cut about old Greer, who was fortunately of a generation that would pass away fairly soon.

At least Kong knew he could count on the healthy young

reactions of the boys, who must be stale with classwork. For the last period on Thursday he recklessly left out practically every piece of equipment the gym boasted. Variety was the best tonic for tedium.

There were some of the boys who saddened him as he threw a keen, healthy eye round the gym. He was almost tempted to think that they might have been spared to study history or something else. It wasn't merely a matter of muscle, it was a question of spirit. The flabby one – Rule; a born malingerer if there ever was one. If he wasn't watched, he would run up to the Danish horse and past it and pant back to the line as if he had made a jump. With scrimshankers like that, the man-to-man approach nearly seemed to break down, and, against his principles, Kong had a hunger to land a whack across the fat rump. The boy was sly, too, sleekit wee eyes and a pious pasty face that you couldn't get through.

Wee Webster was another thorn in his flesh. The kid ran and jumped all right, but there was something hysterical about the way he did it. Big Chadwick had the stuff in him all right, he could do anything he tried. His only trouble was that he tried to make it look even easier than it was. He didn't take it seriously enough.

Kong's eyes lighted with pleasure on the group at the far corner, swinging over the beam. Arthur and Donaldson and Peebles and a couple of others had the idea absolutely bang-on, always had had it. Kong never played favourites, but he couldn't help knowing the good specimens from the duds. Arthur's little crowd were going through the beam work as slickly as a platoon of Guards. You never needed to interfere or tell them anything twice. They just had the right idea, and there was nothing toady about them either. They would carry straight on without any idiotic larking about even if he walked right out of the gym and disappeared. Arthur was a particularly good type. He was one boy who should have been a prefect, in preference to a few of the insanely chosen; Haddow, for instance. Great jumping

Mexican beans. A prefect! The boy was a born clown without a responsible bone in his body.

'All right!' Kong clapped his hands. 'We'll try something else. Gather round, men. We'll see who's on his toes,' he added, with a boyish smile. But before the class reacted, Rule had already repeated his run-and-swerve at the Danish horse, and Kong realized that this was one little problem that had to be tidied up.

'What's wrong?' he asked Stoolie impatiently. 'Are you afraid of it? This kind of horse doesn't bite.' Somebody laughed appreciatively, but Rule looked at him with that sly little innocent expression and said, 'I heard you telling us to gather round, sir.'

'And you just couldn't wait, could you?' Kong asked heartily. 'Right, come on, finish your jump.'

Stoolie looked furtive and uneasy.

'Come on, we haven't got all day, boy! You're holding everybody else up.'

Stoolie waddled slowly, slowly, to the starting line and lumbered up, barely faster, to the Danish horse. He made a mincing little hopping movement when he reached it and said plaintively, 'I was getting off on the wrong foot.'

'Get off on the right foot, then!' Kong curbed his impatience. 'Now watch this, everybody,' he said. 'Rule is going to demonstrate how the horse should be jumped. You don't want to miss it.' Tom Arthur was overcome with merriment. Stoolie trudged back to the starting line, ran up to the horse and actually jumped several inches from the floor. His chest met the horse squarely before he slid back to earth.

'Jump, boy, jump!' Kong shook his head. 'Right, go!' This time he stood by the horse and caught Stoolie's arm as Stoolie unwillingly launched himself, caught one of the grips, and speeded by Kong's pull, started to shoot over the other side face first. Kong leapt forward with superb co-ordination and caught him in his arms before he struck the mat.

114

'You're flabby, Rule, inside and out!' Kong surrendered to the crawling irritation that Stoolie evoked in him. 'Anybody can do that jump.'

'I can't, sir.' Stoolie was stubborn and tremulous at the same time.

'Do you know why you can't do it, Rule? Funk. That's all. Funk. And what is the cure for funking a jump?' He looked round the class for support as they surrounded him, and if it was a pity his eye had stopped at Haddow, well, even Haddow had enough wits to know the answer to that question.

'Give it up and do something else, sir,' Peter said gravely.

'Did I ask you for your opinion, Haddow?'

'Yes, sir.'

'Well I don't think much of it. Your wits are wool-gathering.' Peter hugged himself in joy at the phrase, and continued to stand with a slightly hurt, puzzled expression.

'Come on, shove these on – you, Chadwick.' Kong threw a pair of practice boxing gloves at Big Joe, who started pulling them on with a savage, gloating light in his eye. 'Here, somebody else—' Kong caught sight of Wee Webster deliriously patting Haddow on the back, and Kong smiled a quiet grim smile. 'You, Webster. David and Goliath.'

'Aw, sir!' Big Joe protested. 'I'll not even be able to *see* him.' Jimmy Webster was pulling on the gloves without a qualm, and dancing on his toes.

'Boxing is an art,' Kong explained. 'It's co-ordination that counts. We're all friends here, nobody's going to get hurt.' Haddow was staring at him as if he didn't believe that Kong could possibly exist. There was something sullen and unco-operative about Haddow. 'Right, seconds out. Give us a good clean fight and fight to win!'

Kong joined tolerantly in the laughter as Webster went into a fighting crouch and big Chadwick peered from behind his gloves registering stupidity and fear. The two of them pranced around to shouts of 'Moider 'im, Jimmy!' until

115

Kong impatiently called for them to start fighting. Wee Webster threw himself at Big Joe, who fell back gasping with his arms at his sides. Webster poked a skinny arm at Joe's chest, and Joe started to buckle at the knees. Webster jabbed at his face, and Big Joe wheeled and sank to the mat on his face, with his arms flung out. There were whistles and cheers.

'All right, you've had your fun,' Kong said, with an engaging smile, regretting that Chadwick hadn't had the sense to deliver even a gentle tap — to make the thing more realistic. 'Here, Arthur, you work out with . . . with Haddow.'

Something like fight tension had appeared now. Arthur was light on his feet, putting in some very neat toe-work to loosen up. Haddow was brandishing his gloves like a fool, as usual, and then, after watching Arthur's feet closely, started to do a grotesque shuffle. Then he started leaping in the air, with his fists going up and down like pistons.

'We all know you can play the fool, Haddow,' Kong said sharply. 'Let us see you doing something sensible. Show him, Arthur.'

But Peter was not playing the fool. He changed his step to a *pas-de-basque*, with his eyes unwaveringly on Tom Arthur's face, and when Tom stepped in with a straight right, Peter chanced not to be there. He tapped Arthur's ear before dancing back again, and Kong snorted in exasperation.

Tom Arthur was wearing a hard smile now, and moving forward. Peter started to back-pedal in a circle, and Tom's lip curled as he came after him. Peter had now started to skip backwards, swaying from side to side with both hands stretched out in front of him, and when Tom swung wildly at him, he caught the flying fist between his hands and yanked the glove off. Tom swung the other fist and Peter caught it on the elbow.

'Easy, easy,' he complained. 'You dropped this.' 'Yella!' Tom muttered.

'Behave yourself, Haddow,' Kong called, not smiling. Tom Arthur poked out a left that jolted Peter's chin. Peter shook his head and kept on dancing. When Tom tried the left again, Peter jerked backwards, rolled right over and landed on his feet in a crouch. Tom Arthur stood infuriated as he rose.

'Go on, hit him!' Kong yelled, and almost as Peter drove his glove into Tom Arthur's chin, added, 'Okay, fight's over – no, all right, carry on!' Peter leapt wildly from side to side, and the class began to clap hands in time. Kong was disgusted.

'That's enough,' he said sourly. 'Donaldson and Peebles, you have a go, I want to see some real boxing.' Tom Arthur looked pleadingly at Kong and then threw the gloves at Donaldson, almost in tears with vexation. Peter bowed theatrically at Arthur's back, and Wee Webster darted forward and raised one of Peter's gloved hands.

'Champeen!' he shouted. It was uncanny the way the second-rate element hung together. Kong's pat on the shoulder for Arthur was perfunctory. The boy might have knocked some sense into Haddow if he had only ignored the foolery. Tom was already bitter with the knowledge that he had let the side down. He felt, with a twinge of disloyalty, that Kong might have helped if he hadn't confused him from the ringside.

On the way home, Peter and Davie and Big Joe were walking together, with Jimmy Webster. Jimmy was twitching with delight and reliving his match with Big Joe.

'You're a nut case, Haddow,' Davie said.

'*Une veritable tête valise*,' Peter agreed.

'What do you have to go and get Kong's back up for? "Give it up and try something else." You're just *asking* him to set one of his pet dogs on you.'

'Shut up! What did you expect me to say, Yessir, yessir, three bags full? What's eating you, you're the one that hates his guts.'

'I just don't ask for trouble. You're a fool. Over the

117

head of Stoolie, as well! *He* was asking for it.'

'Listen,' Peter said carefully. 'Stoolie's just a plook. He's nastier than the Kong any day.'

'Well, what's the sense of sticking up for him? He's a fat, creashy slug.'

'It's power, that's what it is. Stoolie's only a plook, but there's nothing he can do to the Kong. The Kong's a plook, but he's got *authority*. So he should lay off Stoolie even if Stoolie is a plook. It just struck me, watching him doing his big, witty gorilla act. Who the hell is the Kong? Just a bloody Ned that got a job as a gym teacher because he failed his Highers, or something. But that gives him the right to crack a hell of a lot of funny jokes, but if *you* crack a joke it's the chopper, Mac. It gives me the boak.'

'Schoolteachers are schoolteachers,' Davie said stubbornly. 'If you were one you would be just the same.'

'Not on your life!'

'How do you know, smartie?'

'I can crack jokes without being a teacher.'

The three others yelled Ha ha ha. Growing hot with irritation, Peter said:

'I'm telling you, that's their trouble. Power mania. They're corrupt wi' it. Do you think they would try the stuff they try on us if they didn't have the belt behind them?'

'Aw, you're away wi' the fairies,' Big Joe said. 'What about the army? They don't have a belt.'

'The same!'

'And the University?'

'The same!'

'Who can belt you at the University?'

'It doesn't need to be a belt . . .'

'Ach, you're dighted,' Big Joe said flatly. Peter struggled hotly for words, but Davie said wearily:

'Oh, God, don't get started again.'

'Do you think the Kong would have the nerve to belt me?' Big Joe demanded, bulging through his blazer.

'No, I don't!' Peter agreed. 'That's exactly what I mean.'

'Ach, you want it both ways. You're dighted, Haddow, I told you, you're dighted.'

'You might as well change the record,' said Jimmy Webster. Jimmy was growing temporarily in confidence. Acceptance in the gang was going to his head, Peter reflected contemptuously. He had an impulse to punch Jimmy's nose, to make him listen to sense about the abuse of authority.

10

It was Joe Chadwick who suggested a mass outing to Millport to celebrate the end of the Highers. Peter embraced the idea without pausing to think of any practical difficulties. Freedom was a pin-point of light at the end of a long tunnel, and it demanded a break-out.

'We'll get everybody in the class,' he agreed. 'And we can climb to the top of the island and have a bonfire of the papers.'

'Eh, no' everybody,' Big Joe demurred, and looked crafty. 'Just a wee gang – you know, mixed.'

'Five a side,' Peter suggested.

'Aye,' said Davie, 'nobody like Stoolie, for instance – your pal, Stoolie.'

'Belt up,' Peter told him. 'How about Jimmy Webster?'

'No, no!' Big Joe moaned. 'You're ruining it. You know what Jimmy's like when there's women about. He goes daft trying to make them believe he hates them. He would just get in the road.'

Peter was forced to agree. 'All right, how about women?' he asked tentatively.

'Just women in the class,' Big Joe said positively. 'That's the idea. They'll be so pleased the Highers are finished they'll let us get away with murder. Are you asking Alice Jackson?' he asked Davie, with a heavy air of casualness. Davie glowered.

'What's the sense of sticking to women in the class? Who have you got? Jackson, wee Enterkin, nothing. Deirdre Campbell, for instance? Byuck.'

'Okay,' Joe said, relaxing. 'I'll take Jackson. You can dig up anybody else you like.'

'Ach, I'll think about it.' Davie was glum and uncomfortable, and being unsubtle by nature, he couldn't help throwing a glance at Peter which made Peter raise his eyes silently to heaven.

'What's up with you?' Davie asked, sullen and pleading at once. 'I don't suppose she would want to come anyway.'

'Oh, it'll be great, going to the woods with my sister there,' Peter cried. 'Just dandy.'

'Who's talking about going to the woods? Nothing funny's gonny happen, see!'

'This must be a different trip you're talking about,' Big Joe said comfortably. 'Get in there, Chadwick!'

'Ach, I don't think I'll bother,' Davie muttered, and Peter said, 'Okay, okay, ask her. Just try to keep her away from me, will you?' Davie brightened up instantly, like an infant who has been denied and then given its biscuit.

Big Joe's idea was the whole Easter week-end, 'At a nice big boarding-house where they don't have any spies in the corridors at night.' But Peter had begun to consider how much money it was going to cost, and what his mother was going to think about it, and even if there was no other objection, he was in no doubt that Jean's mother would never stand for her going away for a week-end with him. He was gloomily uncertain as to whether she would even be able to come for a day. Davie, having got Peter's approval for his asking Christine, at once supported him in everything, and although Joe sulked, they decided they should go to Millport for Easter Monday.

The Highers passed in a dream of unnatural vividness. Every day was the same, with the same concentrated silences and the same frantic knots of conversation to follow. Following the unwritten law, everybody groaned after every paper, but it was easy to tell, for instance, that Tom Arthur's groans about his miserable performance in maths were merely formality, since he was a mathematical freak; and that Davie's groans about maths were groans with truth in them. Davie passed from shattered despair to

121

shattering nonchalance, and his defiant cry that he didn't need a good group to be a car salesman became a sound to avoid.

Peter found the endless post-mortems constricting and claustrophobic, and the questions at home exhausting. His father was on an early shift, and before he went up the street for a pint at five o'clock, he expected Peter to be home with a full report, although Peter knew it could mean practically nothing. It was a matter of filial duty stretched to twanging.

'Did you know all the words?' he would ask, for example, and a shrug or a simple yes was not enough of an answer. He insisted on knowing the details, with a pathetic determination to share the whole experience.

'There was one word, *étang*,' Peter offered. 'I put it down as river, and it means a pond.'

'For heaven's sake!' Samuel was disgusted. 'Anybody knows the difference between a river and a pond. You should have *known* that. You just haven't been sticking in at your homework, that's your trouble.'

'Nobody else knew it either,' Peter explained. 'Except one girl. There's some things you have to guess. Davie had it as a mine-shaft.'

Samuel hooted with unnecessary loudness, in relief that somebody had guessed worse than Peter.

'Poor Davie,' he said. 'Well, if you've failed, he doesny stand much of a chance.'

'They don't fail you for a few mistakes,' Peter assured him patiently. 'Nobody ever gets a hundred per cent.'

'You mean you've passed?'

'I think so. You can never tell, though,' he added, as insurance. 'But I think so.'

'A mine-shaft,' Samuel gloated. 'That's a good one. How are you going to do in the maths? Have you got Pythagorus's Theorem all right?'

'Pythagorus's Theorem?' Peter echoed before he could disguise his surprise. 'What do you know about Pythagorus's Theorem?'

'Don't think you're the only one that knows anything,' his father said sharply. 'The square on the hippotenues is equal to the sum of the square on the other two sides.' He blushed and coughed loudly, and in a flash of insight Peter realized that he had been secretly reading his school-books, to try to find his way into the high-sounding mysteries that were a common language between Peter and Davie. The knowledge made Peter uncomfortable and guilty. It would have taken more insight than Peter possessed to deduce that when Samuel went up to the pub at five o'clock, he carried the results of his inquisitions with him and repeated them with overpowering pride to his old drinking cronies, to whom Peter was a mythical boy wonder.

Emily was also morbidly absorbed in the Highers, but accepted that the actual papers were beyond her comprehension, and expressed her concern in an obsessional terror for Peter's health. At lunch-time, she never ate at all, but put down food for Peter and barely remembered to feed Julie too; and then sat at the table and nervously watched him eating, to make sure that his digestion still worked; and leapt from the table to bring him butter, or salt, or anything that could make the enormous ordeal of eating easier for him. Every morning she saw bags under his eyes and every evening she saw hollows in his cheeks; or sometimes she saw that he was getting fat in the face, and diagnosed swollen glands. Peter had grown so accustomed to this performance in milder doses that he hardly noticed it. When the exams were over, the difficulties he had envisaged about the trip to Millport evaporated. His mother leapt at the suggestion of a good healthy day in the fresh air, and his father awkwardly gave him a pound. Christine thought it was really nice of Davie to ask her to come, and said that she would be able to keep an eye on her wee brother and prevent him from falling off the pier.

Peter had worked round with terrified care and slowness to broaching the subject with Jeannie. Every day, as soon as his father had left for his pint, he had raced to telephone her and give her a more accurate account of how he had fared, and nearly every day he had met her bus and walked slowly with her to within a block of her house. Since meeting her parents he was nervous of seeing Mrs Pynne again, and although Jean assured him that her mother didn't mind him, she was not anxious to test the question too openly. But when Peter finally asked her if she could come with him to Millport for a whole day, she said:

'Phew! I wondered if you were taking somebody else.'

'But how did you know?'

'Cathie Martin told me – she invited me, in fact.'

'Cathie Martin? She's off her head – she's not in it at all.'

'Isn't she? She told me all about it – you, and her brother, and Davie McAllister, and your crowd at school.'

'Oh. Maybe Davie asked her. Hey, are you coming?'

'Are you asking me?'

'Of course I'm asking you. Will your mother not object? I don't want to annoy her. Does she think I'm too young and brainless?'

'I'm going away for the day with the crowd, it's all *right*. Do you think I get locked up or something?'

'Imagine a whole day. Jean, I hate to say this, but I love you.'

'Oh. Oo-oo. Don't hate to say it. Me, too.'

'Say it.'

'I can't, my face goes all silly. I keep writing it in shorthand. Look, it's a phraseogram. Like this. A wee tick . . . then an upward curve . . . then a downward curve . . . and a wee dome thing – the wee dome is you.'

'It doesn't look like me.'

'It does – a dome full of brains.'

'Do it on the back of my hand.'

She traced a design lightly with her finger-nail on the back of his hand, and he clapped the other hand over the place and said:

'I'll be able to look at it now.'

124

'It'll fade away. I'll have to keep on doing it again.'

'You can do it every time you see me.'

'I will, I will.'

The appearance of Cathie Martin in the plan for the outing was no mystery. Cathie was not sensitive enough to need invitations to anything. Her young brother, Sidney, was the same age as Peter, and Joe Chadwick had told Sidney about the plan.

Sidney wasn't one of the crowd, because he went to Allan Glen's school and paid fees and considered himself a sophisticated cut above the local-school peasants, but he prized the acquaintance of Big Joe, and when he reported back to his sister, she instantly reorganized the outing in her own mind. The Martins owned a little tenement house in Millport where the family spent its summer holidays, and Cathie decided that she and Sidney would go down at Easter to open it up and get it ready for summer, use it as a base for the crowd, and take the whole thing over. She and Sidney were waiting at the pier when the crowd arrived. Jimmy Webster was there after all, and Alistair Donaldson, the least obnoxious of the athletic clique, and Lily Enterkin, whose presence reminded Peter how mature and blasé he had grown. He felt even more staggered by his past yearning when he saw that she was paired off with Wee Jimmy Webster, leaving Alistair Donaldson as the extra male. Big Joe sat beside Alice Jackson in the train going down and blandly held her hand, at which Davie, who had spent so much of his youth lusting after Alice, smiled inanely and exchanged supercilious glances with Christine. Peter did not hold Jean's hand. He didn't need to. Merely by sitting beside her he could feel her nearness with every pore.

She sat looking serenely out of the train window and resting one hand on her knee, where her finger slowly traced on the cloth of her skirt a little tick, an upward curve, a downward curve and a little dome.

When they went down the gangway from the steamer at

Millport, Cathie Martin and Sidney were already waving a welcome. Sidney was wearing a school blazer and flannels, and a scarf tucked elegantly into his open-necked shirt. Cathie had a black sweater and her square hips bulged nightmarishly through tight leopard-skin pants. She visibly counted the party and her small petulant mouth shaped a satisfied smirk at the discovery that there was an extra male. Sidney Martin was making the same calculation, with one hand in his blazer pocket and the other elegantly gripping a cigarette.

'Damn bad arithmetic,' he said sulkily. '*Somebody's* had it.'

'Uch, the boat's loaded wi' talent, away and dig one up,' Big Joe said unfeelingly. Sidney puffed deeply on his cigarette and blew smoke down his nostrils with a sneering smile.

'Oh, this crowd's good enough for me.'

'Just keep your eyes off mine,' Joe said blandly, and Sidney answered with a man-of-the-world smile to indicate that he got the idea, but that if it had been anybody but Big Joe, he would have no difficulty in cutting in on Alice Jackson. The party went through the turnstiles and straggled along the promenade, and Peter, in his determination not to be too obvious about Jean, found himself bringing up the rear with his sister.

'Just you watch it, wee brother,' she warned him archly.

'Watch what?'

'I do Pitman's shorthand as well.'

'Look, you're with Davie — how about burying the big-sister act, eh? Just make out you don't know me.' She linked her arm in his and patted his hand. 'There, there,' she said. 'Big sister keep heap big mouth shut. Big sister just not want wee brother get heap hurted.'

'For God's sake don't get cute, Christine.' But he squeezed her arm to show there were no ill feelings.

'Wee brother better watch out for heap paleface,' she said, narrowing her eyes at the crowd ahead. Cathie Martin

126

was hanging affectionately on Alistair Donaldson's arm on one side, and on Davie's on the other. Sidney Martin was walking beside Jean, with his arm round her waist.

'That doesn't mean anything,' Peter said in irritation, because it suddenly did mean something.

'Come on, we'll catch up,' Christine suggested, but Peter shook his head. He was afraid of looking obvious, and he schooled himself to endure the strange torture of watching Sidney squeeze Jean's waist and turn his head to gaze into her face; and the infinitely more awful sight of Jean smiling back up at him and making no move to push his arm away. By the time they arrived at a café, everybody else had already organized three tables pulled together, and everybody was seated except Davie, who was waiting meekly for Christine. Sidney Martin had his chair drawn close to Jean, and the chair at her other side was occupied by Cathie. Sidney was waving one hand, still with the cigarette negligently between the fingers, at a waitress, and calling grandly for eleven coffees. His other arm was flung casually across Jean's shoulders. Jean threw Peter a rueful smile of resignation which angered him irrationally.

When they came to discuss what to do next, Sidney had a great idea. They would hire motor-boats and race them. 'Two in each boat,' he proposed, 'and three in one.' He waved a hand to indicate that the three would be Peter, Davie and Christine. Cold thick rage flooded Peter's mind, and Jean's sudden dumb message of appeal increased it. Cathie and Alistair Donaldson and Wee Jimmy Webster were beginning to hail the idea as wizard, and he faced the utterly impossible problem of stopping this atrocity without punching Sidney's sneering little mouth there and then, and making a fool of himself.

'What a waste of money!' It was Christine, and Peter found himself trembling with relief. 'Take it easy – we can go out in boats after lunch when we're tired.' Davie said good idea, and Sidney was beginning to sneer wearily when Christine spoke again.

127

'We can hire bikes and race round the island.' Jean's face lit up at once, and Peter said, 'Come on, Jean, we'll race clockwise and somebody else can race anti-clockwise.'

'What's the use of splitting the crowd up?' Sidney locked glances of hate across the table to Peter.

'There's too many people in it,' Peter said levelly, and Sidney said, 'Well?' Peter didn't answer. They were all moving out of the café, and Big Joe was refusing to have anything to do with bikes. He and Alice were going for a walk.

'Are we?' Alice asked coolly.

'Sure,' Joe told her. 'I paid your fare, I'm taking you for a walk.' She tutted and said, 'Well!' and meekly walked away with him. Peter could feel waves of hate coming from Sidney as they started to choose bikes, and he hoped Sidney was receiving on his wave-length, too. Cathie Martin and Donaldson set off on the anti-clockwise tour, followed at some distance by Lily and Jimmy Webster. Peter stood, breathing deeply, while Davie and Christine started off clockwise, leaving him with Jean and Sidney Martin.

'It looks as if we're the team with the gooseberry,' Sidney said, to nobody, and nobody answered. He started to make small conversation with Jean. Now is the time, Peter thought, to get rid of him. She only needs to shut him up and say she's with me. But Jean merely returned small conversation. Peter felt betrayed and vicious, and as they rode out of the village, Sidney resolutely kept alongside Jean. Peter, seething and crushed under his misery, clung to the pathetic dignity of refusing to stoop to an idiotic game of cutting in between them. Every second he waited for Jean to drop back, but Sidney matched her slow progress exactly, and on a clear stretch of road took his hands off the grips and rode with one resting on her shoulder.

They had gone half a mile when Jean stopped.

'This bike's no good, the pedals keep slipping,' she complained, her face scarlet. 'I'll go back and get another

128

one.' There was a touch of impatience in her voice, which Peter was sure was directed at himself, and which provoked him to a resentment which was horrible to experience.

'I'll come back with you,' Sidney said, with a smirk of conspiracy.

'No, no! Don't bother, you can just wait here and I'll be back in a minute. Don't anybody come with me!' She turned her machine and pedalled furiously back towards the village. Sidney sat complacent on the grass verge and offered Peter a cigarette, which Peter refused in silence.

'There's too many of us here, you know,' Sidney said, as he lay back and puffed.

'Why don't you beat it, then?' Peter asked him.

'Ah, no, I'm doing all right.'

Peter sat down and stared across the water cursing the stupidity that had led him to hang back at the pier. It had all started there. If he had stuck close to Jean, Sidney would have headed for somebody else. He could find no way of saying that Jean was his girl without sounding pleading, and it was too late to put the situation reasonably to Sidney, who was well in command. Sidney had nothing to lose.

'Some piece, that Jeannie-Peenie,' Sidney sighed. 'I wonder if she goes.'

'Will you shut up?'

Sidney answered with a tolerant sneer. But as minutes went by, both of them became concerned.

'She's had twenty minutes to change that bike,' Sidney said viciously. 'She's probably ditched us.'

'Uhuh.'

'What do you expect?' Sidney demanded thinly, 'when she's stuck with a gooseberry?'

'Uhuh.'

'You do a solo from now on. I'm going back for her.'

Sidney jumped on his bike and started for Millport. With clenched fists, Peter made for his own machine, and then threw it down on the verge and sat beside it thumping his

129

head with one fist. Almost immediately he heard Jean calling him. He looked up to find her riding breathlessly towards him.

'Hurry up!' she shouted. Bewildered, Peter mounted and rode beside her.

'I've been hiding behind the wee hut round the corner for ages,' she gasped. 'I was *sure* you would come back.'

'Oh, Jean!' he wailed. 'I'm a fool, a fool.'

'You sure are, you fool.' She gave him a distracted smile as she pedalled fiercely beside him. 'Do you think he'll catch up?'

'Any minute,' Peter yelled. 'Faster, faster, faster!' They laughed and panted wildly until Jean shook her head from side to side and moaned, 'No, no, no,' and they freewheeled and took in great deep breaths.

'But any minute we'll bump into the other shower,' Peter reminded her. 'It only takes about half an hour to go right round.' He saw Jean scanning the hillside on both sides of the road, and without further discussion they stopped and wheeled the bikes off the road and down towards a rocky part of the shore. They had the machines carefully propped behind a boulder when Jean saw Sidney Martin, and they both lay down beside the bikes, with hands over each other's mouth, until they were sure he was safely past.

'I thought we would never get rid of him,' she breathed, and then pulled Peter's hand back to her mouth and licked it experimentally.

'You should have told him he reminded you of a jellyfish,' Peter said.

'I wish I had thought of that.'

'I was beginning to think you liked him.'

'Oh, Peter! I kept *trying* to think of what to say to put him off, but I couldn't. I'm no use.'

'It's me that's no use,' Peter said moodily. 'I was even getting angry at you because you wouldn't say something to him. Imagine that. It was my job to get rid of him. I

130

should have pushed his face into a coffee-cup and held it there till he drowned.'

'It doesn't matter now. He's gone. Gone! Everybody's gone!'

'It's starting to rain.'

'Well, don't sound so devastated. I've still got a plastic mac.' She pulled it out of her jacket pocket and they laid it over their heads and stared out at the rain on the water. It was only a light shower, with glints of pale sunshine moving over the Firth. After a few minutes they turned towards each other and let the raincoat fall over their heads as they sat uncomfortably twisted and happy.

'You could sit on my knee.'

'I'm all sandy.'

'Sit on my knee at once and don't quibble.'

'Yes, sir.'

'Jean?'

'What?'

'I like saying that. Jean. Jean. Jean. What are we going to do?'

'Go out in a motor-boat?'

'No, I mean what are we going to do . . . you know.' He felt her stir uneasily.

'We don't need to think about anything, just today. It's enough, just to be here.'

'Yes, it is. I think too much, that's what's wrong with me. It's interesting to speculate, though.' He was thoughtful and unworried. 'I suppose it's possible this is merely an adolescent passion, doomed to blaze and then to sink into the darkness, and so on.'

'Don't say that! Oh, Peter, don't say that. It makes me think of being dead.'

'There, there, you're alive. Look. See? You're alive. No, I mean, I try to be rational about it, and then I think, look, I'm only seventeen, and you're only nineteen, maybe it's only a teenage crush. But it's impossible to believe it.'

'Well, then, *stop* believing it.'

131

'I mean, if we were both years older we would take it for granted and we would get married.'

'Oh, wouldn't that be nice!' Jean sighed luxuriously and stroked the back of his neck.

'Of course, the whole thing sounds silly. You don't get married at seventeen.'

'No.' Jean tried to match his thoughtful, serious game. 'But we're getting older all the time. You'll be working soon.'

'No, I won't. The University or the Tech. Three years of idiot serfdom.'

'Well,' Jean sighed. 'I'll only be twenty-two. I can wait. Are you sure you're not worried about me being older than you?'

'Oh, no! Good heavens, woman, when you're ninety-four I'll be ninety-two, with no teeth or anything, chasing you round the house and snapping at you with my gums.'

'Oh, that'll be lovely!'

'Jean . . . you know, I mean it wasn't any of my business, but I keep wondering about it . . .'

She kissed him firmly, and then said, 'Don't worry about it, it never really amounted to anything serious. I mean, we've known each other for *donkeys* – oh, you know, his people are friends of my people, and he's always been *there*. He's quite nice, honestly, but he's just – just *Archie*, that's all.'

'All right, I won't mention it again, honestly. What lovely rain.'

'Yes, it's *private*.'

'I'm sorry, an accident.'

'What?'

'Nothing,' Peter said shortly. 'I didn't mean to touch you like that.'

'Oh, I don't mind, don't worry about it.' She buried her face against his ear. 'I love you. I can say it under here when you can't see me.'

'Again.'

132

'I love you, I love you, I love you.'

Peter held her away from him and said, 'I love you. I was making a silly fuss about touching you,' he added lamely, 'but I don't want ever to take advantage of you.'

'You're *not*!'

'No, I know. I must be inhibited, or something, me with all my big talk about a healthy joy in the human body. And oh, Jean, I do take delight in you, I love the way you move and stand up and the way all the bits of you are fitted together. My skull seems to shrink every time I look at you. I just want everything to be nice and slow and perfect for you – clean and, oh, I don't know . . .'

Gazing from about a foot away into his thin face, with its brow twisted in his efforts to explain his confusion, and weirdly pale in the light that filtered through the plastic, Jean was wrenched with pity and warmth and dim comprehension. She took his hand and laid it over her heart, and she laid her head on his shoulder.

'Oh, Peter. Mmm. Hold me tight. Beautiful, beautiful, Peter.'

'Hey!' Peter said suddenly. 'Oh. I love you. But hey! You get grants for going to the Tech nowadays. A lot of students get married – maybe you even get a marriage allowance. If I got a marriage allowance, and you had a job, we could get married and be poverty-stricken students and eat bread and cheese!'

'We couldn't! Could we?'

'Sure! I would be your kept man. You would have to work overtime to keep me in new blazers and sports jackets. It would be paradisal.'

'You're bonkers,' she muttered cosily, and after a pause, asked, 'Do people really do things like that?'

'What do you mean, do *people*? People don't matter – we don't need to ask what people do. We can do what we like. We're us.'

'Aha. Your mother would like that.'

'Well, my old man would be delirious. He always says

kids should be booted into the cold at fifteen to fend for themselves.'

'Where would we live?' she inquired practically.

'Not with my family, you can bet your life.'

'Oh, with mine?'

'No-o, thank you. We'll buy a tent. Thousands of people live in tents all the year round, they're healthy. We could pitch it on the waste ground.'

'You're not serious, are you? I don't mean the tent, I mean the rest.'

'Sure I am! No, don't be daft, I'm just *talking* again. But I feel better now. If anybody gets funny, we always have our desperate survival plan to fall back on. Hey, I've got a rope-ladder in the old tin hut in the garden. We can always elope.'

'We've got an ordinary ladder.'

'No, a rope-ladder's more romantic. You can keep a bucket of water under your bedroom window. For me to stick my feet in. I *always* stand in a bucket of water when I'm eloping.'

'Oh, Peter, don't lose your rope-ladder.'

'Never. It's stopped raining.'

'I know.'

'Do we go on round the island, or freewheel back to Millport?'

'No, we just sit here.'

'They'll be wondering what happened to us.'

'I'm just not moving from here and that's final, and if I don't move you can't move, so you might as well settle down where you are.'

'Pretty bossy, aren't you?'

'Yes, I am. No, I'm just selfish.'

'Oh, good.'

By the time they returned the hired bicycles and reported to the Martin house, everybody had finished a picnic lunch. Big Joe and Alice Jackson had gone off to hire a motor-boat, by themselves, and Sidney Martin had gone to the tennis courts with Jimmy Webster and Lily Enterkin, expecting the others to follow. Davie winked at Peter, and Christine smiled an accusing smile that said you're the pink limit. But Cathie Martin was disgusted with him, and with Jean. She was still eating rolls with tomatoes. She ate in a practised, greedy style and chewed with her mouth slightly open.

'You're a fine pair,' she said between chews. 'We thought you had had an accident. You can cut some rolls yourself. And you'd better stick to the crowd, everybody agreed to that.'

'When did anybody agree to that?' Peter asked, crushing down his anger.

'It's supposed to be a *crowd*, isn't it? How does anybody know what you're up to if you go and hide?' she insinuated.

'You can have a wee guessing game, Cathie,' Peter said evenly, boiling with anger. 'If you imagine it's any of your business.' And she cried petulantly, 'Well it is any of my business. This is our house, and I'm responsible.'

'You're responsible for damn all,' Peter said quietly, slicing a roll. 'Come on, Jean, we'll eat somewhere else.'

'Oh, yes I am! How will your mother like it,' she asked Jean, in a splutter of venom, 'if she knows you disappeared for the whole day without anybody else there?'

Peter turned from the sink, where the rolls were piled, with the knife still in his hand and black murder in his heart, and the sick consciousness that there was no defence against natural vindictiveness. But Christine was already cajoling Cathie.

'Don't worry, Cathie. Jean's mother will never know how Jean spent the day . . .'

'These things get around!'

'. . . unless some bitch goes to the trouble of telling her, and getting her eyes scratched out with my bare hands, for instance.' A seraphic smile broke on Peter's face. Oh, brother, I love that sister.

135

Sensing steel in the opposition, Cathie reverted to petu-
lance.

'How do you think Sidney felt, looking all over the place
and getting worried?'

'Anyone for tennis?' Peter asked. But part of his mind
remained on Cathie for the rest of the day. Her sisterly
loyalty knew no scruples, and she would be capable of
anything. For the sake of safety, he allowed himself, and
Jean, to be kept close to the crowd, but he stayed close
to Jean too. Sidney worked to establish the fiction, by
suggestion, that the business of the morning with the
bikes had been a childish trick of Peter's, without Jean's
approval, and he oscillated between ponderous wooing of
Jean with bold suggestions that she should stay for the
night, and peevish spleen towards Peter, whom he started
calling Loverboy. Finally, Peter said, in the manner of an
indulgent parent wearied by a nuisance child:

'You know, Sidney, if you loverboy just once more I'll
bash your teeth back round your tonsils.'

'Ha ha ha!'

'That's right.'

Peter was able to endure Sidney's infantile sniping for the
rest of the afternoon without too much concern. He was
still coasting on the sweetness of the morning with Jean,
and minute details of it kept returning to delight him.

They bought bread and butter and chocolate biscuits
and cold meat and fruit and milk for a feast at the Martins'
house before leaving for the last boat from the island, and
it was a relief to have the little kitchen crowded so that the
hostility of Cathie and Sidney was diluted. But when the
time came for leaving, a ludicrously mundane fact arose to
plague Peter again. Sidney Martin was locked in the single
outdoor toilet, and Jean was waiting to use it and to tidy
up before she went for the boat.

'There's plenty of time,' Cathie said. 'The rest of you
stroll down and Sidney and I will come down with Jean.'

'I'll stay here!' Peter declared.

'You'd better go down and book a place in the queue,' Cathie suggested, and Jean nodded agreement.

Everybody else had gone.

'The others can book a place in the queue,' Peter said.

'They're not thinking about Jean,' Cathie protested. 'She'll just be at your back.'

It was impossible to point to anything really wrong with the suggestion. There was a good twenty-five minutes to boat time, and the walk couldn't take more than five minutes. It was also impossible to see much wrong with the idea of staying to wait for Jean, but the vague feeling came to him that she might be physically uncomfortable and shy about it, and he felt that he had antagonized the Martins enough for the day. He walked very slowly down the street to the promenade, looking round to see if Jean was following, and even more slowly along to the pier, where the boat was already in.

When he got to the turnstiles, there was still no sign of her, and crowds were milling round, unsighting him. He was almost convinced that he had missed her when she popped out of the crowd, pink and flushed, and he grabbed her hand and pushed her through the turnstile. They raced to the end of the pier, and it could have been only an illusion that the boat had actually moved several feet, but cheers began to break out in the crowd on the pier and suddenly a passage opened up through the bodies and faces, jerkily seen, smiled and yelled encouragement. Jean was panting painfully as he pulled her wildly by the arm and flew along the space that kept opening before them. Abruptly he found himself facing the edge of the pier, but it was the edge that had no boat at it. The crowd had opened up without thinking, in the wrong direction. And now the crowd had closed again. As Peter jostled back through them he was in no doubt now that the boat was moving. It seemed quite far away.

And everybody was aboard. A gasping moan came from Jean as they stood staring at it across a ten-foot gap and identified Christine and Davie and Wee Webster; and Alistair Donaldson; and Lily. They were waving. Davie was convulsed with derision, and then, as he looked at Peter, the laughter left his face and he looked shattered and cheated.

'Hey, we timed that great.' It was the satisfied voice of Big Joe. He was standing beside Peter on the edge of the pier, with Alice Jackson on his arm. Alice was stamping her foot.

'I'll strangle you!' Christine yelled, and added, 'I'll tell Jean's people.'

'No, don't, I'll telephone!' Jean gasped.

'You'd better tell mine,' Big Joe shouted happily. 'We'll phone Jackson's old lady.'

The boat slid farther away. Davie doubled his fist at Peter in an agony of envy.

'The clock at the Martins's was twenty minutes slow,' Jean cried, when she had recovered her breath. 'But so is my watch!'

'Funny, that,' Big Joe said. He was serene.

'Damned funny,' said Peter. 'Did you have your watch off?'

'No! Only when we were playing tennis,' said Jean.

They walked back up the pier. Just outside they found Sidney Martin strolling towards them. His jaw dropped when he saw them.

'You haven't all missed the boat! You're a hopeless shower.'

'Aye, it's terrible,' Big Joe agreed. 'We'll have to sleep at your place.'

'No kidding.' Sidney threw his cigarette away with a vicious gesture.

'No kidding,' Peter said, and he stared at Sidney with a fist bunched in his pocket.

'We'll see what Cathie says about it,' Sidney mumbled, and Big Joe, with the greatest amiability, went on, 'We're sleeping at your place, so shut up or you'll get a belt in the gub.'

'You're awful, Joe Chadwick,' Alice Jackson was wailing. 'You did this deliberately.'

'Don't natter, Jackson,' Joe chid her casually. 'You knew, all right.'

'You're awful.'

Cathie Martin appeared to be more confused than surprised when she saw them. Peter was convinced beyond doubt that Sidney had planned for Jean to miss the boat and for everybody else to catch it, and that Cathie had quietly given him a hand. She floundered for words.

'What happened, did the boat leave early? There'll be a hell of a row about this. You left in plenty of time . . .' This to Peter. 'This is just a bloody nuisance. There's nothing to eat. We could have a party. I don't know what happened to the alarm-clock. How did *you* miss the boat?' This to Joe. 'Where's everybody going to sleep?'

'Who wants to sleep?' Joe asked brutally, and Alice Jackson cried:

'You're *awful*!'

Alice and Jean were to telephone home, and Cathie offered to go with them as evidence, falling immediately into an attitude of conspiracy.

'But what will I *say*?' Alice Jackson protested.

'Just say you and Jean missed the boat, and you're staying the night with Cathie,' Peter explained patiently.

'But my father'll ask who else is here,' she wailed.

'Do you want us hung?' Big Joe asked her. 'Don't mention anybody else.'

'You don't know my father,' Alice persisted, and Joe begged her to shut up. Peter asked Jean:

'Are you worried?' Although it was said in the company of everybody, it was an entirely private enquiry. 'I'll be all right once I've telephoned,' she soothed him. His heart swelled in the knowledge of how unlike she was to Alice; or to Cathie, or to any other girl.

'I'd better go as well,' Sidney suggested. 'Everybody will know I'm here with Cathie, anyway.' Peter turned on him, bristling with suspicion, but caught Jean's eye and said nothing. 'You two can make the beds,' Sidney said, smirking.

'Don't you dare, Joe Chadwick!' Alice cried, and Peter assured her they would just put on the kettle. It was raining.

'Look,' Big Joe said reasonably, when he and Peter had been left alone in the kitchen. 'This'll be hunky-dory if you like to take Cathie.'

'Oh, Jesus, get knotted,' Peter said without heat. 'You take Cathie, and let Sidney have Jackson.'

'Well, how would you like it if you were stuck wi' your sister?' Joe pursued the point.

'You know something?' Peter asked him. 'I would rather be stuck with my sister than with Cathie. I would rather be stuck with my *father* than with Cathie.'

'Ach, she's all right,' Joe protested. 'You know what Davie says – she lets you do anything. What have you got against her?'

'Look, Joe,' Peter said. 'Chuck trying to sell *me* Cathie. If you fancy her, you can have her. I'll stick.'

'I don't get you,' Joe said. 'I mean, I would swap you Jackson for Jeannie-Peenie. What's the diff?'

'You're hell of a bloody generous,' Peter said.

'Well,' Joe concluded, 'I'm only trying to be helpful.'

'Och, away back to the Wolf Cubs, Joe.'

The rain was teeming when they heard the others coming back from telephoning, laughing hectically as they rushed in from the street. Jean's face was flushed, and raindrops glistened on it. The rain settled down to a steady torrent. Joe found a pack of cards and they played pontoon. Sidney, his spirits recovered, smiled benignly as his sister Cathie coyly squashed on to the same kitchen chair as Big Joe and threw her arm round his neck to keep herself from falling off, and Big Joe merely squeezed her instead of protesting.

'Pontoon is slow,' Sidney suggested. 'How about strip poker?' It was Alice Jackson who silenced him with an angry shout. Peter played in a happy haze while one of Jean's ankles, under the table, rubbed insistently back and forward on his foot. They drank tea and ate dry bread in the yellow light of an oil lamp while the rain swished endlessly outside in the dark, and Cathie finally said:

'Well, it's time for bed if you lot are going to get the early boat. Where is everybody going to sleep?'

'Don't worry about Jackson and me,' Big Joe said. His casualness covered a deliberate challenge, to see how far he could push Cathie, and Alice's cry of 'You're awful' was automatic and tentative.

'You wouldn't desert me, Joe!' Cathie said seductively, standing close to him and shaking her shoulders. Joe shrugged his.

'Jackson's my lumber,' he said. 'I paid her fare.'

Cathie jolted herself into a businesslike attitude.

'All right, that's enough of the kiddin',' she said. 'The girls'll all go in the front room and you can use the box-bed in here.'

'Not on your life,' Sidney said. 'What do you think I am, a sardine? These two can have the kitchen and I'll take the back room. And no wandering about during the middle of the night, either.' He looked threateningly at Peter.

There was a good deal of confused coming and going with pillows and blankets, and headlong dashes into the rain and the dark to the toilet, during all of which Peter never contrived to be alone with Jean even momentarily. Sidney always seemed to be standing beside him. When he sat on a kitchen chair pulling off his shoes, and not particularly unhappy, he remarked to Big Joe:

'This is really hell of a good. Everybody'll picture us having a wild immoral night. Pontoon and dry bread!'

'Well, you could always have had Cathie.'

'But it's you Cathie loves, Joe,' Peter said coyly. 'Brrr.'

'If Sidney wasn't here I would take on Cathie and Jackson at once,' Joe said. 'What do you think of that horrible

141

wee toly – he was trying to get off with Jackson in the telephone-box.'

'Amazing.'

'Do you think we could sneak into the front room?'

'Okay.' Peter stood up.

'Ach, what's the use, Cathie's there. And Sidney's sitting up in bed listening. Listen.'

Through the thin wall at the back of the box-bed in the kitchen, they could hear the repeated creaking of bed springs.

'I wish we could screw Sidney up some way,' Joe said wistfully.

'Well, this might help,' Peter said. 'I sneaked it out from under his bed while he was at the bog.' He reached under the kitchen bed and pulled out an enamelled chamber pot. 'He'll have to wet his feet if he needs it during the night.'

'He could come in here and use the sink,' Big Joe demurred. 'Hey, is there any rope under that bed?'

They rummaged into a clothes-basket under the bed and found a clothes-line. The enormity of it struck both of them simultaneously, and Big Joe broke irresistibly into titters. 'We'll tie his door up,' he whispered, snorting with the effort to stop laughing.

'Shut up!' Peter whispered, and leaned right forward until his face was buried in the clothes-basket, and shook. Sniggering uncontrollably, they fashioned the clothes-line into a slipknot and crept out to pull it tight over the door-knob of the little back room. The other end they dragged back taut into the kitchen and fastened it round the board that ran along the front of the box-bed. Big Joe had lost all muscular control, and was twitching with weakening laughter.

'What if he doesn't need one?' he hooted in a whisper. Peter winked solemnly, and held up a thumb and forefinger pressed together. Then he filled a jug with water from the sink and climbed into the box-bed with the jug in one hand and the massive pot in the other.

'Sssh!' he said. He held the pot close against the wall, raised the jug high above it, and let a thin, ringing trickle of water bounce into the enamel. Joe collapsed over the edge of the bed, his face crimson.

'Gimme it quick! Hee hee hee! You've got me started!'

The bed springs on the other side of the wall creaked violently. Joe clapped a hand over his mouth. Just above the deafening crash of the rain they could hear a door-knob rattling urgently.

'Just a minute,' Joe whispered. 'He'll just open the window.'

'No, they hee hee hee, they keep the windows screwed up hee hee for fear of hee hee hee burglars,' Peter choked into Joe's ear. 'Hurry up, snore!'

They stared at each other with popping eyes and snored.

At the end of April Peter's mother went into hospital for an operation. There was an atmosphere of furtiveness surrounding it that reassured Peter and damped his curiosity. Julie was delirious with excitement and demanded close details of what kind of saws they used to cut open bits of body with bone in them, and Samuel, in exasperation, ordered her to shut up and said that there was just something wrong with her mother's insides and that the doctors wanted to have a look at it.

'But how do they cut you open without all your blood coming out?' she insisted. 'If you make a wee cut this size with a razor blade you can bleed to death. Can I come and watch them?'

'My God,' Samuel moaned. 'You used to be able to shut kids up. Shut up!'

'Well, can I go to the hospital and watch them cutting Mum open?'

'Will you shut your damned mouth? They don't allow kids in hospitals.'

'Why?' Julie shrieked. 'What if I was ill?'

'They would just let you die, stupid,' Peter told her. Julie hovered on a decision to go hysterical, and Samuel stared wearily at Peter.

'For God's sake don't you start,' he pleaded.

'It's not fair,' Julie cried, 'it's *my* mother. I could just stand and watch, I wouldn't be in anybody's way. How am I supposed to learn if I never get seeing anything? Sadie Martin got seeing their cat having kittens.'

'Oh, Christ, I know how it felt,' Samuel muttered to himself.

Life was not too much disturbed by Emily's absence. Peter fell easily enough into the routine of peeling potatoes and preparing food when he came home from school, and Christine threw herself with self-conscious energy into keeping the house tidy. Even Julie occasionally emerged from her speculations about surgery to help. When the absence of Emily became irksome or melancholy, it was always possible to reflect that it wouldn't last long, and when his father was on late shifts, it was pleasant to come and go without being questioned. He returned from a walk with Jean one evening to find Christine kneeling in front of the fire drying her hair, and Davie McAllister on his hands and knees scrubbing the kitchen floor.

'The emancipation of the male sex,' Peter said cynically. Davie's flushed face turned a shade redder. 'Am I interrupting anything?' Peter asked. 'You've forgotten that wee bit in front of the cooker.'

'Oh, bloody smart,' Davie muttered. Peter had the faint sense of intruding. But intruding on what? He couldn't imagine anything more sexless than Davie's relationship with Christine. Even at times like this, when the old man was at the gasworks and Julie was in bed, Christine was in one room and Davie was in the other, knocking his melts out scrubbing floors.

It was the old lunatic lady-and-squire kick, a tradition that Peter regarded as a pretty sickly affair. The two of them just seemed to talk, Davie basking in Christine's favour and Christine basking in Davie's tail-wagging. At the same time, there was something so self-contained and complacent about it that it drove Peter to a mild irritation he didn't understand, and provoked him to sneering at Davie. His sneers had stopped bothering Davie, an even more irritating thing.

And on top of it all, they didn't mind including Peter in their little cocoon. The three of them passed pleasant pointless evenings making supper and talking till past midnight about nothing, trying far-fetched recipes from a

145

cookery book and doggedly eating the results, however surprising.

Part of his irritation came from the fact that ever since the day at Millport, Christine had never brought up Jean's name again, and he found it difficult to mention her in face of this odd silence. Perhaps it wasn't odd, perhaps she refrained from mentioning Jean because Peter never mentioned her. She knew he was still seeing Jean, but the habit of not speaking her name had acquired a solidity that wouldn't dissolve, and it cut Jean off from the cosy company in the parentless house and the talks round the fire.

Their brother's wife, Nan, dropped in on the threesome one evening, to enquire after Emily and see how they were getting on, and she archly commented on Peter's being the gooseberry, at which Peter laughed easily and Davie fell into a trance of embarrassment.

'You might as well be baby-sitting for Alec and me as making up three's-a-crowd,' Nan cooed, and Peter shrugged his shoulders to indicate that he didn't mind. He could see that Nan had been working round diffidently to the suggestion since she arrived, and she was so relieved at his ready agreement that she exhaled a deep breath and forgot to be arch.

'Wee Alec's not any trouble now anyway, honestly, Peter,' she assured him. 'You'll be able to sit and read and forget about him. You can bring *your* girl friend,' she laughed merrily.

'Right, you're on,' Peter said, and she nodded. He wasn't sure whether she assumed he was merely joining in the joke, but his spirits rose as he reasoned that she couldn't complain if he *did* bring his girl friend.

The baby-sitting date was several days away, and he had to put the proposition to Jean by telephone at her office, because she was involved in visits to relatives, and since Peter's father had gone back on day-shift, he felt less casual about leaving the tea-table abruptly to go and meet her bus

146

in the evenings. They reported together at Alec's house at seven on the evening arranged, and Peter instantly divined that Nan had assumed the girl-friend business to be a wee joke.

'Oh,' she said.

Alec was as calm and soothing as always. He accepted Jean with incurious casualness. Nan addressed her instructions about the baby exclusively to Peter, and before they left, Peter heard them in the next room, Nan probably wondering if it was decent to leave two young people together, alone, in a respectable house, and Alec's low easy voice quite as palpably asking if Nan wanted to go out for the evening or not. Left alone, Peter and Jean sat on opposite sides of the fire, slightly constrained.

'Nan will be looking at her watch all evening wondering when the orgy began,' Peter finally said. Jean laughed, not altogether at ease, and said:

'Well, when does it?'

'O-oh.' It was a soft, high-pitched sound, and Peter stretched out both arms above his head and yawned mightily.

'Sleepy?'

'No, I'm just stretching like a cat. A lion, I mean. Grr.' He slid awkwardly off the chair and jerked forward on his knees until he was kneeling in front of her.

'I don't want an orgy,' he said, in a whisper that turned into a croak. He liked the sound of it. 'I like the sound of that,' he said. 'Aaa. Aaa. Louis Armstrong travelling incognito.' Jean looked down at him, passive and waiting for a cue, whatever it would be.

'O-oh. I'm having the orgy now,' Peter croaked. 'Imagine, nobody can see us. The door's shut and the window's shut and we're inside. That's all I want.'

'Your knees will get housemaid's knee.'

Peter jerked himself into a sitting-position on the floor.

'You're awfully far away down there,' Jean said.

'Would you care to join me?'

'May I?'

147

'Be my guest.' He shuffled backwards, and Jean lowered herself to sit beside him. Slowly he raised a hand and slowly advanced it till the fingertips touched her cheek.

'Oh, Jean.'

'Yes,' she breathed.

'Don't let this rugged simple life go to our heads,' Peter said. 'The floor's as hard as hell. Cushions, for you.'

He pulled cushions from the chairs and laid them tenderly on the floor, and she lay back slowly on them.

'Now you can kiss me,' she said.

'Is it all right?'

'Why not?'

'What will Nan think?'

'She'll think the orgy's begun,' Jean giggled. Peter bent over her and her arms went round him. They lay and kissed. Peter kept his eyes open, a thing he described as a form of gluttony. The line of her cheek as he watched it had a perfection that was almost a physical taste. Jean closed her eyes when they kissed. It gave her face a look of innocence and childish helplessness and profundity that appalled and hypnotized him.

'Bones are funny,' he muttered.

'Mm?'

'Look at skulls. They're hard, with dents in them and corners. Your skull is all sharp corners. Here, and here, and here. But your face has no corners. Everything flows into everything else. Like liquid. Liquid flows. That's scientific.'

'It sounds nice.'

Each time his lips touched her lips her hands tightened on him in immediate response. But she was falling asleep. Soon he realized she was asleep entirely. When he moved his arm for comfort she smiled faintly and gave a little sound, but his fingers lightly touching her face failed to disturb her. He smiled down at her and experienced a puzzling sensation of power which he felt must be unreal. He had to make a conscious effort to remind himself that

148

she was female, and in his arms, and that he was in a situation interminably visualized and picked over and reconstructed in conversation with Davie and Joe. It meant nothing. He eased his arm out from under her neck and lay beside her with his chin in his fists, staring at her sleeping face in calm tenderness. She was really very fast asleep. Grinning at himself, he got up and found a magazine, brought it back to the floor, and lay beside her quietly turning it over and reading.

Some minutes later, as he glanced at her face for the hundredth time, he saw moisture, or a tear, slowly emerging from between her eyelids and slowly moving down her cheek. He stared at it, rapt, and then saw the two little lines deepen between her eyebrows as if a very pale shadow of sorrow had crossed her face. He laid a hand gently on her shoulder and patted her as she slept. She stirred, and one of her hands carelessly outflung in sleep touched his arm and held it. Imperceptibly she slid towards into waking, but before her eyes opened, fresh tears began to flood from them, and as she opened them she stared at him without seeing and fell into a long fit of quiet sobbing. She tossed aimlessly on the floor, appearing not to notice him and weeping quietly and uncontrollably. In a wild access of fear and compassion he wrapped his arms round her and held her firmly, but it was as if she were still asleep and dreaming and unconscious of him. Her sobbing finally died away and she lay still for a moment in his arms and looked straight into his eyes, her face still wet with tears.

'What's going on?' she asked him. 'My face is all wet.'

'You've been having a bad dream.'

'What about?'

Peter laughed.

'I wasn't there. Do you not know?'

'No, I don't remember anything. What was I crying for?'

'I don't know, Jean. Don't cry, Jean, don't cry again.'

'I'm not going to cry.' She laughed shakily. 'I didn't know I was crying. Oh, Peter, I fell asleep and left you alone.'

149

'No, I've been here all the time staring at you with insensate lust in my heart.'

'But what's the use of that if I was asleep?'

'Aha!'

'What do you mean, aha?'

'You don't know what I was doing to you while you were asleep.'

'Oh, don't be a mean pig.' She sniffed, smiling. 'Don't you ever dare to do anything to me when I'm not there.' She put her face into his shoulder and punched him in the ribs. He patted her, feeling lordly and wise and baffled.

'Ssh,' she said. 'Have I wakened the baby?'

'No, no, he never wakens. Nan told me.'

There was no doubt that the baby in the next room was crying.

'You've probably given him a nightmare by telepathy,' Peter whispered. They stared at each other with hands over their mouths.

'What'll we do?' Jean whispered.

'It's all right, don't panic, women and children to the boats,' he whispered. 'He probably just wants to be changed.'

'But do you know how to change babies?'

'Of course. I change them into frogs and parasols. And glasses of Guinness, poynggg. Wait here, maybe I can shoogle him back to sleep, or sing, or something.'

There was a low-power bulb gleaming faintly in the bedroom. The baby was wailing purposefully, standing up in his cot and shaking it back and forth so that it jerked across the floor.

'There, there, sleepy bye-byes,' Peter cooed without conviction. The baby paused momentarily from shaking and wailing, and then started again more positively. The two front feet of the cot banged resoundingly on the floor.

'All right, come to Uncle Puncle,' said Peter, loathing himself. The baby stopped wailing as soon as he picked it up, and he brought it into the kitchen trying to convince

150

himself that a little intelligence was all that was required for baby-handling. Little Alec twisted violently round to glare at Jean, and brought his brows down as he studied her without enthusiasm.

'Don't you dare to bring your brows down at your Auntie Jean,' Peter muttered to him. 'She's the most beautiful auntie you're ever likely to see and don't forget it.'

Activity and company appeared to have diverted the baby from its anger. Peter sat down and bounced it on his knee with a thin show of assurance. Jean, torn between perplexity and delight, said, 'Oh, he's *nice*!'

'I'm glad you said that,' Peter remarked in a Goon voice. 'Healthy young women should have a spontaneous affection for babies. I think he's horrible. Sure you're horrible, wee Alec, aren't you? Hurry up, fall asleep and belt up.'

'Don't, you'll frighten him,' Jean protested, and Peter waved her away.

'He only hears the tone of my voice. I could be talking Bantu for all he knows. Babies are ignorant. Sure, you're ignorant, aren't you, wee Alec? Sure, you're an illiterate wee changeling.'

The baby, who was about fourteen months old, uttered several aggressive sounds and punched Peter's face.

'See, I told you he was ignorant,' Peter muttered. 'Come on, we'll change him. Do you want to try?'

Jean put her hands over her mouth.

'What if he fell and broke! I'd be terrified. I'll do it if you want.'

'No, no, I'll manage the monster,' Peter muttered, trying to lay the baby across his knees and pull at its pyjamas. The baby twisted with terrible determination and Jean gasped in terror. Finally Peter laid it face upwards on the floor and set about pulling off its damp clothes. 'Wrapped up like an advanced case of gout,' he muttered. 'It's just a matter of remembering how this thing's folded and doing it all in reverse.'

It took more than half an hour, and at one point a pin

151

jabbed the baby, who broke out into a terrible wail of agony and betrayal.

'Dere, dere,' Peter muttered desperately. 'Feed it. Ram stuff in its mouth. There's biscuits over there.' The baby kept on wailing, and astonishingly threw in a noise that sounded like 'there, there, baby' in the middle of its cries. Jean, trembling with concern and tittering at the same time, knelt beside it and offered a biscuit which wee Alec instantly grabbed and stuffed in his mouth without ceasing his yells. At last he wore out his sense of grievance and Peter lifted him firmly and took him back to his cot. Wee Alec lay and looked up at him, and then in a single movement threw himself round with his head at the foot of the cot, face downwards and snorted noisily into the bedclothes. Peter gingerly pulled out a blanket from beneath him and laid it across his bottom, which was stuck straight into the air, and tiptoed out of the bedroom.

Wee Alec at once yelled bitterly, and brought Peter bolting back into the bedroom in a panic. When he returned to the kitchen, Jean was sitting on the edge of a chair, as if she had been sitting in that position of straining expectancy for hours. Peter shambled across to her, sinking to his knees and dropped his head on her lap. She stroked his hair tenderly.

'You've been in there for *hours*,' she whispered. 'Poor Peter. Is he all right?'

'Mission accomplished, sir,' Peter croaked, and collapsed on the floor with his arms outflung. Jean knelt beside him and stroked his forehead. 'Oh, you're wonderful, Peter,' she murmured.

'I'm rotten with strange, mysterious talents,' he muttered, his eyes shut. 'I've been singing "Tom Dooley" to him. Eighteen million verses.' Jean lay beside him and pressed her cheek to his. 'You're super wonderful cubed,' she said helplessly.

'Don't worry, I'll train you to be as good a mother as me,' he said. He put his arms round her and kissed her slowly. 'This is nice, you on top. It's probably perverted, but it's nice. We'll do a lot of baby-sitting.'

Some minute movement, or cessation of movement, in her body, alerted him.

'Will we do a lot of baby-sitting?' he asked. He felt her head shaking, and she whispered, 'I don't know,' into his ear. Peter sat up and held her back from him.

'Something's wrong,' he said. Along with the twinge of fear, he experienced a mean little sense of triumph at his own quickness of perception. Something's wrong. It had sounded exactly right. He could see himself, living in a situation. Jean looked at him, not denying the suggestion, and the fear swamped the other feeling.

'What is it?' he asked in compassion. 'You don't love me any more.'

Jean shook her head blindly. Not understanding, Peter whirled down into a black pit, but she threw herself towards him and kissed him wildly on the nose and eyes and mouth, keeping her face close to his to avoid his gaze. He allowed himself to be pushed back to the floor and patted her shoulder lightly as she clung to him.

'It's . . . hey, I don't even know his name.'

'Archie?' Her voice, close to his ear, was surprised.

'Archie.' Peter let out a heavy sigh.

'No, it isn't really Archie. Oh, it's not only Archie . . .'

'It's your family.' He felt her head nod against his. 'So,' he said blandly, 'we gotta elope after all. Chuck it, Jean, you'll sever your spinal column if you try to nod and shake your head at the same time.' She laughed tearfully.

'They've found out about Millport,' Peter said after a long silence, during which he had realized that Jean lacked the brutality, or the moral courage, to deliver bad news without help. Jean stirred slightly, still hiding her face, and said nothing. Her parents had never mentioned Millport. But perhaps Millport would do as well as anything.

'That's great.' Peter sat up and spoke in deep disgust. 'That's logic. It's . . . Ach, you would think it was the

153

nineteenth century. But *nothing happened*. It would be easier
for something to happen here than it was at Millport.' Jean
nodded her head in miserable agreement, but with relief
that the worst was over. It was a release to listen to Peter
talking, Peter dissecting the situation, weaving words over
it, picking up the burden that had confused her.

'At least your mother likes me,' he said thoughtfully, and
Jean was startled at his incomprehension, so that she shook
her head without pausing to think.

'She doesn't?' Jean shook her head. 'I thought I had
made my good impression on her.' Peter felt his grip
on reality sliding away. To be disliked by somebody he
deliberately liked was illogical and unfair. It made nonsense
of human relations. Bitterness came to him as he reflected
on the number of blazing buildings from which he had
rescued Mrs Pynne, the runaway steam-rollers he had
diverted from her path, the skull fractures he had sustained
in dragging her from whirlpools.

'I don't understand it.' The comment was hardly adequate.
'Does she really think anything happened at Millport?'

'It's not got anything to do with Millport,' Jean broke
out desperately, lunging at the truth. It was impossible to
say simply that her mother detested Peter. The words
would have associated her with her mother as well as exposing her mother disloyally to Peter. Peter stared at her,
trying to gather up the pieces. To be disliked without even
the excuse of some mythical villainy at Millport was more
terrible than ever. His spirit shrank in him.

'We'll win her round,' he said crisply, and Jean re-
sponded instantly to a note of confidence and cried 'Oh,
yes!' but as instantly was struck with pessimism.

'Don't *worry* about it,' Peter exhorted her, and she
nodded dutifully. He threw out an arm dramatically. 'Time
is on our side!' Jean laughed in spite of herself, and he
pulled her head on to his shoulder.

'I'll never do anything to hurt you, honestly,' he muttered, and when Jean whispered, 'You couldn't,' he said

with a touch of impatience, 'I could easily, I'm a chained beast behind this thin veneer of civilization.' Jean dug her fingers into his back and cried, 'So am *I*.' They kissed in a sudden wild hunger.

'This is terrible,' Peter said. 'You would do anything I wanted.'

'Yes, of course.'

Peter was stunned and humbled.

'Right this minute?'

'Yes.'

'You should be ashamed of yourself,' he said shakily. 'Alec and Nan'll be home any minute.'

'I don't care.'

They knelt and stared at each other, and heard voices on the staircase outside. Neither of them spoke. Without taking his eyes from hers, Peter reached behind him on the floor and found a magazine, which he handed to her. She took it and slowly rose to sink back in the chair behind her, and Peter shuffled backwards to the chair at the other side of the fireplace. With the slow care of a dream he raised himself to sit on it, his eyes still locked with Jean's, and his body suffused with a fire quite new and strange. They were still staring at each other when his sister-in-law came into the kitchen, throwing round a swift glance for signs of sin.

'Wee Alec wakened up. I changed him.' Peter brought his eyes round slowly to Nan, whose suspicions were brushed aside by news of her child.

'Did you do it right?' she asked anxiously. Alec, behind her, shook his head and grinned.

'Well,' Peter said, 'I tried pinning the nappie over his head a few times before I caught on, but I managed to glue it in the right place with treacle in the end. That's where I glued it, the end.'

Nan tutted, but the sharp look left her face. She became the bustler, and Peter abandoned his impulse to refuse to wait for supper, although he was racked with impatience

155

to have Jean alone again, to reconstruct the broken world. He talked incessantly, about changing the baby, about Gutty Greer, about Auntie Sarah. When they left, Jean took his arm and breathed:

'Oh, you're wonderful, super wonderful cubed – what comes after cubed?'

'Wonderful to the power of infinity,' Peter told her.

'Oh, you're a marvel, anyway. I was terrified in case everybody stood and nobody said a word.'

'Huh. I can talk all right. Just press the button. Listen, Jean, I'll not walk you right home. We've got to reorganize our lives.'

'Yes, right.' Jean waited, happy to be told, to have decisions made.

'Everything'll be all right. We'll declare a moratorium.'

'A moratorium,' Jean said. 'There, I've declared it.'

'Don't dare be witty when I'm here to be witty for you. A moratorium is a delaying action. We'll avoid each other for . . . no, twenty years is too long. A month.'

'Right.'

'Don't sound so happy.'

'I'm sorry.'

'It'll be a relief to you.' Peter couldn't quite keep the bitterness from his voice. 'No, it's all right, I mean it. Then we'll see how we feel at the end of a month.'

'Right.'

It would have given him more courage if she had protested that no number of months could make any difference, but he took comfort from her tight grip on his arm.

'I'll go out with other people,' he went on wildly. 'And you'll go out with other people.'

There was a short silence, and then she said:

'I'll have to, anyway. Archie's home.'

Daggers, bolts, red-hot pokers pierced him and he stopped walking.

'Would you rather go out with Archie? Oh, Jean, just tell me, tell me.'

She was at once plunged into wretched uncertainty again. She shrugged her shoulders and made a noise with her lips.

'Oh . . . Archie's quite nice. He expects me to go out with him anyway. Everybody expects it.'

'And you won't have to hide when you go out with him.'

'No . . . it's all nice and uncomplicated.'

The complexities of her feelings wavered before him and eluded his grasp. There was nothing left for him but to take the right attitude and stick to it.

'Good,' he said. 'Well, I'll be seeing you.'

'What?'

'Well, we'd better split up here.'

'Oh, all right . . .'

He refused to waver. He squeezed her arm a last time and turned off down a side street. A few yards later he became convinced that he would regret for the rest of his life not having kissed her good night. He arrived home to find Julie reading in bed and nobody else in the house, but his father arrived a few minutes later, with the warm smell of beer on his breath. He came into the living-room with a certain amount of care, and sat down and dragged his boots off.

'Helluva thing,' he muttered to himself. 'Gold's up a penny a ton.'

'God help the Empire,' Peter riposted.

'Aye, ruination, ruination, we'll have to sell off the plantations.' Samuel smiled to himself, pleased with the little performance. 'God knows what they'll say on Wall Street when I tell them, the poor bastards. Hey,' he looked up at Peter, his eyes focusing with a slight time-lag. 'What's this about this girl you're winchin'? Goin's on at Millport an' everythin', it'll no' do, it'll no' do.' The sound of the phrase pleased him, and he repeated it in an Aberdonian accent. 'It'll no' do.'

Peter's adrenal gland shot a couple of pints into his bloodstream and his skin prickled. But his father was evidently untroubled and merely curious.

'High bloody time you were gettin' married an' goin' out to colonize the frozen wastes or somethin', anyway,' Samuel mused. 'All weans should be booted into the jungle when they're ten. They paint them green, did you know that?'

'White,' Peter said.

'Well, green, white, who the hell cares, they must look bloody stupid. You stick to your lessons and get to the Tech. You stick to the auld square on the hippotenues, that's the game. Where's the tea?'

Peter moved into the kitchen, but his father stood up and leaned on the kitchen door confidentially, in his stocking soles.

'Hey, you got to watch it, you know, kid. How the hell did your Auntie Sarah know you were stuck at Millport wi' some lassie?'

'Auntie Sarah?' Peter was trembling.

'Ach, don't worry, I can sort her out. My God, she's real bitch,' he added in admiration. Peter had the confused sensation that it was because the revelation about Millport and Jean had come from Aunt Sarah that his father had adopted a tolerant attitude in his defence.

'What does Auntie Sarah know about it?' he asked.

'Don't you worry, your Auntie Sarah knows all, sees all, says all. If she said bugger all she'd be easier to put up wi'. You never said anything to us about a lassie at Millport. Weans never tell their faithers anything.'

'Nothing happened at Millport.' Peter kept his face turned away, facing the cooker.

'Well, I hope you've got enough sense,' his father agreed. It was going to be one of his father's good-humoured nights. He went on in a wheedling tone. 'You see, you got to watch yourself if you live in the same planet as Sarah – she's got her telescope trained everywhere. She thought she was gonny give me a helluva shock,' he added, gloating in the recollection of Sarah's failure to get a rise out of him. 'Bert's all right, though. He just lets her run off his back like duck's water. For God's sake don't let on to your mother that there was any hanky-panky at Millport. She would do a wulkie. A wulkie!' He solemnly sketched with his hand the motion of somebody doing a wulkie.

Peter loaded a tray, and insisted, 'There wasn't any hanky-panky.'

'All right, all right. Just keep the heid,' he muttered darkly. 'Sarah'll never rest till you get some lassie in the family way so that she can blame it on Higher Education. Higher Education. You stick to auld Pythagorus, Peter, an' to hell wi' Auntie Sarah. You are,' he leaned back in his chair and looked judicious, 'you are not Auntie Sarah's white-haired boy, did you know that?'

'Huh. I'm not anybody's white-haired boy.' Peter was discomfited but flattered by his father's casual candour.

'I wish to hell your mother was up and out,' Samuel sighed. 'I'm drinkin' too much. Look not upon the wine when it is red. Strong drink is raging. I solemnly promise to honour my father and mother and abstain from strong drink as a haemorrhage.'

'And be a good Brownie, so help me God,' Peter added. His father tittered.

'I solemnly promise to refrain from picking my nose,' he intoned, 'and to shop at the Co-op.'

'Remember the Dividend,' said Peter, 'to keep it holy.'

Samuel burst into spluttering laughter, and Peter, his sides heaving, found himself laughing too. It was strange, to be laughing.

12

During one of his majestic strolls round the English class, Gutty Greer rested his bulk on Peter's desk.

'Now is the arum winter of our mm thingummyjig, eh, Haddow?'

'Yes, sir, definitely.'

'Shades of the hum prison-house begin to close around the mm growing whatsitsname, eh?'

'I thought it was the other way round, sir,' Peter said with excessive respect.

'You have a rare mm talent for being insolent, Haddow, without saying anything the court could pin to you. Did you mm know that?'

'I do my best, sir.'

'Rare talent, my boy. Nourish it, nourish it.' Peter looked round to see if Tom Arthur was going into his black seethe, but even Arthur's secretly fostered hate for him seemed to have withered away in the aimless purgatory that fell on the class between sitting the Highers and waiting for the results. Gutty was clearly bored himself. He made no move to shift from Peter's desk.

'You're more black a visaged than usual, Haddow,' he mused. 'Don't worry, you'll mm get your English.' Peter nodded without excitement.

'What is it, then? The law's hum delays? The pangs of mhm despised love?'

'Ah, yes.' Peter heaved a theatrical sigh, and Gutty brightened up.

'Bliss is it in that dawn to be alive, boy, but to be mm young is um . . .'

'Gruesome?'

'Serves you right, boy, nobody asked you to be young.'

'I know. I was thinking of striding over the moors with unseeing eyes, would you recommend that, sir?'

'Plenty of good um precedents, Haddow. Dying young is widely recommended too.'

'Yes, it's certainly a consummation devoutly to be wished, sir,' Peter agreed. Gutty grunted, heaved himself off the desk, cuffed Peter lightly on the back of the head and ambled down the aisle. The conversation left Peter comforted. But when he walked to Davie McAllister's house with Davie and Big Joe, Davie was in one of his exasperated moods.

'It's just a bloody fake,' he told Peter. 'You're just acting it up. What's the use of kidding? It's just another bloody joke to you.'

'Well, so what?' Peter asked.

'Uch, you make me sick,' Davie dismissed him. 'If you've chucked her, for God's sake chuck looking like a poisoned pup.'

'I don't look like a poisoned pup.' Peter was wounded and stung to anger. 'It's you that keeps dripping about it.'

'You do look like a poisoned pup, honest,' Big Joe assured him. 'So would I, if it was me. Rrrr, what a beaut.'

'Aw, lay off,' Peter said. 'We've just decided to give it a rest. It's a trial separation.' He wished the words hadn't sounded so pompous.

'Okay, okay,' Davie snarled. 'Snap out of it, then!' His contempt hurt Peter more than he would have expected. To be despised by anybody so ridiculous as Davie was hard to bear. He had to force himself to be bland.

'If you don't shut your mouth I'll not let you see Christine again,' he warned Davie.

'Huh. Who do you think you are?' It was appalling to see how Davie's confidence had blossomed inside a few weeks. It left Peter with the feeling of having been outstripped in some permanent race in which his position had always been secure and should have stayed secure for ever.

161

'I'll cast around for new playthings,' he said. 'Play the field. Why should all the other dames in the world be deprived of me?'

Davie wrinkled his lip, but Big Joe jumped on Peter's boast.

'Well, if you horse about wi' other dames, you don't mind if I date Jeannie-Peenie.'

'You?' Peter was winded, breathless with a fresh terror, utterly vulnerable. 'You flatter yourself,' he added lamely, fighting to keep his voice steady. Big Joe turned his palms upwards and said:

'Well, she canny shoot me for trying. I mean you don't object, do you? If you're playing the field. Sauce for the goose,' he added, and it sounded both reasonable and malevolent.

'Just forget it,' Peter said, with a show of weariness. But Big Joe's eyes were far away, looking at a Jeannie-Peenie fantasy, and the crawling horror that possessed Peter was not to be brushed away with words. On the following day Davie asked him, with a casualness that was quite revolting in its spuriousness, for Jean's telephone number, and when Peter recoiled and bristled and demanded to know what Davie wanted it for Davie became quite righteous.

'It's no' a bloody secret, is it?' he asked, and guilt showed nakedly through his display of grievance. There could be no doubt that he wanted Jean's telephone number for Big Joe. It was, Peter felt, the ultimate in treachery, and he cursed his stupidity that had put him in a situation where he couldn't refuse to give it. He was assaulted by intolerable visions of Big Joe dating Jean, Big Joe holding her hand, kissing her, seducing her. The physical reality of Jean, which had been merely a sweet proportion of her importance to him, became overwhelming. His feeling for her, which had grown gently as an affair of personality, which had been un-urgent, and physical more in bold conversation than in actuality, was transmuted into gross physical hunger that sickened him and tortured him.

It was impossible to believe that she would reject Big Joe. It was almost impossible to believe that she would reject anybody. But most of all Big Joe. He saw Big Joe with her, in some vague, dark and private place, and studied by X-ray the operations of Big Joe's greed in the minutest and most agonizing detail. Most horrifying of all was the sound in his ears of Jean's voice, not protesting, but chiding in a tone that thinly concealed delight, her laughter of triumph and joy. Peter tried to force his mind back to sane possibility, but it returned in perverse delight to create the horror afresh and embellish it. Sometimes he attempted to change the picture, to substitute Jean's Archie for Big Joe, but he had never met Archie, and Big Joe was appallingly real. In one terrible flash, he once saw Jean with both Joe and Archie, conducting a Roman orgy and laughing, and laughing especially as one or other of them mentioned Peter's name during their transports.

It was a simple discovery of the commonplace sensations of jealousy. Dimly he perceived that he had not invented this hell; that it was waiting for anybody who could take the trouble to find it. But he failed to convince himself that he was anything but alone. He recalled with an inward cry of pain that a few days ago he had pitied everybody else on earth, who had to suffer a life that didn't include loving Jean. Now he looked bleakly at everybody else on earth, living lives that left out the agony of loving Jean.

It was, after all, merely a glandular complaint, a condition of the body. He could divert it. Cold baths, for instance. To his surprise, he laughed out loud at the idea of doing anything so brainless as taking a cold bath. He saw himself sitting in freezing water and shouting through chattering teeth, 'I shall prevail! I shall freeze to death but under God I shall prevail!'

Instead, he mowed the back grass. His father was astonished into making several surly remarks that were almost approving. There wasn't enough of the grass, though. He started to dig a great hole in the bed beyond the grass, and dump weeds in it. Having begun, he stuck doggedly at the job, but even as he assured himself that he was sublimating his foolishness, he had to stop and lean on the spade and say aloud:

'I'm not sublimating anything. I'm just digging a flaming hole.'

It came as both a complication and a diversion when he went in from the garden to find his father white-faced and twisted with pain.

'Don't look so glaikit, it's just my stomach,' Samuel groaned. 'I'll have to chuck eatin' broken bottles, they're no' puttin' the decent glass in them nowadays.' The fact that he was joking with no normal display of temper convinced Peter that the pain must be intense, and he was racked by his helplessness, but finally produced some aspirin.

'Baking soda would probably be better,' Samuel muttered. 'But to hell, I'll try everything.'

The baking soda finally provoked a massive belch that relieved the pain, but Samuel was still white and exhausted. He determined to visit the doctor, and waved away Peter's offer to go with him. When he came back, Christine and Julie were home, ready for tea, and the table was laid. Samuel dropped into his armchair and held a brief silence to point the importance of the moment.

'It's maybe an ulcer,' he said finally. 'I've had it before, but I thought it was just wind.'

Julie stared in fascination at the region of Samuel's stomach, wondering if he would be cut open to reveal a thing shaped like a sea-urchin. Christine, whom Peter considered was growing almost as skilful as his mother in making conventional noises of absolute tarradiddle, began at once to assure Samuel that it wouldn't turn out to be an ulcer after all. Peter asked if he would have to go on a diet.

'Aye, diet's right,' his father sighed. 'Cut out soup, fries, practically everything worth eating.'

'And drink, Dad?' Christine cooed. 'Oh, Dad,' she added reproachfully, sniffing his breath. 'You've had another wee one.'

For once Samuel failed to smile indulgently at Christine's prattle. But he reacted with the same defensive guilt that he would have shown to his wife.

'I met your Uncle Bert,' he said. 'This'll be a nice wee titbit for Sarah.'

'A poached egg?' Peter suggested.

'Oh, God, a poached egg. All right, I'll be a bloody martyr. Try an' make it taste like steak and chips.' His face twisted again. 'You'd better phone the gasworks later and tell them I'll be in bed for a few days,' he told Peter. 'Struck down in my bloody prime.'

'You'll be fine, Dad,' Christine assured him, and he turned to her peevishly. 'How do you know?' he asked. 'Surely I can get being ill just this once.'

He took to his bed after tea, but found he was incapable of staying there. For the next few days he sat about the house, periodically stabbed with pain and trying to remember at other times to go on feeling fragile and unwell. The most disagreeable result of this was that Auntie Sarah turned up, in her most bellicose mood of Christian charity, to make sure that he wasn't neglected. Peter came home from school to find his father actually in bed, and when he went in to talk to him, Samuel put a finger on his lips.

'Sarah's in the kitchen,' he whispered, and when Peter's jaw dropped, Samuel went on, 'She would never have got past the door if I had been in my right health. Or my right mind,' he added bitterly. 'Jesus, she's having a picnic. She's been flinging the holy saints and the Virgin Mary at me since three o'clock.'

'What is she *doing*?' Peter whispered back.

'Aw, scrubbin' and bashin' the place to death. She'll be back tomorrow. Probably bring a choir of angels with her.'

'I don't get it.'

'Ach, Sarah's been waiting for thirty years to see me on

165

my back, it's a judgment on me for having a Corporation house when she didn't get one. She keeps looking at me and measuring me up for a wake.'

'Will I get rid of her?'

Samuel laughed aloud and then put his hand over his mouth and reverted to whispers.

'Do you think you're Superman? She's got us by the short hairs. God help us all. The Virgin Mary as well.'

'Amen.'

It was true that some force superior to Peter would be required to wrest Auntie Sarah from her grim work of goodwill. Peter's suggestion that she could go home and that he would make the tea brought out the best vintage Auntie Sarah.

'May I never stir beyond that threshold if I don't see that your poor Dad gets tooken care of in his infirmity,' she said, arms akimbo. 'I know where I'm not welcome, but I know my duty as a Christian. What does a boy know about cooking a man's tea?'

'Oh, we get by all right,' Peter mumbled.

'Huh. All right might be good enough for you, but you don't realize your Dad's a sick man. He needs building up.'

'Built up?' Peter murmured, staring innocently at Sarah.

'Oh, I never thought it would come to this.' She lifted a corner of her apron to the corner of one of her eyes in an automatic gesture born of lifelong rehearsal. 'My poor sister dangerously ill in hospital and her poor bairns left with an invalid father.'

'Dangerously ill? Mum isn't dangerously ill, it's just a routine hysterectomy,' Peter protested. Sarah's lips pursed in fury.

'You speak about things you know something about, you know nothing about it, nothing. Nothing! You get your head full of stupid big words you know nothing about, that's all school does for kids, gives them dirty minds. What do you know about being a mother? Women are born

166

to suffer. No man'll ever know how women suffer. And your poor father lyin' there in agony.'

Peter got lost in the cross-currents of logic, and felt that he was being brutally treated for somebody who had been a poor bairn a few seconds ago, but he nodded humbly and tried to look reverent, and Sarah was mollified for the moment.

'I'll make your father's tea myself before I go away, and you see that he eats it all up. Christine can make what she likes for the rest of you when she comes in.'

'I'll manage that,' Peter suggested, but saw at once that this was provocation.

'Christine's well able to make a meal if she does nothing else,' she barked. 'I would go down on my knees before I would let any son of mine interfere in a kitchen where he's got no business to be if he isn't a Jessie. Just you see that your poor Dad eats all this up and that'll suffice you, if you think you can spare the time to do that much for him.'

'Oh, aye, sure.' Peter retreated in rout and buried himself in a book until Sarah exploded from the house on her way home. Then he went into his father's room, where he found Samuel gazing bleakly at a plateful of fish and boiled potatoes.

'Did you notice how she cooked the spuds?' Samuel asked. 'They feel as if she just warmed them under her oxter for five minutes.' He prodded at one of the enormous shiny potatoes, which had the appearance and feel of damp marble.

'I'll make some croquettes, nice and soft, and crisp on the outside,' Peter suggested, and Samuel looked at him in pathetic gratitude.

'Thank God for somebody that can do a woman's work,' he said. 'If you can do that, you'd better away out somewhere after and give yourself a rest. You've been stuck in the house all this week.'

'Oh, it's okay,' Peter said. But it was a relief to emerge

167

again into the outside. The hole in the garden, refilled and glaring like a fresh grave, had used up all his resolutions for mental health by exhaustion. Christine made a half-hearted protest at his going out, but had to admit that anybody who had had Auntie Sarah for a full hour was especially entitled to a break. He decided to try striding across the moors with unseeing eyes, using the streets since there were no moors handy, and on passing a clock, tried not to calculate that if he had come out twenty minutes earlier he would probably have run into Jean on her way home from the office.

Freedom began to oppress him, the freedom of being able to go anywhere or do anything he wanted; since there was nothing he wanted to do very much. It would have been relaxing to drop in on Davie, but not since the revelation of Davie's treachery in the matter of Jean's telephone number. At another time he might have even called for Big Joe, but he would never be able to call for Big Joe again. If Joe was at home, he would talk about Jean. If he was out, Peter would have to endure the certainty that he was out with Jean.

He drifted into the library reading-room and combed through the *Autocar*. Now, ownership of a Merc meant driving past bus-stops where Jean caught sight of him in wild surmise, and he smiled back courteously as he gave it the gun and roared away to . . . the Riviera? San Francisco? Some place where a girl both rich and famous and fabulously beautiful was waiting, longing for him. He cased around in his mind for the girl, but none of them wakened anything more than a surface enthusiasm in him.

Late in the evening, half-dead with boredom, he steeled himself to go to the café where Jean would undoubtedly be sitting with her Archie, or with Big Joe. None of them was there, nobody that he knew except Alice Jackson. He sat beside her, his face stiff.

'Where's Joe?'

'Joe? Dunno. The dump is supernaturally dead.'

'Lemme buy ya coffee, babe.'

'Gee, tanks.'

Alice hardly existed for him as a person. This in itself relaxed him.

'Is it true you cook yourself in a sun-lamp?' he asked her.

'What's the gag?'

'Your legs are always suntanned, even up at the top. We study them in the maths class.'

'You're all awful. I never heard of such . . . Really, you're *awful*.' But she eyed him sideways from under her lashes and over her cup, and Peter said, 'We must be awful right enough. I despise myself. It's nice and rich, though.'

'What?'

'The colour of your legs.'

Alice slapped the back of his hand. 'Where is everybody?' she wondered.

'What do you mean, everybody? I'm here.'

'You. You're usually somewhere else with somebody else.'

'Oh, I'm versatile. You'd be amazed.'

'I just bet.'

Peter wondered what Big Joe talked about when he was with Alice. It hardly seemed possible that they held conversations. Her talk had the light absurdity of a worn-out ping-pong ball; but it took no effort to keep it in the air. He was aware that he puzzled her, and when he made a joke that she understood, she laughed rather readily. When their coffee was finished and the ping-pong ball seemed due for retirement, he got up and told her that he would walk her home. She said 'Oh?' which meant, You're taking a lot for granted, but she got up and came out with him. As they walked through the dusk, she made an effort to talk seriously about the prospects of the Highers, but he waved this away.

'Shop talk,' he said. 'Forbidden. Talk about how gorgeous you are.'

'Oh, you! Nobody can tell if you're joking or not. That's an awful thing to say.'

'I never joke, I'm just naturally funny.'

'I don't get you at all.'

'Hey, you've got a hammock in your garden. We'll sit in it and watch the moon.'

'There isn't any moon.'

'Women, women, always literal.'

'Are you joking about the hammock?'

'I don't joke . . .'

'All right, are you being funny about the hammock?'

'Funny, but serious.'

'My father would chase you anyway.'

'I'm not inviting your father out to the hammock. Come on.'

'All right,' Alice said in despair. 'But be quiet, *please*. I don't know what you want to sit in the hammock for anyway. It's *cold*,' she whispered.

'This is warmer.'

'Honestly, you're awful. We haven't even been on a date, or anything.'

'Will you shut up? Or do I shout and bring your father out?'

'All right, but be quiet, honestly.'

When he kissed her, she writhed towards him in a way that bothered him. It suggested a piece of technique borrowed from watching somebody else. So what? he thought. She ran the fingers of one hand down to the centre of his spine, pressing hard. After five minutes she whispered, 'I'll have to go in now. Somebody might come out.'

'Okay.' He stood up at once. Alice was startled. 'Well,' Peter said, 'you said you had to go in.'

'Oh. Okay.' She stood up, and he held her roughly and kissed her again.

'That's all you get for now,' he whispered. 'Good night.'

'Right enough, you're awful. You're the awfullest boy on two legs. What a cheek.'

'Yes, it's gorgeous.' He kissed her on the cheek and slipped out of the garden gate. None of it had cured anything, but it hadn't done any harm. He decided obscurely that he had got some of his own back at something.

It enabled him, he found, to treat Davie with the right amount of negligence in school next day, and his morale climbed a few points as he observed the old Davie coming to life again; the confused Davie who was sure that something was going on that nobody had let him in on.

'You swallowed the canary?' Davie finally asked him in the maths class. He returned an expression of supercilious puzzlement and disdain, and Davie broke down and said, 'Well, what is it? What's happened?'

'You know, you're never satisfied,' Peter told him crushingly. 'I'll mope again if that'll shut you up.' He looked beyond Davie's shoulder, to where Alice Jackson had just abruptly put her feet down on the floor and twitched at her skirt to cover her knees, catching his eye in silent accusation and conspiracy and perhaps several other things. Peter winked cosily back, and Davie's head whirled to focus on Alice and then back to Peter.

'What's cooking?' he whispered savagely. Peter pushed a delicate yawn on to his finger-nails.

'Done any more pimping for Big Joe?' he asked. It was excessive. Davie's face turned a deep bluish-red and he gritted his teeth. His nostrils went white. Peter was at once stricken with shame. He patted Davie's arm and said, 'Don't be daft, I was only kidding.' Davie stared straight in front of him, but the colour receded and he relaxed. 'You're a bloody fool,' Peter said, in an attempt to end Davie's embarrassment. 'What happened, anyway?'

Davie's familiar sheepish attitude returned.

'Ach, nothing. He phoned her. She said she was washing her hair.'

'My God, the oldest brush-off in the business. Aw, poor Joe. Poor wee Josy-Wosy.'

Davie sniggered and started to choke as Wee Aikie looked

171

round sharply and began to walk up the aisle towards them. More relief and content and self-dislike flooded over Peter than he knew how to handle. His shame at the accusations he had made in his mind against Jean was a pain less only than the pain the accusations themselves had given him.

But it was to be a full day of surprises. At four o'clock he resisted Davie's invitations to come home and listen to some borrowed records because he was anxious to get back to check on Sarah's war of attrition. Davie, thoroughly restored to his proper humility, asked if he could come round and visit Peter in the evening, and Peter shrugged his shoulder and warned him that the old man would be at home to watch him ogling Christine.

A Morris Minor was inching down the street towards him as he approached the house, and it stopped as he drew abreast. The face of Garside, the minister, appeared at the near-side window. Nearside Garside, Peter thought irrelevantly.

'A bit of luck,' the minister said. 'Just the man I wanted to see.'

'Oh, good.'

Garside pushed the car door open.

'Would you care to come in and be comfortable? I wanted to have a wee blether with you.'

'Would it do some other time?' Peter was uncomfortable, reluctant despite himself to decline the invitation. 'My father's sick and I have to get home in a hurry.'

'Oh. Sorry to hear that. Should I come in and – no, maybe not.' He smiled. 'Can you get out in the evening? About . . . about eight o'clock? At the church? I won't keep you long.'

'All right, if you like.' Peter looked blank.

'Good. I hope you find your father better.' Garside let the brake go and slid down the hill. Funny, Peter thought. That was no stroke of luck, he was lying in ambush. He hadn't thought to ask what the minister wanted to talk about. He shrugged his shoulders and went into the house.

Julie was having hysterics in his father's bedroom. It was obvious that Samuel didn't want to know about them. He was lying back on his pillows weary and suffering. Peter yanked Julie out and into the bedroom she shared with Christine.

'Don't bother the old man when he's sick or I'll batter your face to a jelly,' he explained. 'What's up?'

Julie was in the condition when nothing short of smashing something to fragments would really give her complaint expression, but it came out in sobs and jerks that Auntie Sarah had smashed her skull and put it in the dustbin.

'No wonder the old man's sick. He thinks you mean Sarah beat your own skull in.'

'She did, she *did*!'

'Yeah, yeah. Your sheep skull.'

'Well, it *is* my own. She's got no right to touch my things. I'm going to tell Mum about it!'

'That's right,' Peter soothed her. 'You tell Mum and I'll belt you round the conk. Now shut up till I think. She was probably just tidying up.' He looked round the room for evidence. It did seem less strewn than usual. Julie broke into fresh muffled hoots.

'She's thrown out my secret murder codes! They were on bits of paper on the floor in front of my bed!'

'Okay, you can invent a new set. Come on.'

Julie's lower lip trembled and her breath was catching in jerks. She followed Peter into the living-room. Vigorous clanking sounds from the closed kitchen revealed that Auntie Sarah was working off her sense of righteousness on the landscape. Peter opened the kitchen door, and the face of a tigress whirled on him.

'You keep out — oh, it's you. Well, what has the bold Peter to say for himself?' Sarah was girded and ready.

'You're taking too much out of yourself, Auntie Sarah,' Peter said. 'You'll do yourself an injury.'

'Huh! Hard work never killed me.' The implication was

173

clear that hard work would get a clout across the chops if it tried.

'No, I know,' Peter admired. 'But you don't need to tidy the bedrooms as well. Just leave that to us.'

'Tidy the bedrooms, is it? Filthy old bones out of the midden spreading germs and disease in a sickroom. It's a wonder your father hasn't caught jawlock. And may the holy saints forgive me if ever I have to tolerate such impudence from that little clip Julie. I'll skull that little madam.'

'Aye, mhm. Well, it'll save trouble if you don't bother tidying the bedrooms again, Auntie Sarah.'

'I shall do as I think fit, my lad, and don't you give me any of your high-and-mighty school-kid orders.'

'No, you're quite right, Auntie Sarah. Still, don't bother tidying the bedrooms.'

'Oh, but I'll tidy the bedrooms.'

'You'll not, honestly. If I have to put locks on the doors, I'll do that.' Peter was so bland that Julie, behind him, had buried her head in the cushions of the armchair and was having hysterics again.

'By God, I'd take my hand across your face if you were mine,' Sarah gritted. 'You and that bloody stuck-up little madam with her filthy, rotten old bones. You can give your father his tea yourself, I'm not to stand here and be insulted for doing an act of Christian charity.'

'Aye, it's very difficult, Auntie Sarah,' Peter's voice was deep and sympathetic.

'Don't think you've got the better of me, you young clip. I'll be here tomorrow.'

'Oh, jolly good.'

Peter took milk and biscuits into his father when Sarah was gone, sat on the edge of the bed and nibbled a biscuit.

'She's probably doing her best, Dad,' he said. 'But if Christine knew she had been poking in her room she would go off to the moon without a count-down. I'll have to snib the bedrooms from the inside and climb out through the windows before I go to school tomorrow.'

174

'By gum. There must be something in heredity. You know that you and me are the only two people alive in this world that ever sorted Sarah out? I heard every word. Jesus, it was a pant. Haw haw.'

'Well, it's a bit thick . . .'

'Ah, but you don't know anything about it, Peter. Your Cousin Joseph's gettin' married.'

'Good for him.'

'Aw, for God's sake don't act the innocent, Peter. It's helluva sudden. Away out and play, Julie.'

'Oh, no! Joseph's Higher Education has got him into trouble!'

'And broke his poor mother's heart.' Samuel held his stomach carefully while he laughed. Tears ran down his cheeks. 'Aw, but all the same,' he wheezed, 'we'll have to be nice to Sarah.'

'Aye, she's got a terrible cross to bear.'

Peter thought of Joseph and his pale, silent girl-friend and wondered how life seemed to them. Tragic, or exciting? Or just pale and silent? It was hard to imagine excitement there. The whole business was hard to imagine.

He didn't mention Garside's invitation to anybody, since he couldn't imagine the purpose of it. Highest probability was an attempt at conversion, and he knew a pleasurable nervousness at the thought of demolishing this. Davie had arrived by eight o'clock, and Peter merely said mysteriously that he had to go out for half an hour and left Davie and Christine pondering, with something to enliven their conversation while he was gone.

He had some difficulty in tracking down a sign of life at the church, and finally found a low door round at the back which was opened by the minister himself, showing a small room with a Turkish carpet on the floor and a cosy, claustrophobic sense of warmth.

'Oh, aye, come in, Peter,' Garside said, and showed him to a low leather chair. The minister meditated for some seconds and pursed his lips.

'Curious?' he asked.

'No.' Peter was entirely at ease, and proud of it. 'Your move.'

'Aye . . . Aye . . . I wanted to have a word with you,' he spoke in a great hurry and then slowed down, 'about Jean Pynne.'

Peter was on his feet.

'You'll have no word with me!' He heard his voice raised to a shout. 'Keep your damned nose out of it!'

13

'Before we go any further,' Garside said, 'are you prepared to believe me?'

'All right, I don't think you're my enemy if you want to put it that way.' Peter was sitting in the chair, but sitting stiff and breathing hard. 'I'm prepared to apologize without reservation for raising my voice. Anger is a useless luxury. I also apologize if I used bad language. Did I use bad language?'

'I didn't notice.' Garside raised a hand to cover his mouth, and lowered his head. It was important not to smile.

'I quite recognize your . . . I quite recognize that you think it's one of your duties.' Icy dignity. Peter phrased his words slowly. 'But at the same time . . .'

'Mhm?'

'I've forgotten what I was going to say.'

Garside scratched his head.

'I don't do this kind of thing very often myself. I don't know if there's much point in it.'

'I would have thought you would be used to it.' Peter looked straight in front of him. 'But I don't recognize that you're . . . that you've got any special rights, just because you've got a dog collar.' He turned to face Garside. 'Ministers are just the same as anybody else, as far as I'm concerned.'

'But less equal than others, maybe.' Garside laughed shortly at himself. 'Look, I've got myself into this situation. The only thing I can say about ministers is that they spend a lot of time listening to people. If they're not daft, they're bound to learn something as they get on. Is that fair?'

177

'All right, I concede that.'

'Well, I don't know anything about you. I don't know anything against you. The only thing I know is that Mrs Pynne thinks you're getting serious ideas, and she doesn't approve, and she asked me to talk to you. She's very persuasive.'

'What right has she got?' Peter fought in vain to find the cold chain of logic that had melted.

'Och, it's no use talking about rights.' The minister took off his glasses with an impatient gesture. 'She's Jean's mother.'

'I don't concede that.' Peter felt himself slipping backwards and fumbled for a handhold. 'I don't mean that, I mean . . .'

'I know, I know. But you've given her a lot of pain. That's quite simple, anyway.'

'But what about me?'

Garside sighed.

'Oh, I should never have got into this.'

'I'm trying to be reasonable,' Peter said. 'But what's the difference between Jean's mother having pain and me having pain?'

'I don't know, honestly. Surely it's easier to adjust . . . to adapt yourself, if you're younger. It's harder for older people.'

'I don't know,' Peter muttered. 'I've never been older.'

'I don't know either, now that I think about it. But I don't imagine you want to hurt people.'

'No, I don't! But what have I done? I haven't done anything wrong – anything that . . . Oh, I don't get it, I just don't get it.'

'You don't have to do anything "wrong" to hurt people. At least Mrs Pynne has as many rights as a human being as you have.' Garside was fed up with the entire business, and the sharpness in his tone was not addressed to Peter as much as to the way life irritated him. Peter did not make the distinction.

'You mean more rights, because she's older,' he snapped back.

'All right, more.'

'All right, we'll get back to parents being able to sell their children into slavery, or arranging marriages without consulting them. If you're logical, that's what you're saying!'

'It isn't, I promise you. I'm not even saying you're in the wrong. I simply promised to speak to you, and I have. Probably I shouldn't have promised in the first place.'

'I don't think you should.' Peter found heat from somewhere. 'You're on Mrs Pynne's side because she's more important than me, she goes to church, she's older than me.'

'I'm not, I assure you . . .'

'All right, what about rights? Say this, for instance – say there was an atheist living next door to the church, and he was offended at you playing bells in his ear every Sunday morning. Would you recognize his rights, and stop playing church bells?'

'Mm. I've read that somewhere.'

'Well, what's the difference? You've got to answer.'

Garside laughed.

'You can't make me answer. I could have answered you when I was in college. What's that got to do with it?'

Peter, feeling that he had scored a deadly blow, relaxed somewhat.

'It's all the same thing. People's rights. It's got nothing to do with rights,' he went on, getting his teeth into it. 'If people have power, they push other people around. I've got no rights because I've got no power.'

'By golly, though, you can push.' Peter found himself smiling. 'Look,' Garside went on, 'even if you don't see the girl, it isn't the end of the world . . .' but as Peter stared at him, he added, 'Well, maybe it is the end of the world. Oh, to blazes. Honestly, I wish I could do something for you.'

'Tell Mrs Pynne what a good honest young Christian

179

chap I am,' Peter suggested, and Garside let out a bellow of laughter.

'You'll have me roasting in hell. Honestly, will you die if you don't see her — for a while, anyway?'

'I'm not conceding anything.'

'No, I kind of got that idea. But look at it sensibly. You *are* young. I'm not trying to insult you, it's a fact. You've got plenty of time.'

'Things can happen.'

'Nothing very terrible's going to happen, surely. You'll merely feel miserable for a time. Nobody's got a *right* to be happy, you know.'

'No, but they've got a right to try. Anyway, I have arranged not to see her for a while — and it was my own idea, not anybody else's.'

'So I've only made a fool of myself.'

'No,' Peter muttered. 'You've got to do your job, I suppose.'

'Do you have to make it sound like a swear-word?' Garside rubbed a hand down his face as if attempting to smooth it out. 'I hate to say it, but if it comes to a battle of endurance, my money would be on you.'

'If it was a fair fight, maybe.' Peter clung to the sense of doom that he had played with for days on end.

'For God's sake don't talk about a fight,' Garside pleaded. 'I don't think you've given this a serious thought at all. Are you thinking you might marry the girl some day?'

'Yes!'

'All right, don't bite. Has it occurred to you that if you did, you would be related to Mrs Pynne? You *can't* go making an enemy of her.'

'I will if I have to,' Peter said sullenly. 'I don't want to make an enemy of anybody. What am I supposed to do, shoot myself and make everything nice for them?'

'If you talk like that a boot in the behind is all you're worth. Stop feeling sorry for your poor wee self.'

'I'm not sorry, don't worry. I'm not going to shoot

myself either, I don't care how convenient it would be.'

'That's nice,' Garside said drily.

'Well,' Peter said, 'thanks for the little chat. I'm sure it has been most valuable.'

'You insolent pup.' Garside laughed. 'You've got plenty of trouble ahead of you, I can tell you that – whatever you do.'

'Me? All I want is a quiet peaceful life.' Peter was hamming it up again.

But small verbal triumphs were no comfort. Even as he went back over his conversation with the minister and rephrased it here and there to make a better story, perhaps even an hysterical story, he was struck with the impossibility of telling it to Christine and Davie. They would be sorry for him; or they would be fed up with him. Either would be impossible to bear. Black hatred for everybody came over him, and hatred particularly for the overbearing conspiracy of everybody to despise and deprive him.

'I'm wallowing in self-pity,' he said aloud, as he walked down the street, away from the direction of home. A woman passing looked round, startled, and he immediately started to hum quietly, in a despairing automatic effort to show that he had not been talking to himself.

'I'm wallowing, um tum tum tum, wallowing . . .' he broke off and changed it into a whistle. The woman had passed out of sight, but he knew, sourly, that she would know quite well that he *had* been talking to himself, and he felt jolted and exposed, as if somebody had surprised him making faces in a mirror when he thought he was alone.

He returned to humming under his breath, trying to fit the tune of 'Home Sweet Home' to 'If only everybody in the world would mind their own damn business, that's wrong, it should be his own business, it doesn't rhyme but what . . .' The tiny effort of making the song scan was a tiny palliative. But he still felt hugely alone and surrounded

181

by implacable enmity, and it was now so many days since he had seen or heard of Jean that he couldn't resist the conclusion that she, too, had gone over to the other side. Not from hatred, but from gentleness, from her natural desire to please and her inability to be hard or unpleasant to the people around her.

His reading of her character was not entirely true. It was true that she shrank from unpleasantness. Most of the people she had ever known had liked her, and since her demands of life had always been modest, she had enjoyed life without asking for much and without clashing openly with other people over what she wanted. It was easy to interpret her lack of greed as compliance, but this was perhaps the first situation in which mere compliance wouldn't do.

It could still go far, all the same. When her mother had first expressed her concern, carefully casual and humorous, at Jean's becoming too wrapped up in a schoolboy, Jean had smiled and indicated that nothing serious was involved. It wasn't entirely a lie, at first, and when it became a lie, it had been said; and by being said it had acquired official status.

Contrary to Peter's imaginings, Mrs Pynne had no feelings about him at all. What she did have was a nice settled affection for the absent childhood boy friend, Archie Horne, whose father had almost been an old flame of Mrs Pynne's. Not quite an old flame, that was merely a figure of speech. Still, he had liked her. Maybe he had liked her quite a lot, in the old days, among the old crowd. All the boys had liked her. Beach pyjamas had been the last word in daring and chic that year, the year she had married Albert.

It would be wrong to exaggerate the thing, they had simply all been members of the old crowd. But the rest of the old crowd had somehow dissipated and vanished. The Pynnes and the Hornes had always kept up, and it was pleasant to Mrs Pynne to know that another man than her husband could still see her in that light unworn by time.

If anyone had put it to her, she would have cried that it was ridiculous that she could have any unsophisticated storybook nonsense about her tubby little baby Jean and little sober Archie Horne, barely toddling, and kissing the baby. But it had *happened* that way, and it was nice. The two children had grown up in each other's laps, and they had even been on childhood holidays together. Archie was practically one of the family, and he had grown up beautifully.

Still, Mrs Pynne was too sage and intelligent, she knew, to try to force young people, or to try to 'arrange' things that couldn't be arranged. This thing had simply arranged itself, and the sight of it gave her pleasure and peace of mind. If the emergence of Peter irritated her more than it might have, that was not because she had any silly old-woman notions about childhood sweethearts, but because she was concerned for her daughter's happiness and her common sense.

Additional good reasons flitted through her mind and without taking firm shape . . . cradle-snatching . . . loyalty . . . a bird in the hand . . . no, not a bird in the hand, that sounded coarse, it must be something else she meant.

In any case, she had absolutely nothing against young Peter, she had made that quite plain to herself and to Jean. He seemed a very nice child. It was only necessary to mention the thing once, and Jean put her mind at rest. The subject never arose again. At least, Jean didn't bring it up. But against her better judgement, Mrs Pynne developed the certainty that Peter had not vanished, and against her better judgement, she found herself driven to pick at the subject again; just gently; but oftener.

Jean was a good girl, as well she might be. There were no displays of mutiny or nasty tempers in that household. She shrugged off the importance of Peter. And now Mrs Pynne became concerned and even alarmed. But she was no dragon.

'I'm taking your word for it,' she remarked seriously to

Jean, on one occasion. And when Jean nodded seriously and blandly (was it possible that she was capable of concealing anything?) Mrs Pynne went on, 'You told me yourself that there was nothing serious in it, and that's good enough for me. I'll . . .' she stopped, and the topic was dropped, for she had almost said I'll hold you to that, which would have been a silly remark. In any case Jean, too, partly divined the unfinished sentence, and felt unhappy and trapped, without fully understanding how she had been trapped.

It was when Archie finally came home from the army that Mrs Pynne discovered real apprehension. The event that should have cleared everything up turned out to be a puzzling disappointment. Jean was too pleasant and friendly towards Archie to justify any criticism. But perhaps not friendly enough? Or not excited enough?

It was then that Mrs Pynne realized that far from dismissing Peter as an amusing irritant, she had grown to dislike him very much indeed. Having met him only once, and briefly, she could barely recall what he looked like, but she did recall that she had disliked him from the start. She was too wise, of course, to say anything of the kind. It was easier to be particularly enthusiastic about Archie, who hadn't changed a bit except for the better, and leave the rest to be inferred.

It may be that she was in too much of a hurry, but she was nagged by nebulous alarms over what could happen to foolish inexperienced girls who got mixed up with the wrong people, and Jean's unexcited acceptance of Archie's homecoming, which might have seemed merely normal before, now looked like downright apathy. She asked her daughter searchingly if she was still seeing Peter, and when Jean said no, it was said so flatly that Mrs Pynne couldn't really believe it.

'It's time you were settling down,' she remarked one evening, when she had Jean alone.

'Oh, there's plenty of time for that.' To hear her own

words in Jean's mouth was dangerously exasperating.

'Does Archie feel the same way?' she asked with some asperity.

'I haven't asked him.' For all her habitual compliance, Jean had a flip, shrugging manner when she was uninterested in going on with a question.

'I may be your mother, but I'm not blind,' Mrs Pynne remarked, determinedly jolly. 'I've been watching Archie, and I know the signs.'

'Well, they can't be on my wave-length.' Deprived of the escape she craved, Jean escaped into sullenness.

'Don't start being deliberately stupid. Even Archie's people know there's something in the wind.' What a silly phrase that was.

'I'm not marrying Archie's mother and father, if that's what you mean.' Jean spoke coldly. Her knees were trembling.

'Don't take that tone with me.' This was also the wrong tone, but Mrs Pynne had her limits.

'All right, but I don't want to talk about it. Everybody's always expecting me to do something,' Jean muttered.

'They're entitled to! You're not an orphan, remember.'

'No.'

'Anybody would think young people nowadays had nothing to do with their families. Parents are entitled to expect something.'

Jean stood up. She knew that the strength was draining out of her, and that the meaningless tears that would spring to her eyes would ruin her.

'I don't care,' she said. 'I'm not going to marry anybody. Ever.'

Mrs Pynne had overplayed her hand, and the knowledge was acid and unbearable. She struck Jean a ringing blow on the cheek.

The tears that had almost betrayed Jean were suddenly forgotten. Whatever triumph there was, was hers. Her voice was quite steady as she said:

185

'I'm going to bed.'

In the darkness, she nursed the trivial pain almost with joy. She had won. The smack on her cheek could not be wished away. Her mother would not be able to bring the subject up again after so terrible a descent into violence.

Mrs Pynne, horrified at herself, didn't view it so simply. Her horror was horror at having handled the thing badly. After a day in which the whole business was meticulously ignored, she was able to resume her commanding position, bolstered by a strong conscience, because Jean must take the squalid responsibility for having provoked a scene.

But Jean, perceiving how the battle had been turned against her again, clung to the memory of being struck. It would not be forgotten. She talked and even laughed and was pleasant to Archie, and held on to this one comfort. She could never even share it with Peter, since that would be disloyalty to her mother. But it was there. Perhaps, much of the time, she didn't even think about Peter at all. And perhaps he would have understood that. He didn't know, anyway.

By this time, having walked off his talk with Mr Garside, Peter was leaning on the Dougans' gate, talking to Veronica Dougan and for minutes on end not even thinking about Jean. Having given himself a long interval to hum the minister out of his system before he should face his family, he had met Veronica on her way home and was gently stunned into anaesthesia by her conversation.

'Do they still let you out yourself at night?' Veronica prodded him. She leaned back on the gate and waggled her shoulders as she looked up at him, in a way that was probably alluring and mysterious. 'Any boy as tall, dark and gruesome as you, it's a wonder some female doesn't kidnap you if you go out without a lead.'

'Och, women are not interested in me. And, frankly, I am not remotely interested in women.' It had a nice, disenchanted ring that pleased him.

'Hey, nark the patter about remotely interested, you're

186

not foolin' this kid, somebody's gave you the good old brush-off. Ach, don't let it get you down, Peter. San ferry ann, san ferry ann! There's better fish came out the sea than ever kicked a blether. That's what the old man always says, fat lot he knows about it. Easy come,' she snapped her fingers and curled her lip, 'easy go, pardner.'

'Is that why you got engaged?' It was balm to listen to Veronica flattening the world out, parcelling it up and trampling on it. There was also nothing wrong with watching her eye him up and down and weighing him like an interested butcher.

'Huh! No future in it, Peter. I have informed Johnny that from here on in he's got the chuck.'

'Aw. That's a shame.'

'Ach, this kiddo's not cut out for it.' She snapped her fingers and did a quick dance-step. 'I'm strictly a good-time gal. Maybe there's something wrong wi' me. Live it up, that's me. And you should see his old lady. You've heard of Dracula's daughter. That's Dracula's mother. But not for Veronica. Can you imagine that big slob? He had it all fixed up in his tiny mind that we would go and *live* with her.'

'Well, you have to live somewhere.'

'Okay, I'll take the gas chamber. Ach, it's just a gag, gettin' engaged. I reckon it's strictly from a confidence trick. You like the way some slob dances, and the next minute you're stuck wi' ten snottery-nosed kids and a life-sentence. And Dracula's mother as well.'

'You're talking through a hole in your hat, Veronica. You'll get married, all right. It's your destiny.'

'Hey, is that a proposition?'

'Do you think I'm frightened?' Peter said recklessly.

'I don't know about you.' Veronica eyed him narrowly. 'No, but I mean, tell us honestly, Peter. I mean, when you go out with some slick chick, what do you do, just talk a lot of stuff out of books? You know, highly intelligent conversation. Ha, that's a laugh, highly intelligent conversation –

187

I'm just thinking about that big slob Johnny, he's got as much patter as a deaf Indian totem-pole. Strictly from Braille . . . Well, you haven't answered my question.'

'What was the question? Oh. Yeah, yeah, highly intelligent conversation. Sure. I'm the all-time champeen at highly intelligent conversation.'

'And that's all?' Veronica was seeking assurance on a point of etiquette.

'No-o. *I'm* a Braille champeen as well.'

Veronica shook her head in wonderment.

'No, honestly, no offence, Peter, I just can't picture it somehow. You just don't look the type, don't get me wrong, you're quite a pin-up in a gruesome way but honestly, I can't picture it. Anyway, I bet you're nothing like Johnny-o. I bet you do it kind of refined, like.'

'Sure. Like this, for instance?' Peter, wondering if he was taking a hideous risk, but at the same time made bold by Veronica's cheerful brutality, put his arm round her and pulled her close. She stood against him unresisting and looked up at him. She wasn't surprised, merely speculative.

'Okay, okay, end of demonstration,' she said, and he released her. 'Yeah, you're a slick operator, all right.'

'And you'll get married, all right,' Peter said, easy and unruffled. 'You can't dodge it.'

'Ach, get lost. Can you see me feedin' three kids wi' one hand and givin' myself a home perm wi' the other?'

'But that's what husbands are for. Your husband can give you the perm.'

'Now you're talking,' Veronica said slowly. 'You begin to interest me strangely, my friend. I will give your proposition careful consideration. Hey, that got you worried, Peter.'

'Me? Worried? Yah!'

He watched her go to her front door and wave derisively at him, and then walked along to his own gate. But before he could turn into the garden, a hand was laid on his arm.

188

He turned to find himself confronted by a strange, tall young man whose face was hardly familiar at all, but by association, he immediately identified him as Johnny, the silent fiancé who had trailed in Veronica's wake on New Year's Eve. Quick fear set Peter's pulses prickling.

'It's you she's gone for.' Johnny made it a statement.

'Not at all.' Peter tried to keep his voice from shaking, and on an inspiration added, 'Keep your voice down, my father's ill.'

Johnny was properly impressed at once.

'Are you sure you're telling me the truth?' Johnny's teeth were clamped tight, but whether in rage or misery, or in a conscious simulation of both, it was hard to tell.

'Don't be daft,' Peter whispered. 'We've known each other for years – Veronica's just like a sister to me,' he added wildly.

'I don't get it.' Johnny's teeth unclamped and he relapsed into bewilderment and despair. 'She's went and thrown me over.'

'Tough luck.'

'Do you think she'll be in the house herself?'

'Oh, there must be somebody else there. It's late.'

'I know.' Johnny looked round numbly for succour. 'I don't want to bother her. I've got to get my ring back,' he added in aggrieved tones.

'Oh, aye?'

'Well, it cost fifteen nicker!'

Peter whistled his admiration.

'Aw, it's no' me, it's the old wife.' Johnny tried to offer a defence. 'I don't want the bloody ring. She'll kill me if I don't get it. Do you think old Dougan's in?'

'Are you worried about him?'

'I'll do that old bastard.' Johnny's attempt at bravado was hollow and failed to convince. 'Hey, you wouldny like to go in for me, would you?'

'Me? Oh, no, for God's sake.'

'Would you come along wi' me?'

Peter was stiff with embarrassment and horror.

'What's worrying you? It would look silly if I came.'

'Would you wait here? I don't like to ask you.'

Peter couldn't understand how he could help by waiting, but was so relieved at not having been persuaded to go with Johnny that he agreed eagerly. Johnny begged to be assured that he wouldn't run away, and this made Peter feel masterful and impatient. He brusquely ordered Johnny to hurry about it, and waited as the pale young man tiptoed to the Dougans' front door and gave it an inaudible knock.

'Louder!' Peter whispered. Johnny banged the door once, and recoiled at his own audacity. The light went on in the front hall, and the door opened. The silhouette framed in the light wasn't Veronica — Ria, probably. There was a low murmur from Johnny, and a sharp answer from Ria. Johnny stepped back a pace, shrinking, and murmured again. Then Ria disappeared and her raised voice could be heard inside the house. When Veronica appeared at the door, Johnny raised a hand, either in explanation or in defence, and gabbled something.

'I know who sent you.' Veronica's voice was clear, loud and contemptuous. 'You would jump in the canal if *she* cracked the whip!'

There was another mutter from Johnny, slightly louder this time, and edged with bluster. Veronica was engaged in an odd gesture with both hands clasped together before her, and then she raised one of them and moved as if to strike Johnny, who crouched back.

'You're welcome,' she snapped, and flounced into the house and slammed the door. Johnny looked round him in confusion and then trotted out to where Peter was waiting. He was near to tears.

'Could you give us a hand, Mac?'

'What for?'

'She's *threw* it at me. I'll never find it myself.' And as Peter burst into startled titters, Johnny added, 'It's no laughin' matter. It cost fifteen nicker. Och, I'm fed up wi' this.'

The two of them crept into the Dougans' front garden and peered at the rank grass for the glint of jewellery, and Peter, who had become violently uninterested in the engagement ring and was convinced that search was useless and pointless, became aware that Johnny's grip on dignity and manhood had snapped. He was weeping quietly as he moved over the grass on his hands and knees. Peter then became aware that it had grown darker, and realized that the light had gone out in the Dougans' living-room, and that Ria and Veronica were sitting at the window watching the search. More than ever he wished that he had never heard of Johnny.

'Away you go and get a mine detector!' Ria Dougan shouted.

'Just ignore her, she's as common as dirt!' Johnny sobbed. 'You shut your mouth, Ria Dougan!' he yelled back in the same breath. Ria answered with a hoot of unkind laughter, which Peter thought he heard Veronica trying to shush. But the window upstairs was already opening noisily, and a head poked out.

'What's going on out there?' It was the querulous Mrs McGill, querulous partly from twenty years spent living upstairs from the Dougans. Johnny shouted back, by now quite abandoned to tears:

'You mind your ain business, see?'

Peter crouched low in an effort to be invisible, and stared bleakly at the grass, which very nearly was invisible. Johnny was snivelling to himself, 'The bitch, the bitch! Fifteen nicker! I'll do somebody for this. I would do that old rat Dougan for a start. Rat. Rat. He's an old rat.'

Johnny's desire materialized at once, for Mr Dougan abruptly appeared out of the darkness as he came in at the gate.

'What is it, what is it?' he snapped, and Johnny leapt

round convulsively, sobbing, 'Don't think I'm feart! I'm no' feart, see!'

'What's the game?'

'She threw my ring away!' Johnny wailed. Mr Dougan struck a match and remarked in a frozen voice, 'There it is. Pick it up and get yourself off my premises.'

It was typical of Mr Dougan, Peter felt, that he should order the ring to be exactly where he struck the match. Johnny picked it up and stared at it through his tears, and muttered, 'It wasn't me that asked for any trouble. I'm fed up wi' this – wi' the lot of you,' he added, keeping well back from Mr Dougan, who stood in a dignified pose and pointed the way out. Mr Dougan ignored Peter, having no time for complications, and Peter sneaked round behind him. In the brief time since Johnny had first knocked on the door, Christine and Davie McAllister were standing on the pavement outside, mildly curious.

'What the devil's going on?' Christine muttered to Peter.

'I was helping to look for some lost jewellery.'

Johnny was still standing beside him, sniffing heavily and regathering his composure.

'Aye, help!' he said bitterly. 'Don't think you can kid me, it was you that loused me up all right. You're the one that done it. Well you can have her, see! I hope she does you the same as she done me. You can *stuff* it, the lot of you!' Johnny shambled splendidly off into the night. To his intense irritation, Peter found Christine hustling him into the house, where he was going in any case.

'What have you got yourself into next?' she demanded, when they were inside, and Davie McAllister was standing around wondering whether to look baffled or disgusted.

'Nothing, nothing!' Peter's voice was high-pitched. 'Lay off, lay off! Now just listen carefully. Veronica's chucked her boy friend, and she threw his engagement ring at him, and I helped him to look for it. That, is, all. Get it?'

'Come on, brother,' Christine retorted. 'What did he

mean, you could have her? For heaven's sake, Peter, you're not getting mixed up with Veronica Dougan next!'

Peter looked at Davie, who lifted his eyebrows and his shoulders as who should say, Well, are you? Peter put his hands to his head and swayed in a Yiddish motion of resignation and despair.

'O-o-oh God,' he moaned.

14

Miss Cumberland, the science teacher, was big-boned and
had short grey hair and the look of a born spinster who had
never thought of being anything else. Weary of trying to
keep a sense of urgency alive in the curriculum during the
purgatory weeks between the Highers and the results, she
was relaxing with a discussion on the nature of time. Peter,
who had never devoted any effort to considering this, found
himself being wooed into pure intellectual speculation for
the first time in weeks. He was slightly nettled to find that
Tom Arthur, the all-time clean-cut athletic pimple, seemed
to be more hep to the jargon than he himself was. Arthur
was a science-fiction maniac, a thing that would never have
occurred to Peter and which annoyed him for a reason he
couldn't analyse.

  'Sure, it's a fact, miss,' Tom was saying, 'that if you
travelled faster than the speed of light, you would get
younger and younger and the clock would run backwards.'

  'Do you fancy that, Arthur?' Miss Cumberland, hard to
ruffle, was more interested in Tom Arthur's reactions than
in the theory itself.

  'Sure thing.' Tom's reaction to a question was to dig
doggedly into any prepared position available and defend it.

  'What would happen,' Peter inquired, 'when – just a
minute, say you were exactly seventeen years old, and the
clock turned back seventeen years? Would you just go pop!
No Arthur?' Tom Arthur made a downward gesture with
his hand to knock this interruption out of existence, and
said, 'Haddow has to be funny about it.'

  'It's not a very funny possibility,' Miss Cumberland said

drily. 'Anyway, Haddow, are you convinced that past time is lost for ever?'

'Yes. I *think* so. Except in your memory.'

'That's old-fashioned,' Tom Arthur scowled. 'If it was lost, it would mean that the whole universe gets destroyed every second and then rebuilt every next second.' Alice Jackson, who was improbably in the Higher Science class, cast her eyes to heaven and shook her head.

'Where did you read that, Arthur?' Miss Cumberland asked, alerted. 'Have you been dipping into Dunne?'

'No, everybody knows that,' Tom Arthur tutted. 'It was in a story in *Nebula*, for one thing.'

'Good old *Nebula*,' Miss Cumberland murmured.

'Anyway,' Peter objected, 'all that stuff about dreams being wanderings in time. Freud has already proved they're the products of the unconscious mind in conflict with its environment, or something.'

'Huh. Or something!' Tom Arthur was heavy with triumph. The whole thing set off aimless trains of thought in Peter's mind and he found himself wondering what reality was. He found himself drifting away from it, and began to doubt that he was himself, or that anybody's identity was an acceptable idea.

What was real about his being trapped, not only in this body and in this place, but in this self? His identity was so fragile a thing that it was laughable to think of it producing effects or suffering effects. If he were somebody else, he could begin everything again and be accepted without any of his past. He speculated idly on the possibility of selves floating from body to body, and soon found himself so confused and withdrawn, that he was compelled to telephone Jean at four o'clock. He half-expected her to answer that she had never heard of him.

'My astral body has been floating round the Equator,' he began. 'That's the explanation for this call. I couldn't find out who I was. Do you know who I was?' It was the kind of statement that frivolously fed his self-importance because it suggested strange intellectual adventures that must stir her to bewilderment and therefore admiration.

'Yes, *I* know who you are,' she answered, quite satisfactorily. 'I wish I had been round the Equator with you. Was it lonely?'

'Oh, I'm inured to suffering,' Peter declaimed.

'I've been wondering how I could get in touch with you,' Jean said. 'I don't know – maybe this is silly . . . I wondered if you would like to meet Archie. Is that a silly idea?'

'Oh. Uch, I don't know. Maybe I would like him.'

'That would be nice.'

'No, it wouldn't. I don't want to like him. Oh, I'm talking like an arrested juvenile again. All right. I don't know what good it can do, honestly, Jean.'

'No. Well . . . Oh, I don't know either. Maybe it would do *some* good, though. You know . . . I thought we might meet in that café at Anniesland . . . tonight? I've just got to do *something*.'

Peter detected the protest in her voice, and said:

'All right, half past seven?'

'If you're sure you want to.'

'Oh, the lamb to the slaughter.'

'No, not that. I'm glad you phoned.'

'Ah. So am I. Even although the month isn't up.'

'Oh, yes.'

But when he was slowly preparing himself emotionally to leave the house and meet Jean and Archie, something else happened. His father, sleepy from two pills, had retired to bed and indicated, with only a twinge of martyrdom, that he could be left alone. Julie was going to a birthday party, and as soon as Christine had helped her to look pretty, Christine left the house too; probably, Peter reflected, on a date with some goon of her own age, whom she could later discuss with Davie McAllister and make Davie feel important and miserable.

Determined not to be early, Peter was just getting up

196

to leave for Anniesland when the front door flew open and little Julie burst in. She was still prettied up for the party, and she wore a tight, bright smile. Peter glanced at her without much interest.

'Forget something?' he asked casually. Julie shook her head, still smiling the unnatural smile.

'What's up, then?'

'Nothing.' Julie's voice was bright and hard.

'Well?'

She shook her head again, still smiling. Then the smile abruptly drooped. Tears spurted from her bright eyes as if they had been tightly corked and building up pressure. She stood in the middle of the living-room floor and her mouth opened to jerking sobs and sniffs. Peter, sensing some tiny tragedy that would get in his way, was overcome with weariness at having relations.

'I can't make out a word you're saying,' he complained.

'I . . . hate . . . Sadie . . . Martin . . .' Julie now abandoned her control and jammed her knuckles in her eyes.

'Well, I hate her big sister, so what?'

'I knew it was last night all the time! I knew!'

Premonition of genuine villainy came to Peter.

'What, the party? The party was last night?'

After the relief of her first outburst, Julie was able to gasp and blubber her story. The birthday party had been last night, but Sadie Martin had insisted that it was tonight, and Julie had finally been overwhelmed by Sadie's assurances. When Julie arrived at the home of some girl called Hetty Morgan, who was throwing the party, Mrs Morgan hadn't been able to stop laughing at the comedy of some little girl arriving twenty-four hours late.

It was evident that Julie had walked home with her firm little smile gripped between her teeth in case anybody should ever know what a fool she was. Peter awkwardly patted her shoulder and said, 'Don't howl, there'll be plenty of other parties.'

'I'll never go to a party again in my life! Sadie Martin's a . . . a . . . a *shite*!'

'Sh, sh, the old man'll hear you.' But Julie had launched herself in a magnificent movement at the armchair and was weeping away her broken heart and her smashed pride. Peter looked at her in weary bewilderment.

'Well,' he said, 'I have to go out.' Julie didn't appear to hear. He went to the hall, lingered in indecision, and then went out by the front door. But by the time he had got to the gate, he knew angrily that it would be impossible to leave her. Damned sisters, he thought. And damned Martins. What am I supposed to do, take her with me for Archie? Oh, great. He went back into the house. Julie was still in the chair, still weeping.

'Come on,' Peter said, 'I'll take you to the pictures.'

'I don't want . . . to go to the rotten pictures.' The voice came muffled from the arm of the chair, but then she looked slightly upwards, her weeping slightly lowered in volume by a new thought.

'I'll take you to the pictures in town. The Odeon, or somewhere.'

'It's probably a rotten programme.' Julie stared straight in front of her, her fists covering the lower half of her face. 'We wouldn't get in to the balcony, anyway.'

'All right, wash your face and come on.'

Julie sat for some minutes, loath to abandon her bereavement, before she got up and trudged to the kitchen to wash. By the time they were on the bus for the Odeon, her tears were forgotten and she alternated between speculations on whether they would get a front seat in the balcony and deep, malignant promises that she would get Sadie Martin if it was the last thing she ever did.

Peter watched the programme also alternating in his feelings; between misery and disaster at having stood up Jean, and nobility at having sacrificed all for duty. He was also bothered by the knowledge that he had spent all the money he had been saving for an end-of-the-month

Saturnalia with Jean, but he didn't know whether to feel disgusted or proud about this.

As far as Julie was concerned, the evening had been turned into a triumph. He was forced to join in her exaltation at the defeat of the ghastly Sadie Martin, and if his agreement was absent-minded, Julie didn't notice. She was buoyed up by her painstaking calculation that the outing, including fares and special ices and chocolates, had cost fourteen-and-six, and this in itself was a large element in the story with which she was going to bludgeon Sadie Martin next day.

By the middle of the following morning, Peter had partly swung round to a mood of righteous anger at Jean for suggesting so insane a thing as a triangular meeting. If she had as proper a sense of the obligations of love as he had, she would have straightened Archie out with kind firmness by this time. He bolstered himself with such reflections while he groaned at the imprisonment of the classroom which prevented him from getting out to telephone and win her sympathy with Julie's sad story.

When he got home for lunch, his father was at the table, dressed, and in a rancid mood.

'Feeling better?' Peter asked, and Samuel turned on him with curling lip. 'Don't you start,' he warned Peter. 'If I'm dying, I'll die on my feet.'

Auntie Sarah glared out from the kitchen.

'You leave your father alone!' she snapped. 'It's always the same every time you come in, nothing but trouble. If you can't help, don't hinder!'

'Aye, right,' Peter said, but his father took him up at once with, 'Aye, I should bloody well think it's right.'

'What did I say now?' Peter demanded, trying but failing to shut himself up, for he saw that Samuel was like his normal self, and subject to explosive rage if he was crossed or even questioned.

'You talk too damned much!' Samuel came bang in on cue. 'All I ever get in this damned house is arguments and questions. Just once, shut up and do as you're told.'

Peter breathed heavily and forced himself to silence.

'Where the hell did you get to last night?' His father couldn't leave it alone. Peter shrugged his shoulders.

'Is that an answer?'

'I thought you said it was all right to go out,' Peter mumbled, knowing that any answer was likely to lead to more unpleasantness. Auntie Sarah was poised at the sink, with her left ear pointing smugly in the direction of the living-room. But Julie, whose lifelong habit it was to become invisible when Samuel was in one of his tempers, spoke up.

'He took me to the pictures because I was blubbering because Sadie Martin said Hetty Morgan's party was the night before and I went last night,' she said.

'Some bloody tarradiddle,' Samuel muttered, and then, reluctantly changing his standpoint, added, 'Well, that's the least you could do.' It sounded like an accusation. Christine arrived at that point, and with the superior maternal air she sometimes used, said:

'Tut, tut, are you two at it again?'

'You shut your lip, girl!' Samuel shouted at her. Christine coloured and her eyes glinted at this unheard-of humiliation, right in front of Auntie Sarah. Samuel, snorting, coloured too, but there was no way of withdrawing the words. They sat down to table in a dense numbing silence, avoiding one another's eyes.

Julie, who was incapable of protracted silence, broke this one.

'You should have seen Sadie Martin's face. I fixed her but good,' she gritted, half to herself. Everybody, even Samuel, turned to her with excessive bright interest.

'Oh,' Julie added, with an instant change of manner, falling into a sneer that was supposed to be an impersonation of the loathsome Sadie. '*She* said her rotten big sister had a rotten message for you, Peter. Some rotten pal of her rotten big sister called Peeny-Jeeny got engaged. Peeny-

Jeeny!' Julie sniggered at the stupidity of the names worn by friends of the rotten Martins.

'What the hell kind of name's that?' Samuel asked, glad of a neutral subject that could cure the atmosphere.

Peter had eaten a lump of vapid potted meat and was halfway through one of Auntie Sarah's special quarter-boiled potato boulders. He continued to chew it, setting his lips in a smile that felt odd-shaped and ugly.

'Oh?' he said. He avoided Christine's quick glance, and lifted another piece of dank potato.

'I bet it was a lousy party, anyway, Julie,' Christine babbled. Peter leaned back in his chair and drummed his fingers on the table.

'Oh,' he said. 'My nails are dirty. Excuse me, folks.' The ordinary actions of pushing back his chair and standing up were novel and difficult, his arms and legs embarrassing lumps of flesh that had never before learned to operate. He made his way to the bathroom and started to whistle, but his lips were dry and no sound came until he had licked them. He locked the bathroom door behind him and leaned his forehead on the pebbled glass. Then with a startled sense of objective revelation he discovered that he was going to be sick. He knelt on the floor before the lavatory bowl and vomited with awful violence. He reached up to the wash-hand basin and turned the cold tap full on to drown the noise.

When he returned to the table, Auntie Sarah was standing beside it, rubbing her hands on a dish-towel and glaring at him with compressed lips.

'People in some homes have the manners to sit at the table when people have knocked their pans in making good food for them!'

Auntie Sarah was very far away and too trivial to be bothered with. He felt drained and weak and calm, but suspected that his calmness was the numbness from a knife-slash before the blood has spurted.

'I don't feel hungry, Auntie Sarah.'

'If you didny eat a lot of dampt sweeties at that school you might have an appetite for decent healthy food!' she barked. Was it possible that she smelt blood and was inflamed for more?

Samuel, irritated that any of his family should provide Sarah with an opening, glared at him too.

'Eat your dinner and be glad you can enjoy it,' he said. Peter shook his head.

'Eat your damned dinner!' Samuel was over the edge of his exasperation again. Peter stood up.

'I want to get back early to school,' he said. He forced himself to move quickly to the door, for Samuel was half-rising.

'You'll eat your dinner first!' he ordered Peter, who shook his head and went out. 'Come back here!' Samuel shouted. Peter left the house with the hounds of hell at his shoulders and didn't look back. The news about Jean he would digest later. First he had to suffer his head-splitting rage at the oppression and callousness of his own home. There was no dignity anywhere, it was impossible even to suffer without being bullied. Thinking with surrealistic clarity he couldn't think of anybody he didn't hate to the bottom of his soul. The human race was organized in total war on him.

The condition of mental clarity remained as he lived out the afternoon, and his brain operated at headlong speed. It hurtled through everything he knew and everything he had experienced. Maybe, he thought, I'm actually drowning. He thought of drowning and rejected the idea at once. Eventually, he decided, he would have to stop thinking and adopt an attitude, become a recognizable person and not this breakneck jumble of postures that presented themselves to him. He would surrender to permanent despair. But as he contemplated this, Davie McAllister turned to him in the maths class and asked:

'What's two hundred squared?' and Peter answered, 'Forty thousand oblonged,' and Davie's simple sense of humour drove him into strangled sniggers.

He would be bright and gay and not, give, one, teetotal, damn for anything. But he pictured himself being bright and gay haa haa ha, inventing new space-rocket fuels and making high-pitched jokes about them while everybody else in the lab looked sideways at him and sent for a plain van and a strait-jacket. Wearily, he laughed at his own postures, but his frenzy was real and not to be dismissed although he could find no way of reducing it to silence in his mind so that it could be endured.

He reflected again on the mystery of time, and projected himself forward ten years, brisk, successful, polluted with money. A white lab coat. Long-legged girls in white lab coats, with their hands stuck deep into the pockets, cool grey eyes and burnished careless hair. They meant nothing, it was like going through a Technicolor performance of being a person. Life stretched before him like a grey dusty corridor of time, half-lit and echoing muzzily with old dead memories. Living on memories, Jesus, he thought. At seventeen. I haven't even had time to *get* any. But another part of his mind instantly presented him with his memories, and he knew he couldn't live with them.

He would telephone Jean at four o'clock. He would pretend to have heard nothing, and simply tell her the sad story of Julie's party. But he couldn't sound casual. Already, merely at the thought of telephoning, he was experiencing the tremulous apprehension of stage-fright. He would telephone and be baffled and amused. What's this nonsense I've heard? Even better, he would telephone and say, Let me be the first to congratulate you, and good-bye. And good-bye for ever? Or I hope you'll be happy and don't worry about our adolescent flirtation, it was good for kicks while it lasted? Easy come, easy go. No, it's been swell knowing you. Not swell, it would sound phoney. No bones broken? No . . .

It was impossible to telephone, but it was more impossible to think of a whole evening, a whole night, of mounting insanity. He had to borrow fourpence from Davie

203

again, and Davie handed it over with only a small protest. But the nearest telephone-box was halfway home anyway, and before he reached it, he met Auntie Sarah. He saw her in the distance, hurrying along, but on catching sight of him she slowed down, and finally approached him with measured tread and a preternatural air of gravity. The look she bent on him was so mournful and compassionate that her fat little face was almost disintegrating under its weight.

'Poor Peter,' she said. She pursed her lips, shook her head and stared over his shoulder.

'What's up?'

'Your poor dear father has passed away.'

'Don't be daft,' Peter said.

Auntie Sarah could not be riled. She crossed herself quickly.

'It's a mercy he felt no pain at the end,' she sighed. 'I gave him the final rites myself.'

'You what? What the hell are you talking about?' Peter shouted.

'Ah.' Sarah sighed again. 'Poor orphan weans.'

'Shut up!' Peter roared at her. He had already started running towards the house. 'Final rites!' he gabbled aloud at himself. 'Passed away?' In the two-hundred-yards run to the house he was gasping for breath, and the long muscles of his thighs twitched under him. He threw himself at the front door and discovered that he had forgotten his key. He found himself sobbing inanely and muttering aloud, 'The window. Locked. Damned nonsense. Open, open, hell!'

The only unlocked window that was accessible was the window of his father's bedroom, with the wooden coal bunker standing beneath it at the back of the house. At his first attempt he slid uselessly down from the bunker and heard himself moaning, 'This is stupid!' All the blinds in the house were down, and when he had scrambled with his fingertips to prise up the window, the paper-blind in his father's room bellied inwards and back again and ripped as his foot caught in its cord.

His father's figure was quite still under the bedclothes, with the sheet drawn up over his face. 'It's not true!' Peter wailed, and a sleepy muffled voice answered, 'Oh, God, what's up now?'

Peter jerked the sheet back and his father blinked up at him. Peter crumpled on his knees beside the bed and rested his head on one hand. He found that tears were streaming down his cheeks.

'You've just passed away,' he said. His voice caught on something in his throat. 'Auntie Sarah gave you the last rites.'

'She's fine and bloody previous,' his father muttered, still half-asleep. 'What the hell's going on in this house?'

Peter succeeded in describing his meeting with Sarah, his dash for the house, his entry by the window of the death chamber. Samuel had propped himself up feebly in bed.

'By God, she's a pant, you canny whack Sarah,' he pronounced. 'I took two pills after dinner. By God, I needed them after these spuds of Sarah's, you were bloody clever leaving yours. Here, I've noticed these pills dope me up, I must have went out like a light.'

'Sarah'll be disappointed,' Peter managed to say. He had risen and was standing at the window, trying to roll the torn blind up.

'Oh, will she no'? She'll be away dyein' her face black for the funeral. What the hell are you *greetin'* at?'

Peter kept his face turned away.

'I thought you were dead.'

'Well, you'll be disappointed as well.'

'Aye, sure.'

'Well, you would get it all your own way.'

'Oh, sure.'

'Ach, don't be daft, Peter, you and me are too much alike, that's our trouble. God, I'm hungry.'

'Will I make you something?'

'Oh, aye. Would you do that? Something nice, Peter?'

'What?'

205

'I never knew you were sick at dinner-time, it was Sarah that got me down. Christine telt me. Honest to God, what do you want to go and boak for? This lassie you had at Millport?'

Peter waved his hands. 'What does it matter?'

'It matters a hell of a lot if you've got it that bad.'

'I'll see what's in the kitchen.'

'Okay. Naw, just a minute, Peter. Well, look at me when I'm talking to you. Honest, I'd be as well talking to my pipe.'

'Okay, I'm looking at you.'

'God, we'll be startin' another argument in a minute. Did Sarah really get you down?'

'Uch, the trouble wi' me,' said Peter, 'is that too many things happen to me.'

'Well, you're bloody lucky. Bloody lucky.' Peter caught an intonation of wistfulness and regret, and it jolted him. He didn't want to think about it.

'You'll rise above it,' Samuel told him. 'You're better than the lot of them, you've got brains, even if you never use them. Don't let it get you down, tae hell wi' the lot of them.'

Peter laughed uncertainly. But he discovered that his brain had stopped racing some minutes back. He would go into the kitchen and make something. A scrambled egg, maybe, if there were any eggs. Something. He would make it nice. He would phone Jean. Or if it was too late, he wouldn't phone Jean, he would phone her tomorrow.

Just a minute, what was he panicking about? If Cathie Martin had told her young sister to tell Julie to tell him that Jean was engaged, what kind of credibility did the story have? Cathie couldn't have heard anything since last night, and last night he was supposed to meet Jean and Archie. It couldn't have happened then. Could it?

Did a girl invite her lover to a café to meet another guy and tell him she was marrying this other guy? Did girls do things like that? Could Jean do things like that? Listen, even if she was going to marry this Archie, she would have to break it gently, she was too soft and gentle to expose herself to a scene, to an argument. Jean wasn't like that. Had she gone and got engaged to Archie just because Peter hadn't turned up at Anniesland? What kind of damned drivelling nonsense was that?

If she had, he might as well ditch her straight off. Or no, he would do something about it. Something. What was all the panic about, she wasn't *married*, was she? The mental energy that had tortured him all day channelled itself into pure aggression, and he broke an egg on the edge of a bowl with savage efficiency.

'I shall prevail!' he snarled at the yolk. 'And if I don't I shall still prevail. They don't know,' he added, as he jerked a fork round the bowl, 'that they're dealing with Haddow, the terror of the Pecos. Bang flaming bang bang.'

He took the egg to his father, who shuddered at it and began to eat it greedily.

'By God, though,' Samuel said, 'Sarah's a corker. What'll she say when I shout boo at her tomorrow?'

'Ah, it's a shame to make a fool of her,' Peter said. 'She does her best.'

'Aye, aye. She's got a terrible cross to bear.'

Peter pursed his lips and set his arms akimbo.

'It'll break that poor woman's heart,' he cried.

'By God!' Samuel spattered scrambled egg over the bed-clothes. 'Maybe she'll try to bury me anyway.'

'I'll deal with Sarah,' Peter said, and he rubbed his hands together.

'Ah, I doubt it takes a man to handle that one,' said Samuel. 'Uhuh? Aye, maybe you *are* man enough. Do you fancy yourself as a man?'

'Just stick around,' said Peter.

THE END

A SELECTED LIST OF FINE NOVELS
AVAILABLE FROM CORGI BOOKS

THE PRICES SHOWN BELOW WERE CORRECT AT THE TIME OF GOING TO PRESS.
HOWEVER TRANSWORLD PUBLISHERS RESERVE THE RIGHT TO SHOW NEW
RETAIL PRICES ON COVERS WHICH MAY DIFFER FROM THOSE PREVIOUSLY
ADVERTISED IN THE TEXT OR ELSEWHERE.

All Corgi/Bantam Books are available at your bookshop or newsagent, or can be ordered from the following address:

Corgi/Bantam Books,
Cash Sales Department,
P.O. Box 11, Falmouth, Cornwall TR10 9EN

Please send a cheque or postal order (no currency) and allow 80p for postage and packing for the first book plus 20p for each additional book ordered up to a maximum charge of £2.00 in UK.

B.F.P.O. customers please allow 80p for the first book and 20p for each additional book.

Overseas customers, including Eire, please allow £1.50 for postage and packing for the first book, £1.00 for the second book, and 30p for each subsequent title ordered.

NAME (Block Letters) ....

ADDRESS ....

....